THE PARIS TRIP

Beth Good

Thimblerig Books

Thimblerig Books

Copyright © 2024 Beth Good

All rights reserved

The characters and events portrayed in this book are fictitious. Any similarity to real persons, living or dead, is coincidental and not intended by the author.

No part of this book may be reproduced, or stored in a retrieval system, or transmitted in any form or by any means, electronic, mechanical, photocopying, recording, or otherwise, without express written permission of the publisher.

ISBN: 9798324821302
Imprint: Independently published

What Real Readers Are Saying About Beth Good's Romances: (all the following are from genuine 5-star Amazon reviews of Beth Good romcoms)

'This is another excellent story from Beth Good, which I'm so pleased I was able to fit into my Christmas reading schedule. If you're looking for a novella that will make you laugh, smile and is great for the run-up to Christmas, then look no further.' - Rachel Gilbey, from Rachel's Random Reads

'I've read most of Beth's books & like all her others this one doesn't disappoint. It's a nice love story.'

'I've given this five stars because it didn't just make me smile but actually managed to make me snicker (and try to read bits out loud to my husband).'

'The story speeds along at a very quick pace and each chapter wants you to keep reading more!'

'A fabulous and funny Christmas romance.'

'A nice book to curl up with over Christmas time.'

'Brilliant book, a MUST read. Loved it all and cannot wait to find more from this author - laughed and cried in places. Recommended. '

'I really enjoyed this book! It has some really funny parts and some twists that I definitely didn't expect! I definitely recommend this book '

'What a wonderful little book to read on a cold winter's day, it warms your heart. '

'Not your typical Christmas romance story!'

'A lovely little book, full of Christmas spirit. An easy to read, romantic and funny story that was great to curl up by the fire with.'

'Great characters you just had to root for.'

'I would recommend this book to my friends. I lost myself in the story, it was lovely with a very happy ending.'

Other gorgeous and amusing romances by Beth Good

The Cornish Colouring Book Club
The Oddest Little Chocolate Shop
The Oddest Little Christmas Shop
The Oddest Little Romance Shop
The Oddest Little Christmas Cake Shop
The Oddest Little Cornish Teashop
The Oddest Little Book Shop
The Oddest Little Mistletoe Shop
The Oddest Little Beach Shop
The Oddest Little Gingerbread Shop
The Oddest Little Cornish Christmas Shop
The Oddest Little Flower Shop
Winter Without You
All Summer With You
A Very Cornish Christmas
Purely Yours

With Viki Meadows
Christmas at the Lucky Parrot Garden Centre

PROLOGUE

If he'd been prancing through Château Rémy in scarlet heels, sporting a devil's tail and a flashy red cape, Leo could have understood why everybody he passed was turning to stare at him, apparently amazed by his long-overdue return to the family home.

As it was, he was dressed sombrely in dark clothes, as befitted the occasion, and making his way quietly and respectfully through these dimly lit corridors thronging with grieving friends and relatives.

There really was nothing remarkable about him today. He'd shaved off his trademark beard and moustache, ignoring the severe pangs this cost him, and even tied back his long hair with a black ribbon, to look less 'wild'. Yes, that was the word his grandmother had used to describe him last time he was home. *You look like a wild beast, Leo.* Conscious of not wanting to upset her, he had taken steps to tame his appearance before getting on the train first thing that morning.

Yet still, at every corner, these friends, relatives and hangers-on ogled him, wide-eyed and prurient, whispering among themselves like snakes hissing in the darkness.

'*Ah, c'est Leo… Leo Rémy.*'

At last, he reached the room where his brother lay in state, like a dead king.

The door stood open, waiting for him.

Leo halted and swallowed. His hand went to the knot of his unfamiliar tie, wishing he could loosen it. Tear it off it, in fact. But some things were simply impossible. They could only be faced and endured.

Like the body of his older brother.

He squared his shoulders, accepted a handshake from old Alfonse on the door, who doubtless had been standing there for hours like a guardsman, and stepped into the room.

Francis had been laid out on the dining room table, its length now draped in black velvet. Like Leo, he had been dressed in his best suit. Though Francis's was an austere three-piece with black waistcoat and tie. No doubt *he* was untroubled by the knot held firm against his throat. His brother's shoes completed this picture of urbane professionalism. Expensive black leather, highly polished, not a speck of dirt to be seen.

It didn't look like Francis. At least, his face was the same. Noble, patrician, his hair thick and black and parted in the usual way. But the rest of him…

No, this didn't look like Francis at all.

His brother would have hated that formal suit, which no doubt their weeping grandmother had picked out for his funeral. He had preferred jeans and tee-shirts in the summer, and jeans with hoodies in the winter. And always trainers on his feet. Even when he had worn a suit, for weddings and funerals, he'd paired it with trainers. Whomever those shoes had belonged to, he doubted it had been Francis. Perhaps they had been bought specially for the occasion.

The last shoes Francis would ever wear. And he would have hated them.

His throat choked with sudden, inappropriate laughter, and he wished he could make a joke about it.

To Francis.

'Hey, nice shoes... You up in court, bro?'

But he couldn't.

Francis was dead and Leo would never get to mock him again. Never argue with him again. Never have a brother again.

'I'm very sorry for your loss,' a voice said at his elbow. Some distant relative from Bordeaux, a man he barely knew, put a hand on his shoulder. 'So tragic. To be taken so young... How old was he, Leo? Thirty-three? Thirty-four?'

'He was thirty-six,' Leo replied thickly, dismayed by the emotion clogging up his throat.

'Do they know how it happened?'

This was the last thing he wanted to talk about.

But they expected him to crack, didn't they? To rip off his tie and head for the nearest bar...

'Pilot error seems to be what they're going with. It should have been a routine flight. He was flying solo back from Bordeaux when –'

Leo stopped, unable to go on, and bowed his head.

'I'll leave you alone with him.' The relative, whose name still escaped him, discreetly slipped away

Francis had managed the family business well.

But now he was gone, and their father had nominated Leo in his place to oversee their finances.

He could refuse, of course. Walk away.

But he knew his father wouldn't bother sobering up and coming to Paris to manage things for himself. No, he would simply run the estate into the ground and eventually be forced to sell the château and the vineyard in Bordeaux to cover his debts.

And what would his grandmother and poor frail Nonna do then?

They were all relying on *him* to pick up the reins where Francis had dropped them on his death. Because if his profligate father took charge, the family could be ruined within a few short years.

When he turned to leave, Liselle was waiting for him on the threshold, her large dark eyes shimmering with tears.

After more than five hours on the train from Nice, she looked wild and untamed, and yet still classically beautiful, with her long, flaming Titian hair that had caught his eye from the first moment he'd seen her in a night club in the South of France. She had sat for a portrait the next day, and they had become lovers soon after.

It had not lasted, not least because she was so much trouble. But Liselle was tenacious, he had to give her that, and was now his manager, though she still sat for him occasionally.

'Oh, my poor darling,' she cried, casting a quick, horrified look at Francis over his shoulder before shuddering dramatically. 'I'm so, so sorry. You should have waited for me. I would have come with you to see him. But your grandmother kept asking me questions... I couldn't get away.'

'It doesn't matter.'

'I'm here for you now. Whatever you want, just tell me. My poor Leo. Will your father come to the funeral?' she asked.

'No. My grandmother managed to track him down and let him know his eldest son was dead. But he still refused to pay his respects.'

'What a horrible man.'

Leo shrugged. 'All he said was that I must take over where Francis left off. That I would have to come home permanently to run the family business.'

'What will you do?' she whispered, wide-eyed.

'My duty to the family,' Leo said grimly, and loosened the knot on his tie before it could strangle him.

'Give up painting?' She sounded horrified.

'I don't have any other choice.'

Liselle stared. 'But of course you do.' She tugged urgently on his sleeve. 'Darling, let's leave. Straight after the funeral. We'll take the train back to Vence and your studio, and your father can go to hell.'

'With my blessing,' he snarled. 'But if I simply run away again, what will happen to the rest of my family? He'd destroy everything within a year.' His teeth ground together at the trap closing about him. 'No, I have to run the business in Francis's place.'

'What about Bernadette? Why can't she take over?'

'She could, absolutely. But my father barely tolerates her living at the château. He'd never give her the family business.'

Liselle looked shocked. 'But she's your *sister*.'

'My mother's child, yes. But he didn't father her.'

'Oh.' She blinked in surprise at that revelation, then said robustly, 'Well, if you're staying, then I'll stay too.'

Leo glanced at her briefly, not sure if that was a good idea. Their relationship was on the wane; he knew it even if she didn't. But that hardly seemed worth arguing about right now. Not with everything else falling to pieces around him.

'We can talk about it after I've buried my brother,' was all he said, tight-lipped. 'First though, I need a stiff drink. Come on…'

CHAPTER ONE

Three years later

'Right, listen up, everyone!' The tour guide clapped her hands a few times above the excited rumble of conversation and then seized the microphone to get their attention, booming out, 'Your final session of free time in Paris begins *now*!' Her fanatical gaze roved across their faces, studying each one in turn. 'Hello, people... *Are you listening*?'

Three rows back, sitting bolt-upright, Maeve gave the tour guide an encouraging smile. *She* was listening. Pen poised above her notebook, she was also ready to take copious notes, as she always did.

Better safe than sorry.

'From here, you can explore the Louvre museum and galleries, take a cruise on the River Seine, relax in the lovely Tuileries Gardens, or even treat yourself to a slap-up meal at the exclusive Paris Ritz. The choice is up to you. But please remember, people, you only have six hours. We meet back here at five o'clock *sharp*.' Betsy paused. 'Any questions before I let you go?'

Maeve stuck her hand in the air.

A collective groan went up from her fellow travellers, and she glanced about at them, unable to suppress an inner flicker of annoyance.

Perhaps she had asked rather a lot of questions on this tour. But it wasn't her fault that so much was left unexplained. Besides, the coach tour was almost over now. Tonight they would be heading back to the ferry and the white cliffs of Dover. So one more itty bitty question could surely not hurt...

Betsy pursed her lips. 'Yes, *Maeve*?' Her eyes had narrowed, and her tone was distinctly unfriendly. Which was unfair, given that she hadn't even heard Maeve's query yet.

'When you say five o'clock sharp –'

'I mean, not five past five. Or ten past five. And definitely not *half past* five.' Betsy glanced at Petunia, who had proved herself notorious as a latecomer when returning from other so-called 'free time' excursions, which simply meant times when they could explore alone rather than with the tour guide in charge. 'Our sailing back to Dover is fixed in stone, I'm afraid. So please note, we won't be waiting for *anyone* who misses the 5pm rollcall. Don't say I didn't warn you...'

5pm rendezvous at the coach. DO NOT BE LATE!

Maeve scribbled those last four words in large

block capitals in her large, leather-bound travel notebook, which also usefully accommodated her passport, travel documents, and even her mobile phone in a handy pocket.

As she fastened the clasp on her notebook and thrust the whole thing safely down into her backpack, she caught sight of her reflection in the window next to her seat. Her blonde hair looked neat and unfussy, a shoulder-length bob that made blow-drying quick and simple in the mornings before she had to dash out to school. She rarely wore make-up, except for a little flattering foundation when term had dragged on too long, and had not even bothered with lipstick that morning, feeling confident enough to go *au naturel* for the last day of this wonderful short break. She could have wished her eyes were a little brighter or more vivid; her particular shade of blue had always struck her as insipid. But she looked ready for anything, and Maeve took that as a win.

Sliding out of her seat, she met Petunia's hard gaze and felt a sudden urge to reassure her less well-organised fellow traveller.

'Plenty of time before five o'clock,' she said encouragingly, pulling on her jacket. 'I'll aim to be back here half an hour early though, just to be sure.'

'Of course you will, Little Miss Perfect,' Petunia muttered and pushed past her down the coach steps.

Taken aback, Maeve stared after the other woman in surprise.

That was rather uncalled-for, she thought, blinking. She was certainly not perfect. Far from it, in fact. She hoped she hadn't been giving off that impression, though she also knew from experience that her insistence on dotting every i and crossing every t could be irritating to less-organized people. Most people managed not to be mean to her about it though.

Still, maybe Petunia was just having another of her 'dodgy tummy' episodes; these had been a feature of their tour, even causing unpleasant odour issues when the onboard toilet began to malfunction. Not that anyone would have said anything to Petunia's face, of course. But Maeve had spotted a few hankies clasped to noses and requests to turn up the air con.

She'd never been on a coach tour before, and it had been a revelation. On a whim, desperate for a break from her usual 'stay home and vegetate' summer holiday, she had paid for this five-day sightseeing and shopping trip to Paris. And it had been wonderful so far, despite a demanding itinerary.

They had spent a whole day exploring the vast, imposing palace and formal gardens at Versailles; climbed hundreds of steps up to the famous white basilica of Sacré Coeur; taken in dinner and a show at the exotic Moulin Rouge; and even spent a leisurely afternoon wandering around the fascinating Latin Quarter on the Rive Gauche.

Today was their final day though, and she was very much looking forward to a more artistic day visiting the Louvre and viewing its priceless paintings and *objets d'art*.

Maeve taught Maths in a North London secondary school. She was not particularly artistic, knew next to nothing about art and paintings, but had always been in awe of creative people like her best friend Sally, who taught art in the classroom opposite hers. She might be at home discussing symmetry and mathematical shapes with her school students, but she had no idea how people managed to make beautiful works of art.

Artists were such curious and fascinating creatures. Where did all their ideas come from? How did they learn their craft? Was it natural or did it involve hard work too? Could *anyone* become an artist?

There was a family legend that her maternal grandmother had been a Parisian artist, or perhaps an artist's model, she wasn't sure which. But since her mum had abandoned Maeve when she was a toddler, she knew next to nothing about that side of the family, except a few hazy details that her dad had reluctantly provided. Hence the alluring shroud of mystery around this French grandmother.

One day, she had resolved, she would investigate her family tree. She'd even brought her grandmother's last known address with her on this trip, thinking perhaps...

But it would have been ludicrous to turn up on some unknown and possibly long-gone Frenchwoman's doorstep, wouldn't it? So she had not acted on that impulse, burying it deeper with every day that passed.

'Maeve will know the answer,' someone said close by, and she turned, instantly eager to help.

'Yes?'

'Which way is the River Seine?' Mr Endersley asked in his thick Yorkshire accent.

His dainty wife added with a smile, 'We fancy the idea of a boat trip down to the cathedral of Notre Dame and back. Such lovely weather for going on the river, isn't it?'

'What a good idea. Though don't forget the sunscreen this time,' Maeve said, glancing at Mr Endersley's reddened forehead. 'Those open-top boats are suntraps.' She paused, biting her lip as their query sunk in. 'Actually, I'm sorry, but I don't know how to get to the river from here,' she admitted. 'We'd better ask Betsy. Or look at a map. I've got one in my rucksack.'

Mr Endersley frowned. 'Eh? But we heard you telling someone you was born right here in Paris.'

Oh dear, Maeve thought, seeing a few interested

glances turning their way.

'I was born here, yes,' she agreed hurriedly. 'But my parents took me to live in the UK as a baby and I've never been back to France since. Until now, that is.' She flushed, catching Mrs Endersley's look of disbelief. 'So my birthplace is purely a technicality, I'm afraid.'

Betsy came bustling past, intent on some errand of her own, and the Endersleys turned to ask her for directions to the river.

Without waiting to make sure everyone got to where they wanted to go, Maeve slipped away towards the Louvre, which was thankfully so famous and well-signposted she couldn't possibly miss it.

A group of giggling French girls swarmed past her and she stood aside for them, listening with a stab of curiosity to their swift rattling French.

French. Her mother's native tongue.

Not having known her mother beyond the age of three, her grasp on that language had grown sadly more tenuous as the years passed. Of course she had taken French at school, but only to age sixteen, and had forgotten much of it since then, having concentrated on her favourite maths and science subjects after that.

Maybe after this holiday she could sign up for a French evening class. There had been some embarrassing moments over the past few days, struggling with a language she really ought to know better. Though her work at the school was so demanding, she didn't have much free time for leisure pursuits.

The amazement on Mrs Endersley's face came back to her as she joined the long, snaking queue for entrance to the Louvre.

Perhaps it was strange that she'd never visited France before, considering that Paris had been her birthplace. But her life was so busy... And she had intended to visit the Parisian building where, according to a scribble on the back of a photograph, she had been born.

She'd found the photo in a dusty old album left behind by her mother and studied the smiling, fair-haired young woman cradling a baby – Maeve herself, her dad had confirmed – standing in front of a very French-looking apartment building. Her grandmother's residence, apparently. She'd even managed to locate the address on a map of Paris. But she hadn't plucked up courage to go there during this tour, and now it was too late...

Anyway, her mother had abandoned her and Dad to run off with another man. They had never heard from her again, and her father had raised her alone in London. So she didn't owe her mother's family anything.

Besides, she didn't know if her grandmother was still in residence in that tall building with its white shutters and balconies with terracotta pots of colourful geraniums. She might have moved home or even died by now. People didn't live forever. There might be strangers living at that address. It would have been too horribly embarrassing to knock at the door and be confronted with an uncomprehending French stranger.

This last-minute Paris coach tour had been an attempt to get back in touch with her roots, she suspected. But that side of it had been a bit half-hearted, which was unlike her. So she'd stuck to the itinerary like everyone else and tried to push those ideas of reconnecting aside.

It had been a silly notion anyway, looking up her long-lost French relatives, and she wasn't generally given to frivolous ideas.

So that was that.

End of.

Maeve spent an exhausting but utterly marvellous few hours traipsing around the vast, echoing galleries of the Louvre, wandering beneath gloriously decorative ceilings that gave her a crick in the neck just staring up at them. She stood motionless for some time, ignoring the buffeting crowds all around her, to admire the Winged Victory of Samothrace on the Daru staircase and the beautiful, smooth-marbled Venus de Milo, apparently dating from one-hundred-and-fifty-years BCE. She studied the imposing Coronation of Napoleon with polite interest and bit her lip at Psyche Revived By Cupid's Kiss, which made her feel very far from sensible for a moment.

And, of course, she diligently waited her turn to stand for a few dizzying seconds in front of the Mona Lisa by Leonardo da Vinci.

That beguiling smile...

After all the hype and dramatic build-up, she'd half-expected to find the world-famous painting ordinary. Too much of a fuss made about nothing. It was only a bit of paint daubed on a canvas, after all.

Instead, she was bowled over by the painting's subtle, mysterious beauty and its air of undisclosed secrets. She came away from viewing the Mona Lisa with a sense of having had her world enlarged, even though she couldn't say exactly how or why. But she was glad she'd taken the time to queue up and view da Vinci's masterpiece.

She took lunch in one of the swish Louvre bistros, despite needing to use her credit card for the bill once again. This was what she'd been saving for, surely? The chance to treat herself after years of careful parsimony, mending rather than replacing, eating and living simply. Maeve wasn't sure she believed in astrology one hundred percent, but she was a Virgo, and her general star sign description did tally with the way she preferred to live. Clean, careful, simple, thrifty.

She wasn't so keen on the idea of Virgos as fussy, nit-picking perfectionists. Yet, with a grin, she had to accept it wouldn't be a totally unfounded accusation...

Lingering over coffee, since she still had a good hour before the coach was due to leave, she wrote a few chatty postcards to colleagues at the school – though to their home addresses, as school was out for summer. Finally, to her best friend Sally, she wrote more candidly of her odd reaction to the Mona Lisa portrait, and ended with a smiley face icon, finishing, *Wish you were here!*

Though she was rather enjoying being on her own, in fact.

School was a madly busy environment, and although she lived alone now that her father had passed away, the building that housed her small North London apartment was often noisy, with slamming doors and echoing footsteps in the stairwell, and always a child somewhere either shouting, laughing or crying. Every other flat in the building seem to house a family with children, many of them quite young. It was nice to be surrounded by so much vibrant life. But sometimes she longed for peace and quiet, and dreamed of a little cottage somewhere in the country, with a walled garden and perhaps a stream running through it. Ridiculous, really, as she knew it would never happen. Not on her salary as a teacher!

Finishing her postcards, she stuck a French stamp onto each one, double-checked the addresses, and then hurried round to a post box near the Louvre. She had politely enquired from a passer-by where she could post her letters and postcards, and marked the place on her little map. The road was busy but the pavement was thronging with tourists. She found herself constantly sidestepping or bumping into people, and was glad to turn a corner into a side street where it was relatively quiet.

The late afternoon sun beat down on her shoulders as she swung her rucksack off her back, rummaged inside for the postcards before slipping them into the postbox in the wall.

The sound of muted sobbing made her turn in surprise. An elderly lady, possibly in her late seventies and very elegantly dressed, was seated on the kerb a few feet away, clutching her ankle. Tourists will walking around her, paying no attention.

Still zipping up her rucksack, Maeve hurried over. '*Excusez-moi, Madame... Est-ce que je peux vous aider?*' she stammered in her rusty French, though her language skills had much improved even on this short trip to France, words coming back to her that she hadn't even realised she knew.

As the woman lifted a tear-stained face towards her, frowning into the sunshine without a word,

Maeve tried again in English. 'Erm, have you fallen? Can I help you?'

'Oh, you are kind, Mademoiselle,' the lady said in good English, but with a charming French accent. She lifted a shaking hand to shield her eyes from the sun. 'Yes, I took a bad step and twisted my ankle. I've been here some minutes... Nobody else has stopped to help me.'

'How horrid.' Maeve felt awful for her. 'Can you stand?'

'I'm not sure.'

'Here, take my hand and we'll find out.' Maeve helped the old lady to her foot to her feet and supported her, one arm around her shoulders. 'How's that?'

'*Bien*, let me try a step or two... *Ah, non!*' The lady winced, unsteady on her feet and unable to do much more than hop. It was clear her ankle was badly twisted.

'Oh dear. Can I fetch someone for you?'

'*Merci, oui.* My grandson has a car. He's meant to be meeting me soon, in the next street along, but I'll never get there in this state.'

'I could go and find him for you.' Maeve didn't much like the idea of leaving her alone though. 'I know... Do you have a mobile phone? Perhaps in your handbag? You could call and let him know what's happened. Then he could come and collect you.'

'How silly of me. Yes, of course.' She bit her

lip. 'My phone, it's in, erm... *ma poche.*' The lady had reverted to French, clearly in too much agony over her twisted ankle to find the English words. With a pained frown, she fumbled in her jacket pocket, finding the phone and calling the number. 'Will you wait with me until he arrives, mademoiselle? I'm sorry to be such a nuisance.'

'No, of course I'll wait,' she said, then muttered, 'If he's not too long.' She was feeling slightly anxious and wished she could check the time on her phone. But the phone was in her rucksack, and it would look rude to stop and rummage about for it. She'd noted the time as she left the museum to post her letters though and knew that she'd need to be back at the coach quite soon or face ridicule from her fellow travellers. Especially after being so stern with Petunia about not turning up late again.

Though she could hardly leave this unfortunate lady hobbling along the street alone, could she? And there would still be time to make the deadline if she walked briskly.

The lady was speaking rapidly into her phone in French, presumably to her grandson. There was a pause, then she tutted loudly and spoke in a more agitated fashion, spitting out words that Maeve couldn't quite follow, but they sounded almost angry.

Perhaps her grandson couldn't pick her up immediately.

Worried again about the deadline approaching, Maeve felt a flicker of dread and hoped he wouldn't keep them waiting too long. She strongly disliked being late for anything. Besides, it would be too awful if she missed the coach leaving and had to make her own way home. Apart from anything else, her suitcase was already stowed on the coach, ready for the usual Customs inspection at Calais, so she would have no clean clothes until she got home.

'He's on his way,' the old lady said, putting away her phone. She was looking relieved. 'But how rude of me. I'm Madame Rémy.' She held out a hand, and Maeve shook it. 'Might I know my rescuer's name?'

'I'm Maeve Eden,' she said, smiling. *'Enchantée, Madame.'*

The noisy racket of a motorbike approaching didn't attract her attention until it slowed and abruptly swerved her way. Then, out of the corner of her eye, she caught a leather-clad arm reaching down to grab her rucksack, sitting beside her on the pavement.

'Hey!' she shouted in panic, making a grab for the bag as she suddenly realised what was happening. But she was still shaking Madame Rémy's hand, and in the precious seconds that it took to gently disentangle herself, the bag had been stolen and the motorcyclist was revving away.

'Thief! *Voleur!*' Incensed, Maeve dashed after the motorcyclist, who had mercifully been forced to slow as a car swerved in front of him. 'Come back here!'

To her relief, her rucksack was still dangling from the rider's hand. As the rider struggled to negotiate the blockage, she lurched forward, making a grab for it. At that moment though, he lifted it away from her and simultaneously opened up the throttle. In the next few seconds, he sped away down the street, the roar of the engine deafening.

Maeve, who had thrown herself headlong after the biker in one last desperate attempt to retrieve her property, lost her footing on a loose grating.

With a despairing cry, she tumbled forward, cracking her head on hot dirty tarmac…

CHAPTER TWO

She came to with an aching head, blinded by full sunshine in her face, being lifted out of the road by two men. One was a burly, middle-aged gendarme, judging by his uniform, moustachioed and wearing a grim expression. The other man was lean and dark, in black jeans and black shirt, somewhere in his early thirties. His dark hair was surprisingly long for a man, silky strands brushing his shoulders.

Maeve focused on that silky black hair without comprehension, blinking in pained surprise as she tried to process who these men were and why they were manhandling her.

'What... Whatever happened?' she muttered as they lowered her onto the alcove seat in some very welcome shade. Her legs were shaky and she put a hand to her aching head, which felt as though someone had tried to split it open with an axe. 'Good grief. Feels like I... I cracked my skull.'

'Stay still and try not to speak, Mademoiselle,' the silky-haired man told her in such fast-paced French she could barely follow what he was saying. But it seemed to be along the gist of,

'You've banged your head. And don't move too much either. It could be dangerous.'

Maeve didn't argue, for she did indeed feel sick and dizzy. She wasn't even sure how she'd got there. The two men moved away, muttering together, possibly about her, and she closed her eyes with a groan, struggling unpleasantly against nausea.

After a while, she found it possible to open her eyes without pain lancing through her head, and her breathing became less laboured. She studied the quiet Parisian street in baffled silence, not recognizing a single thing and having no clue what she was doing there.

Gradually, memory came back to her and she recalled the coach tour, the Louvre visit, the elderly lady with the hurt ankle, and she jerked upwards, staring in consternation down the street. 'My rucksack. I remember now. There was a motorcyclist.' Panic ripped through her. 'He... He stole my bag. Oh no!'

Both men was staring at her blankly. But she'd been speaking in English. They probably had no idea what she was saying.

Painstakingly, in stammering French, Maeve sat up straighter and tried to explain more calmly and clearly what had happened. It was hard to think of the correct words when her heart was thumping with panic, but she tried her best. 'There was a lady. Madame... something. Rémy, that was it! Madame Rémy. She'd fallen in the street. I stopped to help her.' She paused, wincing as she recalled her own painful fall. 'And while I was looking the other way, a motorcyclist came along and stole my bag.'

Glancing around though, she couldn't see Madame Rémy anywhere, and wondered with a stab of betrayal if the woman had been in on the theft, maybe part of some Parisian bag-snatch gang. And the old lady had seemed so nice too.

Goodness. Had she only pretended to have fallen over to distract Maeve while her bag was stolen?

The man with black hair seemed to have accurately gauged her thoughts. He shook his head, bending to check her over with cool, efficient hands.

'Madame Rémy is my grandmother,' he said in excellent, barely accented English, and flashed her a wry grin when she studied him in surprise. 'Yes, I speak English. My grandmother was horrified when that motorcyclist stole your bag. And I did try to stop him, pulling my car in front of the bike. But he still got away.'

Maeve recalled the car that had swerved into the motorcyclist's path. So that had been him. 'Well, thank you for trying, at least.'

'You're welcome. But look, don't worry… This gendarme was on the corner and saw the whole thing. He's already filed a report, so other police will be looking out for your thief.' He stopped to study her face, frowning. 'Meanwhile, you must let us help you, mademoiselle. You have a nasty swelling on your forehead and ought to be checked over at a hospital.'

Maeve thought that was a good idea. She probably ought to be seen at a hospital, as her head was throbbing. She might even have concussion after hitting her head on the pavement. And she felt guilty now about suspecting that poor old lady of being involved.

'How is your grandmother?' she asked meekly.

'I don't think her ankle is badly hurt. Just twisted. But I put her in a taxi and sent her to hospital with my sister anyway, while you were unconscious. Just in case she needs an X-ray.'

'Goodness,' she said, blinking. 'how long was I unconscious?'

'Not long. But we made you lie still until we were sure you hadn't broken any bones. Don't you remember?'

'I don't remember much,' she said frankly. 'Except letting go of the bag and banging my head. Which reminds me, if you do catch the motorcyclist, I'll need my bag back urgently,' she added in French, looking at the gendarme.

'Of course, mademoiselle,' the gendarme agreed, and took out a small tablet, which he proceeded to turn on. 'Your name?'

'Maeve Eden.'

'And can you describe this bag, Mademoiselle

Eden?'

'A rucksack. It contains all my money, my travel documents, my phone, my souvenirs... Oh, and my passport!' Shocked, the full weight of what had happened sinking in, she clasped both hands to her cheeks and stared up at them in horror. '*My passport*! I won't be able to get back to England without a passport.' Then she remembered something else and her eyes widened. 'Oh crikey, the time! What time is it? Erm, *quelle heure est-il?*'

Madame Rémy's grandson checked his watch. 'A quarter past five.'

'Quarter past – Oh Lord!'

Maeve struggled to get to her feet and began hobbling away, her head throbbing painfully. Then she stopped dead, realising she had no idea which way to go for their rendezvous point. Right, and then left, and then right again? She'd marked the rendezvous point in her travel notebook and on her city map. But both the map and notebook were in her rucksack. And her rucksack was somewhere in Paris, no doubt being emptied of her precious belongings at this very moment.

'Mademoiselle, please... You need to sit down.' The man in jeans had come after her. 'You're confused and in no fit state to go anywhere.'

'But the coach tour... I have to get back to my coach, don't you see?' She was speaking in English again, her brain too frazzled to try communicating in a foreign language. 'The coach was due to leave for Calais at five. Rendezvous at five o'clock sharp, Betsy said – she's our tour guide – so I must find her and make her wait. Or I'll miss the boat back home to England.'

'But, mademoiselle, even if this Betsy has waited for you and the coach is still there, you don't have a passport,' the man pointed out gently in English. 'So there's no point attempting to reach Calais.'

She gulped. 'Oh.'

'Don't worry, I'm sure it will be a simple enough matter to sort this out. First, you must give the gendarme a full description of your bag and its contents, then I will help you contact the British Embassy.' He paused, looking a touch impatient when she said nothing but continued to look about wildly, as though wishing Betsy and her coach tour would appear and rescue her from this disaster. 'But hospital before the Embassy, yes? You are not looking well, mademoiselle.'

She could see the good sense in that. 'I suppose I should go to a hospital, yes,' she said slowly, and batted away a stupid tear. Whatever was the point in crying? She never cried. Except perhaps at funerals or over old photographs. She was in shock, that was all. And the bang on the head wasn't helping. 'I expect Betsy won't have waited for me, anyway. Five o'clock sharp, she said. Not five past. And certainly not a quarter past.

Besides, even if you drove me to the coach right now, by the time we arrived...'

She was babbling, she realised, and moaned in despair. But the gendarme calmly led her back to the alcove seat and took her statement, noting down her name and British address, and what little she could remember of the theft, even taking the man's name too, as he had been a witness too.

'Leo Rémy,' the man told him calmly.

'*Merci*, Monsieur Rémy.' The gendarme paused, studying him curiously, then added what sounded like, 'Leo Rémy? The artist?'

'*Oui, c'est moi.*'

Leo Rémy. The artist.

Maeve blinked, wondering what he meant but it hardly seemed a good time to ask. Besides, her head was aching again. Perhaps she really did have concussion.

Once the burly policeman had gone, reminding her to call at his police station in a day or two for any updates, Leo Rémy helped her towards his car. It was indeed the vehicle that had slewed across the path of the motorcycle, a sleek black car with blacked-out windows.

'Hospital first,' he reminded her, helping Maeve into the front seat of the car as carefully as though she were an invalid.

To her chagrin, Leo insisted on accompanying

her into the hospital casualty department, a visit made even more awkward by her complete lack of documents. With no way of proving her identity or nationality, and with no method of payment available to her, Maeve struggled to assure the receptionists, nurses and doctors in turn that she had an NHS card guaranteeing free health care in France and would produce it as soon as the police caught her *voleur*. (Assuming they ever caught him or retrieved her belongings, that is, she thought grimly, but tried to stay positive.) The receptionist in particular had not seemed very confident in what she was saying and, in the end, Leo had to intervene, using his own bank card to pay for her treatment and ignoring Maeve's repeated demands to be told his bank details so she could reimburse him as soon as humanly possible.

Once payment had been made, she was treated with impressive speed and efficiency, and only discharged from the emergency department once the doctors had concluded she was showing no signs of concussion. But she was given a list of worrying symptoms to watch out for – blurred vision, headache, dizziness, confusion or drowsiness – and told to come back for another check-up if anything didn't feel right within the next few days.

Refusing to leave her to make her own way there on foot, Leo drove her to the British Embassy, even though it was late at night by then. But she had nowhere else to go, did she?

It was clear he didn't want to leave her there, especially with the place mostly in darkness, but she'd decided enough was enough. The man was a perfect stranger, and although it was very kind of him to be driving her about like a taxi service, she was chafing at the bit to feel like less of a passenger in life and to take charge of her own destiny again.

'*Merci*, Monsieur,' she told him, holding up a firm hand as he attempted to follow her to the embassy entrance, 'but I'll take it from here. You've been very kind.'

Leo began to protest, but sighed and gave a weary shrug when Maeve glared at him. '*Bien*, but please take my telephone number, at least.' He handed her a business card. 'In case of any problems.'

'Thank you. And... well, *thank you*,' she said, flushing as she considered how rude she'd been. It wasn't like her to be rude. But she had suffered a bang on the head and a tremendous shock, so maybe she should allow herself a little leeway on this occasion. 'I'm really very grateful for all your help today, Monsieur Rémy.'

'Leo,' he corrected her, shook her hand, and headed back towards his car. '*Au revoir, Mademoiselle Eden. Bonne chance.*'

She hesitated as he walked away, suddenly

uneasy, and had to restrain herself from calling him back.

It was ridiculous, of course. But now that the coach tour had well and truly departed for Calais, having probably reached it and the ferry by now, Leo was the only person she knew in Paris. Well, him and his elegant grandmother, Madame Rémy. And watching as he drove away with a final wave of his hand left her feeling distinctly alone and friendless.

CHAPTER THREE

Her hands in her jacket pockets, Maeve waited with a fake smile on her face until his car had disappeared out of view before making her way to the door. She didn't want him to suspect how vulnerable she felt. Which was silly. If she couldn't accept help now, of all times, when could she? There was being independent and there was being pointlessly wilful, and perhaps this time she was erring on the wrong side of stubborn.

The embassy did indeed look shut for the night, with only a few dim lights visible through narrow windows. But there were two uniformed security guards patrolling outside the closed front entrance door to the embassy who gave her sharp assessing looks as she approached the building.

One guard barred her way, saying in English, 'Sorry, Miss, but the embassy is closed now. You'll need to call the out of hours helpline.' He pointed to a sign on the wall.

'I don't have a phone.'

He looked taken aback. 'I suggest you come back in the morning, then.'

'But this is an emergency.' Briefly, she explained her situation, and the man listened carefully, and then turned away to make a quick phone call.

When he came back, he shook his head, looking glum.

'Sorry, Miss,' he repeated, 'but no one's free to see you tonight. There's a private embassy party going on and most staff have the night off.'

Fury flashed through her. 'Marvellous. I do hope there's dancing. And fruit punch.'

The guard pulled a face. 'I can see you're upset. But nobody's actually dead, you see, so... '

'I might be dead if I have to hang about the streets of Paris all night with nowhere to sleep,' she pointed out. 'I have no money and no documents.'

'I understand that, yes.' He shuffled his feet, looking embarrassed. 'Look, the best I can suggest is for you to wait outside here until first thing in the morning. Not ideal, but that would guarantee you being seen as early as possible. Besides, perhaps someone will become available before then if you wait? You'll be pretty safe here. Especially with us about.' His grin died at her stern expression, and he glanced nervously up at the clear dark skies above the city rooftops instead. 'At least it's not likely to rain tonight.'

With only a perfunctory word of thanks, she stomped away down the street, cross and dispirited, before realizing that she still had nowhere to go and no money. She walked for some time, trying to put off the inevitable. But there was only one thing she could do, unless she wanted to spend the whole night outside. She was growing chilly and felt bone-tired. Besides, Leo's card was burning a hole in her pocket. And the last thing she needed was a hole in her pocket on top of everything else…

Swearing under her breath, she returned to the guard and asked with restrained politeness if she could use his phone to make a local call.

'Hello?' she said rather breathlessly when the ring tone stopped. 'Is… Is that Monsieur Rémy?'

There was a short silence. Then Leo asked in a deep, abrupt voice, 'Maeve?'

Briefly, trying to sound calm and in control, though in fact she was frankly terrified and exhausted, Maeve explained her situation.

'It seems no one can deal with me until tomorrow morning. Meanwhile, I've no money and nothing to wear except the clothes on my back. I know this is a huge inconvenience but you said if I needed help that I could call you. And I was just wondering if…' She tailed off, horribly embarrassed. Good grief. What on earth was she thinking, asking this Frenchman, this complete stranger to help her out? She must've been mad even to consider such a thing. Maybe it was the bang on the head… 'I'm sorry,' she stammered, 'I shouldn't have called. It's nothing to do with you,

Monsieur Rémy. Please forget what I said.'

'No, of course I'll help you. It would be my pleasure, Mademoiselle.'

Even though she'd asked for his help in the first place, Maeve cringed inwardly, wishing she had the strength to decline. But she was simply too tired and distressed to turn him down. She'd always been fiercely independent and loathed relying on other people. But right now she badly needed someone to lend a hand, even if it was only to offer her a bed for the night. And maybe a cup of tea.

Goodness, she would *kill* for a nice hot cup of tea.

'I'll come back and collect you,' Leo went on smoothly. 'You can stay here with us. We have plenty of room. Are you still at the Embassy? I'm on the other side of the city from you, I'm afraid, and in my pyjamas now. So it'll take maybe an hour to sort things out here and come to get you. Can you manage alone for an hour?'

'Absolutely. I'll walk up and down, or around the block a few times. Oh, but you are amazing… Thank you so much. You're sure it's not an inconvenience?'

'Not at all.' Leo sounded amused rather than annoyed. 'I'll let my grandmother know at once. She's gone to bed but I'm sure she'll still be awake. She's been fretting about you ever since she got home. Trust me, this news will cheer her up.' And with that, he rang off.

She handed the phone back to the security guard. 'I've found a bed for the night,' she told him, and saw the man's brows shoot up. She didn't know what he was thinking but she could guess by the cynical look in his eyes. 'Thanks for your help,' she added shortly, determined to stay polite. 'I'll be back first thing tomorrow.'

He touched his cap. 'Goodnight, Miss.'

Maeve set off on a leisurely walk around the block, keeping within well-lit areas only, as she didn't like the idea of standing around on a street corner. The last thing she needed was to be mistaken for someone touting for trade. Though the guard had assured her it was a respectable area, so she ought to be safe enough.

She walked as slowly as possible without actually grinding to a halt, sometimes whistling or humming under her breath to appear cheerful to passers-by, and constantly checking over her shoulder. Lightning might rarely strike twice but she still felt vulnerable since being targeted by a snatch-and-grab biker.

Respectable the area might be, but her heart was thumping the whole way and it was hard to stay calm. The occasional motorbike that came zooming along the quiet Parisian street made her stiffen and draw back against the wall, glaring after each unfortunate rider in case it was her thief. But nobody else attacked her. Passers-by mostly ignored her, in fact, absorbed in their own thoughts, hurrying home from a late work shift or some evening entertainment, and fifteen minutes later she was safely back outside the embassy.

The guards grinned as she passed them again, heading around the block for a second time, walking more briskly now and swinging her arms, for the night was growing chilly and she was only wearing a light summer jacket.

Thank goodness she'd chosen jeans for today's excursion to the Louvre rather than shorts. It might be full summer, but it still would have been a bit on the nippy side, strolling about the capital at night with bare legs.

I'm in my pyjamas...

Had Leo Rémy really said that on the phone?

She felt guilty at the thought of having disturbed him on his way to bed, poor man. But also knew a jolt of curiosity, envisaging him in some stylish, belted dressing-gown that stopped mid-thigh.

Good Lord.

Her mind needed to be cleaned out with wire wool.

At last, on her fourth time around the block, feeling weary and bored, a car pulled up sharply behind her in a side street.

Startled, Maeve jumped back from the kerb, fists up and ready to do battle with some unknown assailant. Struggling for a stringent French phrase to use against some would-be attacker, she was embarrassed to see Leo Rémy gazing coolly back at her through the open driver's window.

'Get in,' he said unceremoniously, for his large, expensive vehicle was blocking the narrow street and another car had already come up behind them, the man behind the wheel sounding his horn despite it being past midnight.

'Parisian drivers are so impatient,' she grumbled, climbing in beside her rescuer, and then bit her lip. 'Oh, I'm sorry. That probably sounded horribly rude. You're a Parisian driver too, aren't you?'

Leo shot her an enigmatic look, accelerating away with barely a glance in his rear view mirror for the car behind. 'Put your seat belt on,' was all he said.

So, fumbling with her seat belt, Maeve found herself back in Leo Rémy's increasingly familiar car, this time heading at speed through dark Parisian streets with no real idea how she was going to get through the next day or maybe two until this mess was sorted out. Somewhere out there, the coach tour would even now be on a boat back to England. If only she hadn't gone round that corner to post her postcards. If only she had headed back to the coach earlier, or even at the last minute, and never walked down that stupid sidestreet...

They exploded out of an empty side street onto a far busier avenue, bright headlights blinding her as Leo threaded a path between swiftly moving vehicles without even slowing. Someone else honked a horn at them but Leo didn't pay any attention, overtaking aggressively.

She wondered where all these people were going at such an early hour of the morning. Did nobody in Paris go to bed?

'You drive awfully fast,' she said out loud, without really thinking through how that would sound.

Rude, she realised a split-second late, grimacing. Very, very rude. And ungrateful. Yet again.

But it was said now.

He hesitated before answering, 'This is my normal speed.' He sounded mildly surprised.

Maeve tried not to say anything else about it. She pressed her lips tightly together and stared straight ahead. But as he weaved like a maniac through a busy intersection, almost hitting another equally fast-moving motorist and practically scraping the side of a lumbering night bus, she blurted out, 'Do you have many accidents?'

'Never.' There was a short silence as he slowed for a red light ahead, which kindly turned back to green before they reached it. Though 'slowed' didn't really sum up the jolting change from insanely fast to almost dead-stop, returning to insanely fast at such a pace that Maeve could have sworn she felt her brain hit the back of her head and rebound, wobbling painfully. 'Well, perhaps *once*.'

'Perhaps? Either you had an accident or you didn't.'

'It was the other driver's fault.'

'Oh, naturally.'

He flashed her a sharp look. 'You know I'm doing you a favour, *oui*?'

'Yes, of course. Sorry.'

She felt ridiculously tearful again, and clasped her hands in her lap. Her empty hands. No purse with cash and cards to help her navigate the world like everyone else. No phone to check for messages or social media updates. No notebook crammed with important times and dates and instructions so she wouldn't be late for whatever came next. Not even a bag containing a modicum of make-up, plus her sunglasses, lip balm, hand sanitiser, crossword book and other vital knick-knacks.

'I didn't mean to criticize you,' she went on. 'In fact, you've been marvellously kind, taking me in like this. I was just trying to distract myself.'

'No, I'm the one who should be sorry.' Leo slackened off his pace, turning a corner and heading uphill at a more reasonable speed. Which was still too fast for her. 'I had forgotten how much slower the British drive. No wonder you were scared.'

'Not scared,' she said at once, sitting up straight, lips pursed. 'I just thought maybe you were in training for a Formula One race.'

He laughed then, a hoarse bark of genuine amusement. 'Now you sound like my grandmother.'

She sneaked a shy look at him, studying his lean, hawkish profile. 'You know the UK well, then? I suppose you must. You speak very good English.'

'My mother is British.'

'Oh, really? Will I meet her? And your father?'

'My father hasn't lived with us in years.' Leo was looking ahead, not at her, but she sensed a shift in atmosphere, his hands tightening on the wheel. She instantly regretted having made him uncomfortable. Her insatiable curiosity again, always asking questions… 'And my mother is dead.'

'I'm so sorry.' Now she felt awful.

'No need to be. It was all a long time ago. Anyway, I wouldn't worry about your lost passport. I'll drive you back to the embassy tomorrow morning and I'm sure it will all be sorted out soon enough.' He paused, frowning. 'But even if it takes another day or so, we're very happy to put you up at Château Rémy. I left my sister Bernadette sorting out a guest room for you. I hope you'll enjoy your stay with us.'

Maeve stared at him, taken aback. Château

Rémy? That sounded rather grand. 'It must be a big house,' she said cautiously. 'I'm very grateful to your sister too. Are there many people living there, or just you, your grandmother and Bernadette?'

He bared his teeth in a wolfish grin. 'I wish! No, we always have a full house at the château. Cousins, siblings, hangers-on.' When she said nothing, feeling awkward, he glanced at her sideways. 'I wasn't including you in that category, of course. You are very welcome to stay. If you hadn't so kindly stopped to help my grandmother, none of this would have happened to you. You would have been on that ferry back to England by now, *n'est-ce pas?*'

He really was rather good at reading her mind, she realised, which made her a little uneasy.

'True, but I think that debt has been well and truly repaid by now, don't you think? You and your family have been more than generous, Monsieur Rémy.'

'Leo, please. But let's not talk about my family. Between you and me, talking about my family gives me a headache. What about you? Is there anyone at home you need to contact? Mother? Father?' His dark gaze flashed to her ring finger, which was bare. But he still added speculatively, 'A boyfriend or husband expecting you off the boat tonight?' He paused. 'Or a girlfriend, perhaps?'

This made her gurgle with laughter. 'No, no boyfriend or husband. And no, I'm not gay, so no girlfriend either. Plus, my parents are both dead.'

'My apologies,' he said gravely. 'I didn't mean to pry.'

'Oh yes, you did.'

'Well,' he murmured, head on one side as he considered that possibility, 'maybe a little.'

'Oh, *un peu?*'

'*Peut-être,*' he agreed smoothly, his lips twitching.

'You are insufferable.'

'It has been said.' Unexpectedly, Leo slammed on the brakes and reversed at speed into a tiny parking space, leaving the car bumper to bumper with others in the narrow Parisian side street. 'Here we are. Château Rémy is just around the corner. I'm afraid we sold off the parking area to generate cash, so we have to park wherever we can now.' He got out of the car, and she scrambled out after him, peering about the dark street in confusion. 'Follow me, mademoiselle.'

They walked across the road from his parking place and up a steep, narrow, cobbled alleyway. Maeve blinked. Could she see turrets up ahead?

Sure enough, the looming shapes in the darkness were revealed to be turrets, surreal and unlikely in a busy Parisian street, somehow squeezed in between stately apartment buildings and modern office and shopping blocks. The turrets, picked out by multiple spotlights set at ground level, were topped with red-tiled circular roofs above high stone walls blanketed in thick, ivy-like creepers.

Like something out of a fairy tale, she thought, glancing at her host's back.

Who *was* he?

CHAPTER FOUR

Leo Rémy... The artist.

That was what the gendarme had said on the street near the Louvre, his expression one of recognition and perhaps even grudging respect.

So Monsieur Rémy was well-known in Paris, at least. And as an artist.

But what kind of artist? The traditional sort who painted portraits and landscapes? Or the wacky experimental type who bunged a load of bricks in a wheelbarrow and called it 'art'?

Maeve knew which sort she preferred. A painter who stood musing for hours in front of an oil painting, a paintbrush between his teeth... That was the old romantic image of an artist, and one she revered and instinctively approved of. That kind of art was born from many hours of hard work, endless canvases painted and thrown aside in despair, alongside a lifelong study of the great masters...

But there was something unsettling about Leo Rémy that made her suspect he was the other type. A wheelbarrow of bricks artist.

She followed in silence as he trod swiftly up the

uneven cobbled path, picking his way unerringly in the dark where she found herself stumbling. Then he ducked his head through a crumbling, narrow archway and led her around the back of some enormous building – the château itself, she guessed – while she trailed after him, feeling weary and a little lost, constantly missing her footing in the dark.

Where on earth was he taking her?

The path went on and on into gloom. High walls glowered down on them from all sides. Eventually, she realised they were skirting a garden. In fact, her eyes gradually adjusting to the darkness, she realised it was not even a garden. Just a narrow strip of yard separating the massive château from its nearest neighbours, consisting of a few ironwork benches and chairs set beside plants in troughs to lend a splash of greenery.

At last, they passed a row of tall, cream-shuttered double windows at ground level before reaching another arched entranceway, this time opening on an inner courtyard.

'This way,' he told her without glancing back.

This inner space was also cobbled, but made more welcoming by adequate lighting, allowing her to see several huge-leaved fig trees growing up against the walls, while bushy geraniums sprawled from stone urns set in pairs at intervals, marking out a pathway that led to a dilapidated-looking door.

Around the periphery of the courtyard, spotlights dazzled her eyes as they picked out a dozen or so windows on upper storeys.

Above their heads, the Parisian night sky glowed a soft dark orange, and she caught the muffled beep of a car horn on one of the streets below, the only reminders that they were in the heart of a great European city and not in the countryside.

Maeve stopped and turned on her heel, taking in these beautiful surroundings with surprised awe. So this was Château Rémy? 'It's very big, isn't it?' she murmured. 'Though I suppose that's why you call it a château.'

Leo, who was wrestling a large key out of a small inner pocket, flashed her a bemused look. 'I don't call it a château. It *is* a château. It's been a château for some four hundred years.'

'Goodness. And have the Rémy family owned it all that time?'

He hesitated, then shrugged. 'No, you've got me there. We did change the name. The Rémy family bought this place a few generations back. But it's a very old building.' He was wrestling again, only this time with the lock of the dilapidated back door. Cursing in French under his breath, he rattled the door handle and struggled with the iron key, which was long and ornate, looking like something out of the eighteenth century. 'And bits of it… keep… not working.' As he said this, the ancient-looking door handle came off in his hand. He bared his teeth, staring down at it. 'Or simply fall apart.'

'Oh dear.'

'Ah, the English and their mastery for understatement.' Leo bowed his head for a moment as though gathering his strength, and then pulled a mobile phone from his pocket. The screen lit up as he made a call. Somebody answered at the other end and he had a rapid-fire conversation in French with a woman. Who then hung up.

Replacing the phone in his pocket, Leo took a step back and looked up, craning his neck as he studied the upper stories. A light came on above and the sound of thudding feet could be heard.

Seconds later, the door was unlocked from the inside – with some difficulty, as it seemed the handle had become detached on the other side too – and flung open.

A young woman in her late teens or early twenties looked out at them, curvaceous and clad in a tightly belted gold dressing-gown with silky white pyjamas underneath and the unexpected addition of muddy hiking boots.

She had a round face and very pale skin, like a porcelain doll, with sleek dark hair exactly like Leo's, except it fell to the middle of her back in an elegant black shower. They shared the same dark brows and thrusting nose and impatient, thinned lips. His sister?

'What the hell, Leo?' The young woman spoke in French, though the rest of her short brutal speech was lost on Maeve, startled by the speed and ferocity of the woman's utterances. But she was clearly angry and resentful at having been roused at this late hour. No need for a translation to work that out.

Leo heard her out without any change of expression, then nodded over his shoulder at Maeve. 'Bernadette, allow me to introduce you to Mademoiselle Maeve Eden,' he said in pointed English. 'She's our guest tonight, so try to be polite.'

'Oh.' His sister regarded her with brief interest, a touch of hostility in her gaze. 'A new girlfriend?' she asked him in French, her tone sardonic.

Well, really...

Maeve decided to embarrass the other woman by ignoring her rudeness. 'Hello, I'm Maeve,' she said in slow, painstaking French, 'it's very kind of you and Leo to let me stay here tonight.' She seized Bernadette's hand and shook it before his sister could protest, giving her a big brave smile. 'My French isn't very good, I'm afraid. I hope you can understand me.'

At least, she hoped that's what she was saying. It was hard to tell, especially as the other woman didn't bother responding.

Bernadette pulled her hand free and transferred her unfriendly stare to her brother. 'Liselle is still in bed. She's been asking for you all day. Apparently, you haven't been to see her for days and you're ignoring her calls and texts too. For God's sake, Leo, just go and speak to the girl. Make her understand it's over, so the rest of us can get on with living our lives.' She turned back inside, then paused and added casually over her shoulder, '*Enchantée*, Mlle Eden.'

Then his sister stormed back up the stairs, her boots rapping on the uncarpeted stairs; for all the world, Maeve thought, like one of the Billy goats crossing the wooden bridge in the old folktale. Though that, she considered more carefully, would probably make her the troll living under it…

'I must apologise for my sister, Miss Eden,' Leo told her, bending to retrieve some screws that must have fallen out when the door handle broke, a frown of concentration tugging his brows together. 'She's not much of a charmer, I'm afraid. But I doubt anybody else is awake at this hour.'

'I hope you'll inform your sister that I'm *not* your girlfriend,' Maeve said with just the right amount of indignation, holding herself stiffly.

Leo looked amused. 'You caught that, did you? I thought you didn't speak much French.'

'It was hard to miss.'

'In that case, I'm sorry. I will certainly tell her. Though I'm sure she meant it is a joke.'

Maeve felt a little stab of annoyance. Why would

it be a joke? 'Excuse me?'

Without answering, Leo gestured her inside and shut the door behind them, again having to wrestle with the lock. Thankfully, this time it worked.

'I'll need to come back and fix this properly before I go to bed,' he muttered, then realised she was staring at him. 'What? Oh, *that*... Sorry, I've not been in the habit of asking women out on dates lately. Too busy, I guess.'

'Really? So, who's *Liselle*?'

He raised his brows. 'Is that any of your business, Miss Eden?'

She blushed fierily, and was glad he probably couldn't see her face that well in the dimly-lit hallway. 'Erm, no, sorry. You're right, that was uncalled-for.'

Her toes curled in embarrassment, which she now discovered was actually a thing. What on earth was wrong with her? She was ordinarily polite and well-behaved, especially with strangers. But there was something about this man that seemed to be lowering all those internal barriers she had taken years to erect. Well, in the morning, she would hurry back to the embassy as soon as possible and be out of their hair for good. Begone, Monsieur Rémy...

'As I said,' she added, stumbling over the words, 'this is very kind of you and I'm grateful.'

'No need to keep thanking me. You're very

welcome.' He nodded her towards the stairs. 'After you.'

She preceded him up the stairs and into a honeycomb of narrow, poorly-lit corridors with high ceilings, some hung with unlit chandeliers, some festooned with cobwebs, the walls decorated with dusty gilt-framed portraits of long-dead ancestors, each one bearing the name of the ancestor underneath on a gold scroll. Lights gave off a dull glow at intervals. The walls appeared to be painted a dull, glowering red where they weren't panelled in dark wood.

'Which way now?' she asked at the end of one corridor, her voice echoing in the enclosed space.

'Follow me,' Leo said, heading rapidly up another set of stairs, glancing over his shoulder to be sure she was still behind him. They passed through huge doorways and along corridors broad enough to drive a car down, and up and down staircases until she was flagging and quite unable to remember the way they had come in.

'How big is this place? We seem to have been walking for ages.' When he shot her an ironic look, she added guiltily, 'Sorry, but I've been up for hours and I'm bloody exhausted… If you'll pardon my French.'

He gave a rough bark of laughter. 'Your French is pardoned.' Stopping abruptly before a low door, he pushed it open with his foot and gestured her inside. 'Your room, my lady.'

He snapped on the light.

Wonderingly, Maeve stepped inside, looking about herself. It was a small attic room with a sloping ceiling.

Going straight to the window, which had no shutter but a tatty curtain on a rail, she looked out over the twinkling lights and dark roofs of Paris at night.

She guessed they must be high in one of the turrets. Perhaps at the very top, from the way the ceiling curved in on itself with ancient, exposed beams. He had called her 'my lady,' and although she knew it had been a silly joke, it put odd thoughts into her head. She wasn't much given to fanciful notions but rather liked the idea of being a princess trapped in a tower.

Rapunzel, Rapunzel, let down your long hair... Except her practical, shoulder-length hairstyle wouldn't get her very far during a rescue attempt, alas.

He watched her with a half-smile. 'I apologise for the long trek. I know you must be incredibly tired. But the only habitable rooms are already occupied, so we had to prepare an attic room instead.' He paused. 'I believe the bed's a little lumpy. But I hope it won't be too uncomfortable.'

She tested the bed with a hand. Yes, it was a little lumpy, and the furniture was old and ramshackle, and there were even packing cases and tea chests in one corner, partly covered with sheets. But the bed was a four-poster and had been made up with a lacy white cover and several large pillows, and the shaded light overhead was reassuringly modern.

Set against the wall opposite the bed was a heavily scratched dressing table with a cracked mirror, but someone had set fresh lilies in a glass vase there, filling the tiny room with their sweet, cloying scent. Plus, two fluffy and generously-sized white towels had been left on the bed for her personal use, which was thoughtful. She also noted with astonishment that the paperbacks stacked on the bedside cabinet were all in English. Talk about attention to detail!

'This is marvellous, thank you. Though I wish your grandmother hadn't gone to all this trouble for me. She was hurt this afternoon and should have been resting her ankle… I feel really bad.'

'Please don't concern yourself. My sister prepared the room for you. My grandmother merely directed her what to do. Besides, her ankle is much better.' As she lingered over the towels, he pointed down the corridor. 'I'm afraid there isn't an ensuite. But there's a good-sized bathroom with toilet just down there. Though if you prefer a shower, there's one on the floor below. Whichever you use, please remember to open the windows to let the steam out. It's an old-fashioned house and we haven't had any ventilation or air conditioning fitted.'

'Of course.'

He went to the door, glancing back at her. He was looking tired too now, and she felt guilty at having forced him to drive halfway across Paris to collect her, then kept him up with all this. 'Is there anything else you need?' he asked.

Maeve thought longingly of her suitcase, no doubt sailing merrily across the Channel by now, deep inside the belly of the coach she'd missed, containing all her lovely clean clothes and bathroom essentials. But she didn't want to appear rude by saying anything negative, so shook her head and smiled. 'No, this is brilliant. Thank you so much.'

'You said you'd been parted from your luggage.' As he looked her up and down, she wondered again if he was a mind-reader. 'Of course... You don't have any clothes. Including pyjamas.'

'It's alright, I'll manage.'

But he was frowning. 'I'll ask my sister if she can spare something for you. I daresay she won't have gone back to bed yet. Meanwhile, I'll bid you goodnight, and see you in the morning. No doubt you'll want a lift back to the embassy.'

'I don't want to put you out.'

His brows rose. 'It's too far for you to walk, and you don't have any money for public transport. It would be ludicrous not to offer you a lift. Besides, my grandmother wouldn't hear of letting you leave Château Rémy under your own steam.' He ran a hand through his hair, fatigue in his face. 'Goodnight, Miss Eden.'

'Good night, Monsieur Rémy.'

'Leo,' he reminded her.

Slightly nettled, she thrust her chin in the air, saying, 'Maeve, then.'

'Goodnight, Maeve,' he said softly and closed the door behind him.

Maeve stood there a moment, listening to the unfamiliar silence of the ancient château around her, and the muffled sounds of the city that continued even in the middle of the night. Slowly, she began to remove her shoes... Then the enormity of everything that had happened that day struck her. She sat down heavily on the bed and burst into tears.

'It'll be alright,' she sobbed under her breath, trying and failing to comfort herself. 'Everything is going to be all right.'

A knock at the door brought Maeve upright in a flash, horribly embarrassed.

'Um, hang on a tick... I mean, *un moment, s'il-vous-plaît.*'

Hurriedly, Maeve rubbed at her damp face and sniffed a few times, wishing she had a pack of travel tissues to hand, mortified to be caught weeping over something as insignificant as a missed bus and a stolen passport. But the tissue pack had been stowed neatly in her rucksack, so was now in the possession of criminals. No doubt that horrid biker was gleefully blowing his nose on her tissues right now, dreadful man…

'*Entrez!*' she called, struggling back to her feet.

CHAPTER FIVE

The door creaked open to reveal a elderly woman. She struck Maeve as being at least ninety years old, her face creased with fine wrinkles, her springing hair snow-white and wonderfully wild, her back stooped as she leant on a silver-topped cane. She was wearing a knee-length, dark-green woollen dress – despite the warmth of the summer night – a heavy silver crucifix glinting about her neck as she shuffled forward, one hand outstretched.

'*Ah, ma petite...*' Her cloudy hazel eyes were nonetheless still keen and intelligent, reminiscent of Leo's own penetrating gaze. 'Don't cry, my little one,' she told Maeve in French, her voice husky and guttural, like an ex-smoker's. 'It's not serious. You are safe now.' Her smile showed a row of teeth far too white and too perfect to be real. 'You are home.'

Home?

Maeve was baffled. Had the old lady mistaken her for somebody else? Or maybe her own powers of translation had reached the natural limit.

Politely, Maeve allowed the woman to take her

hand in a surprisingly strong grasp. '*Bonsoir, merci*... Gosh that's quite a grip you have there,' she added in English, too exhausted to reach for the right words in a foreign language. It had been one hell of a day, and the universe was apparently not yet finished with her. 'I'm Maeve.'

'Maeve,' the old lady repeated, smiling and nodding as though she already knew this.

To clarify matters, Maeve said slowly and loudly, 'Leo said I could stay. I'm just here for the night.'

'Leo, *oui, ah oui*.' The old lady's smile broadened. She really did have an extensive range of unblemished teeth, Maeve thought, smiling back at her. 'You will help Leo,' she added with a knowing wink. 'You will be his Muse.'

'His, *what*?'

Now Maeve was sure that her French had deserted her. Because that made no sense at all.

A 'Muse' was someone – usually female – who inspired an artist to create and often 'sat' for portraits as well. In the nude sometimes, if the Pre-Raphaelites were anything to go by...

As soon as she'd downed her obligatory coffee and croissant tomorrow morning, she'd be out of here and likely never see Château Rémy again. She'd have a job becoming anyone's Muse under those restricted circumstances. As for stripping off...

The only removal of clothing likely to happen

under this roof was when she jumped into a hot bath, a plan which seemed doomed to failure at this rate.

But the old lady was adamant.

'Yes, his Muse. That Liselle... Ah!' The explosive sound encapsulated both disbelief and laughing derision. 'That girl is finished... Done! She was never his Muse. Bah... She thought she was, but we all knew different. Now it is revealed...' The small dark eyes bored into Maeve. 'But you, little English...'

'Me?'

'Yes... *You* will bring out his paints again.'

'His... paints? Yes, if you like.' Had Leo lost his paints? What on earth was this conversation about?

Her brain was too befuddled to make head nor tail of it. But she smiled back anyway because she didn't want to be rude.

'*Bienvenue, p'tite!*' The old lady drew her close, warm and perfumed, and kissed her on both cheeks before exclaiming, 'Maeve! Maeve!' with a prophetic cry that echoed around the room.

'Yes, that's my name. Maeve.' The old lady wasn't letting her go, she realised, as she gently attempted to extricate herself. 'I'm terribly sorry, but if I could just...'

'Maman, what are you doing here?' a voice demanded.

Maeve was relieved to see Madame Rémy again,

now in a pink cotton dressing gown and slippers, a glass of water in her hand, standing in the doorway.

Rescue had arrived, it seemed.

At first sight of Madame Rémy, the old lady relinquished her grasp on Maeve and hurried away, leaning heavily on her cane. Muttering something in French, she was ushered from the room by Madame Rémy, who apologised profusely to Maeve in English. 'I'm so sorry. My mother… You must forgive her. She is very elderly and isn't always aware what she's doing.'

'*His Muse!*' The old lady threw over her shoulder before disappearing.

'Go to bed, Maman!' Tutting, Madame Rémy handed Maeve the glass of water. 'Here, I forgot to ask Bernadette to make sure you had water. Such a warm evening.'

'Oh, thank you, yes. But please don't worry about your mother. It's very good to see you again. I hope your ankle is better.'

'Much, thank you.'

'I'm so glad. And thank *you* so much for letting me stay tonight.' The old lady was already tap-tap-tapping along the attic landing with her cane. Maeve peered round the door after her. 'Your mother's lovely. And I'm not really sure what I'm doing either, most of the time,' she added in an undertone. 'So… I guess that means she must be Leo's great-grandmother?'

'Yes, she's ninety-two. Can you believe it? Wait for me, Maman! Don't try to manage the stairs alone...' Madame Rémy gave a dry laugh, and touched her arm. 'But you must be desperate for sleep. We'll see you at breakfast, I hope?'

'Yes, thank you again.' Maeve closed the door and leant against it on the other side, listening as the two women made their slow way back through the honeycomb of passageways to who knows where.

Almost too tired to move, she bent again to remove her shoes and wiggle her poor aching toes about, and was just considering a much-needed expedition to locate the bathroom when someone else knocked at the door.

'Oh my goodness, what now?'

Her nerves fraught, Maeve threw open the door and glared at her new visitor, half-expecting some other ancient member of the family come to impart wisdom in the middle of the night. But it was only Leo's glowering sister, a stack of clothes huddled untidily in her arms, holding out a brand-new toothbrush still in its packet.

'My brother asked me to bring you these. There's toothpaste in the bathroom,' Bernadette said sullenly, 'and shampoo, of course.'

'*Merci*,' Maeve sighed, drumming up a weary smile. She really was very grateful. These people had been so kind to her and yet she could barely keep her eyes open.

Bernadette shrugged, handing her the bundle of clothes, and stomped back along the landing in the same direction her grandmother and great-grandmother had taken just minutes before.

Maeve peered up and down the passageway. 'Anyone else want to come and speak to me?'

There was no reply.

Grabbing a clean towel, she staggered along the landing to the bathroom, which turned out to be huge, despite its low, sloping ceiling, with a freestanding antique bath with gold taps set on a raised platform, and an old-fashioned screen between the bath and the toilet.

There were no curtains at the window but the glass was frosted. She pushed it open, remembering what Leo had told her about the steam.

'Ah, at last...' Running herself a bath, she was delighted to find the water tolerably hot and climbed in for a quick dunk of her hair and an overall wash. Closing her eyes in the warm scented water after scrubbing all her bits, she allowed herself to soak for five minutes of pure unadulterated relaxation, and then jumped out, towelled herself off briskly and brushed her teeth with the new toothbrush.

Two and a half minutes of assiduous brushing, as was her twice-daily habit.

Being robbed in broad daylight and left stranded in a foreign country without a passport was no excuse for poor dental hygiene.

Bernadette's night clothes were a little on the large side, but they were better than sleeping in the top she'd worn all day or, worse, in the all-together. There were limits, after all, and she *was* British.

Stumbling wearily back to her bedroom, she heard a strange cry from somewhere below her in the house and stopped dead, startled.

Was that a cat? Or perhaps a *woman,* crying?

Maybe she had been too brusque with the great-grandmother and upset the poor old lady. But her intuition told her it was somebody completely different. Nobody she had met so far in the Rémy family, she suspected, listening to the soft distant sound of sobbing.

As she got ready for bed, the crying continued, muffled but unmistakable. Sometime later, she heard footsteps, a rumble of voices, and the slamming of a door. Then silence.

At last she slept.

Maeve woke just after dawn and padded barefoot across to the tiny window in her fairy tale turret bedroom to stare out across Paris.

Last night, she had been too dazed to make much of the tiny lights dancing all over the city's velvety glow. By daylight, the view was miraculous. Parisian roofs, balconies, office buildings and elegant apartments filled the skyline. The sky was a deep, gorgeous, shining blue. No clouds, very little wind, judging by the still treetops she could just see in the yard below.

A perfect summer's day, in fact.

She wiggled her toes and thought with brief longing of her absent suitcase. It would be back in England by now. Dear old Blighty. How they must have stared in astonishment when she failed to make the rendezvous and they had to leave France without her. Maeve, who did everything by the book, had missed the coach. And not even contacted Betsy or the tour company to explain why. In the end, they must have decided she was *dead*. Because absolutely no other explanation would fit...

What would happen to her luggage now? They would hold it for her at one of their offices, perhaps. She needed to look up the phone number of the coach tour company as soon as possible. Of course, she had the number in her rucksack. All the numbers she might need in the event of an emergency, along with names, websites, protocols. But she no longer had her rucksack. Or her smartphone, for that matter. It was all a bit of a disaster. But nothing that couldn't be sorted out once she was given permission to travel back to the UK.

She hated the idea of everyone laughing at her, and almost wished she had died. Well, maybe that was a tiny bit extreme. Nobody wished they were dead just to avoid embarrassment. Especially when she would never be forced to hear their chuckles or witness their barely concealed smirks.

With any luck, she would never see any of her fellow travellers again. But it was still humiliating to imagine what they'd said behind her back...

Soon, she would be home again, checking through the book marking she still had to do before school started again in September, and perhaps eating a heart-healthy reduced sugar biscuit.

Except that her house keys had been in her rucksack too, she realised, her heart sinking even further. Her neighbour Mrs Fletcher always kept a spare set, of course. So she wouldn't need to pay a locksmith to break in for her.

It would simply be an awkward conversation, that was all.

'But where's *your* key, Maeve?'

'Well, I was robbed by a young man on a motorbike. He stole my rucksack, which contained my passport and money and phone and keys... I had to rely on the kindness of strangers. One of them was a very good-looking Frenchman. An artist, in fact. And yes, Mrs Fletcher, I know I shouldn't have accepted his offer of a bed for the night, but what choice did I have? Besides, he lived in a simply vast château and it was a four-poster bed...'

'Oh my goodness, Maeve. And did anything *happen?*'

She drew a deep breath and squared her shoulders. Maybe that was a very *small* cloud in the distance, a tiny patch of white scudding across the Parisian skyline. Where there was one cloud, others might follow, and before you knew it, the sun would have gone in and it would be pouring down.

At least, that's how British weather worked.

But maybe French weather was contrary. Or hadn't got the cloud memo.

She would need to make something up.

'But where's *your* key, Maeve?'

'I dropped it into the Seine by accident, Mrs Fletcher. I was distracted while on a lunchtime pleasure cruise. One of the other passengers was a young child with a red balloon, you see, and her balloon popped very loudly right next to me just as I was examining my key fob while holding it out over the water…'

'Oh my goodness. How unfortunate. Well, it's lucky that I keep a spare set hanging in my kitchen then, isn't it?'

'My thoughts entirely, Mrs Fletcher.'

Yes, it would be awkward.

She disliked awkward things. Like having to tell a little white lie to avoid an over-complicated conversation. Awkward things made her nervous and even sometimes gave her digestive issues.

She hugged herself, turning away from the beautiful view of the blue Parisian sky. That tiny cloud had faded away before it could reach their part of the city, and she knew it must be about breakfast time by now. She wished she'd invested in a watch before coming to Paris but had assumed her smartphone would do the job perfectly well on its own.

She also had an app on her phone that reminded her when to meditate, and told her every time she logged in that she needed to relax and not worry so much. She was missing that app right about now.

It was hard not to worry, given her situation. Whoever designed that app had probably never lost their passport in a foreign country and been parted from their luggage and had to stay in a strange house of sobbing women…

Had she imagined hearing that lamentation in the night?

'Focus on the positive,' she told herself, channelling the relaxation app. 'The Embassy will sort it all out for you, Maeve.'

Having washed and dressed in Bernadette's rather over-generous clothes, she went downstairs to find out where breakfast was being eaten.

The château, she realised, was big, but not as huge as it had seemed last night, being led her through countless corridors and up-and-down staircases. Leo must surely have gone the long way round, she thought, exploring the ground floor and finally popping her head round an open door to what had to be the breakfast room, judging by the delicious wafting scent of food and lively chatter of voices.

She cleared her voice, feeling like an intruder, and the conversation died to silence as everyone turned to stare at her…

CHAPTER SIX

'Ah, *Mademoiselle Eden.*' Leo's grandmother rose in welcome, indicating a chair to her left. 'I trust you slept well. Please, join us.'

In the centre of the dark, wood-panelled room, its ceilings so staggeringly high she imagined they must need a crane to change the lightbulbs, stood the longest breakfast table Maeve had ever seen. It could probably seat an entire football team, she thought. Maybe the opposition as well.

Not all seats were taken, though. Some stood empty or were just spaces with no chair set there. Leo, who was eating his breakfast at the far end, looked up and raised a hand in welcome, his mouth full. Beside him, a young man with purple hair and an earring gazed back at her and put down his croissant. 'Hello,' he said in French, studying her with undisguised curiosity, 'so you're our mystery guest.'

Maeve smiled, unsure if an answer was required.

Seated in the middle of the long table, two young women sat opposite each other, both glowering round at her.

One was Bernadette, Leo's sister, whose sharp gaze took in the clothes she'd lent Maeve in the night before her mouth quirked and one brow rose steeply. The other woman was older, maybe in her mid-thirties. She had long Titian hair, with flawless skin and large glowing eyes, gold jewellery glinting at her throat and in her ears. She had a generous mouth, eyes outlined in black kohl, and wore rather too much blusher, especially for a summer's day. Long scarlet-tipped claws drummed on the table as she looked Maeve up and down, and then transferred her glare to Leo, who ignored her.

There were also several other people at the breakfast table, none of whom she recognised from last night, except for the very old lady who had visited her in the night. Leo's great-grandmother.

'*Bonjour*,' Maeve told them all politely, feeling very much on show. 'Thank you for letting me stay. The bed was so comfortable. And I love the view from the window. You saved my life last night. I'm really very grateful.'

'The bed was comfortable?' Leo repeated, his eyebrow arched in much the same way as his sister's. 'I'm glad to hear it. Though I'm not sure any of us believe you.'

'Leo, enough,' Madame Rémy warned him, and smiled benignly as Maeve sat in her allotted seat. A cup was pushed towards her and filled with steaming coffee. 'Do you take milk? But of course you do... You're English. The English are so funny.' Madame Rémy glanced at the wicker breakfast baskets set at intervals down the middle of the table. 'Um, we have homemade croissants and fruit, and a selection of cold meat and cheese if you want something more substantial.' She paused. 'We do not do sausages, I'm afraid.'

'Bacon and eggs,' the young man next to Leo said in thickly accented English, adding in French, 'That's what the British eat for breakfast. Bacon and eggs. And "black pudding".' He pronounced it delicately in English, and then shuddered.

Bernadette shot the young man a disbelieving look. 'Black... pudding? ' she repeated. 'What is that?'

'Some kind of sausage made with blood, I think,' the young man replied in French, and they both gave cries of horror and amusement.

Over this exchange, Leo said calmly but clearly, 'English only, please. Let's be polite to our guest. Her French is...' His gaze lifted and locked with Maeve's, and his mouth twitched. 'Minimalist,' he finished at last, and then looked down at his plate, spearing a small piece of what looked like Camembert with his knife.

'I've never eaten black pudding,' Maeve told the assembled family, and felt herself blush as all eyes turned towards her. 'Or bacon and eggs. At least, I don't eat them for breakfast. Except maybe a few times a year, when I'm on holiday.' She hesitated. 'I suppose I'm on holiday now. Though, bacon and eggs are probably a bit thin on the ground in Paris. But I do love croissants. Home-made though? Who makes them?'

Everyone pointed or looked at Bernadette.

'They take a long time,' Bernadette said flatly.

'Well, I'm very impressed. I'd love to see how you make them. And whatever that sliced meat is… It looks delicious. Like, um, pink waxed paper. I shall have some with a croissant. And maybe a piece of fruit too.' She smiled determinedly as a very elderly gentleman opposite her pushed a wooden fruit bowl in her direction. It scraped across the table in the silence. *'Merci, monsieur.'*

The old gentleman raised a shaking finger. He looked about eighty-five years old, maybe older. 'Alfonse,' he told her in a deep voice. 'I am Alfonse. Pleased to meet you, Mlle Eden.'

'Yes, quite right, Uncle Alfonse… I apologise for not introducing Mlle Eden to everyone.' Leo pointed to each person in turn around the table. 'Maeve, you already know my grandmother, Madame Rémy, and this is her mother, my great-grandmother, whom we all know as Nonna. And the gentleman who passed you the fruit bowl is my great-uncle Alfonse, Nonna's brother-in-law.'

'The others are all dead,' Nonna muttered in

French, her bright gaze on Maeve's face. 'All dead.'

Alfonse grimaced and nodded. 'All dead,' he echoed gloomily.

Maeve felt awkwardness strike and heard herself tell the old man, *'Je suis desolée,'* meaning she was very sorry. Though for what, she wasn't quite sure. There was no evidence any of them had died an untimely death, given his own advanced age...

Leo nodded to the young man on his left. 'And this is my cousin, Jean. Pay no attention to him. Nobody ever does, and it's by far the best policy.' The young man protested, but laughing. Leo indicated his sister. 'You met Bernadette last night. And the two young ladies to your left are Sophie and Marie, yet more of my cousins, though not on Jean's side of the family. They're seventeen and here on a visit from Bordeaux. We own a vineyard there.'

The two young ladies, who looked to be twin sisters, giggled and waved shyly at Maeve. They reminded her of girls at her school back in the UK, though more sun-tanned, both with long, slightly unkempt chestnut hair worn loose, in pretty summer frocks.

There was a delicate cough from the one person at the table who had not been included in this round of introductions.

Leo took a sip of his black coffee, his gaze steadily on the table. 'And the lady with the tickly throat is Liselle. She is not related to anyone here.'

'God, Leo, you are such a bastard,' Liselle said in such perfectly enunciated English that it was almost impossible to detect an accent. She rose, throwing down her napkin, and stalked dramatically from the room, tossing back a wave of thick Titian hair as she did so. On her way, she flashed Maeve a dismissive look. 'You're welcome to him, Mademoiselle. Just don't let him break your heart, that's my advice.'

And with that, she left the room.

They sat in silence, listening to the click of heels on the uncarpeted stone flags as she headed out.

Maeve didn't know what to say. But something seemed to be required, as everyone was now looking at her. Even Leo, whose gaze was steady and sardonic.

'Oh dear,' she said at last.

Nonna gave a low, mischievous chuckle. 'I told you,' she said in French, pointing at Maeve. 'Liselle... she is *finished* here.'

Shaking his head, Leo got up.

Maeve looked at him nervously. 'Are you still okay to run me to the Embassy?'

'Of course. But enjoy your breakfast in your own time first. My study is just along the hallway. I'm sure Bernadette will point you in the right direction once you're ready to leave.'

He left, and Maeve bit into a ripe pear, looking about the table and wishing she knew what on earth all that tension with Liselle was about.

You're welcome to him, Mademoiselle. Just don't let him break your heart, that's my advice.

Could the dramatic redhead really believe she was Leo's new lover? It seemed ridiculous, and yet...

She ought to ask Madame Rémy about it. But she would be gone soon anyway. Perhaps it was better to smile and ignore Liselle's outburst. Yes, that would be the British thing to do.

'Mmm, this pear is so delicious,' she said, dabbing at her mouth with a napkin, and turned politely to listen as Madame Rémy agreed and began enthusiastically praising the local fruit suppliers.

Another half an hour and she would be free of this château. And the Rémy family. And Leo's tangled love life...

The man at the embassy was equally polite but adamant as he handed her a stack of papers to sign. 'I'm afraid you'll need to fill these out and come back in a week or two.'

She was aghast. 'A week or two? But I can't. I mean, I don't have any money, for starters. Where am I going to stay?'

'Didn't you say you stayed with friends last night?'

She blushed angrily. 'Friends is pushing it. More like bare acquaintances. And it's one thing to beg a spare bed for a night, and quite another to throw myself on their charity for a fortnight.'

'I quite understand.' Mr White pursed his lips, a tall, reedy man in a dark suit, his receding hairline an unfortunate indication of early-onset baldness. 'Well, I'm sure your bank will advance you some emergency cash.'

Since she had already made a further call to her bank Lost Card helpline, using Leo's mobile, on the way to Château Rémy last night, and been told her bank balance wasn't in the best shape for large-scale borrowing, this was a blind alley. But the bank, having already stopped her lost cards yesterday when she first reported them, had grudgingly agreed to loan her a few hundred until she could get home, via an emergency code at a cash till. But if she was to be stuck here for two more weeks, she would need far more cash than that...

'Not enough,' she said tightly.

'Then I suggest you go back to your friends and ask for additional accommodation. Maybe if you were to offer to pay in kind?'

'Sorry?' She stared, horrified.

'You could wash up and tidy the house in return for bed and board,' Mr White explained mildly. 'Just a suggestion.'

'Oh.'

He frowned. 'What did you think I meant?'

'Nothing,' she muttered.

His eyes widened and his brows soared. 'Oh.'

'Forget it.'

'Well, yes...' He cleared his throat and shuffled his paperwork. 'I'm very sorry about the delay. But an anomaly's been thrown up, you see, and –'

'A *what*?'

'An anomaly.' Mr White met her eyes frankly. 'We found you on the system. But a red flag went up when we tried to issue you with an emergency –'

'*Red flag*?' she interrupted him, dumbfounded. 'What on earth are you talking about?'

'There's been some query over your status as a British citizen, I'm afraid. You were born here in Paris, weren't you?'

'Yes, and I was taken to the UK as a baby. So what? I've always had a British passport. Nobody's given it a 'red flag' before.'

'Well,' he said delicately, 'it seems your UK citizenship may have been issued in error.'

'I beg your pardon?'

'We're investigating the issue. No need to get worried. It will probably turn out to be a mere formality. These things sometimes do.'

'Only *sometimes*?'

He cleared his throat and glanced meaningfully at the clock on the wall. 'Leave it with me and we'll get back to you. We'll need your contact details though and an assurance that someone can vouch for your whereabouts while this is resolved.'

'Are you joking?'

Mr White grimaced. 'I wish I was. But the French don't take kindly to foreign nationals without passports wandering the country freely. Your friends from last night... Will they agree to house you?'

'I... I don't know.'

'Perhaps you could phone them?'

'My phone was stolen. Along with everything I had. I told you all this.' She had tears in her eyes and was choked up. 'Oh, this is... intolerable.'

He watched her for a moment, looking conflicted, and then pulled some tissues out of the box on the table and handed them across to her with the weary air of someone who'd done the same thing a thousand times. She wondered how many other people had sat where she was sitting and been flatly told no, you can't go home.

'Here, please don't be upset.' He hovered, frowning. 'Do you have a number for these people?'

'Rémy. Their surname is Rémy.'

'I can ring them if you like.'

'Do we really have to do this? I mean, *two whole weeks*? Isn't there a way to resolve this more quickly?'

He shook his head. 'Sorry.'

'For goodness' sake.' Reluctantly, she fumbled for Leo's number, still in her pocket, and passed it to him. 'I can't believe this is happening. I'm a British citizen. I have documents in my name. I rent a flat. I... I had a *British father*, for God's sake. Though he's passed away now.' She blew her nose, watching as Mr White punched Leo's number into his phone. 'Could you at least try to contact my father's family to confirm it? I may have some cousins somewhere...'

Oh, why hadn't she made more of an effort to keep in touch with her father's side of the family?

'It's not that simple,' Mr White muttered, but did not elaborate further, as Leo had answered at the other end.

A swift and brief conversation in French followed, ending abruptly. Mr White shrugged and put down the phone.

Maeve stared at him. 'Well?'

'Monsieur Rémy has agreed to put you up while we sort this out and to vouch for your whereabouts. He's on his way back.'

'Oh, how embarrassing.' Mortified, she dropped her head in her hands.

Mr White waited a moment, and then said uncomfortably. 'I have another appointment, I'm afraid. You can wait outside for Monsieur Rémy.' He went to the door and opened it. 'Someone at reception will prepare his paperwork. He'll need to provide ID details and sign a release form before you leave.'

Stunned, Maeve forced herself up out of the

chair. 'This is really happening, isn't it?' But at the door, she halted beside him, stammering, 'You're sure you… you haven't made a mistake? Got me confused with someone else, maybe?'

He gave her a perfunctory smile. 'Good luck, Miss Eden.' He shook her hand. 'Hope springs eternal.'

CHAPTER SEVEN

'You have to let me do something in return for your hospitality,' Maeve insisted. 'I'm not a brilliant cook, but I'm willing to help out in the kitchen. Or wash up. Or do the laundry. Whatever you need, really.'

She was sitting in the inner courtyard of Château Rémy, sheltering under a striped umbrella from the blazing summer sun. At the table sat Madame Rémy and Nonna, while Bernadette, a few feet away, was down on a kneeler, tending to the plants growing in urns around the courtyard. It was a little oasis of peace in the centre of a busy city. Every now and then she would hear a car horn or sounds of raised voices from the streets below. Yet here in the courtyard it was peaceful, somehow apart from the busy metropolitan life going on around them.

Maeve still felt stunned by what had happened. And not entirely sure she understood. *An anomaly*, Mr Whitehead said. *A red flag.* Some kind of error that meant her British citizenship was now in question. She had no idea how that was possible.

All the way back from the embassy, she had sat white-faced and sickened, while Leo tried to reassure her, insisting that it must simply be a clerical error or a computer cock up, and that she would soon be on her way back to the UK. And that was the most logical way to approach her situation. Except she wasn't feeling very logical right now.

Frankly, she felt more like bawling her eyes out or going back there and begging Mr White on her knees to let her back into the UK.

Britain was the country where she'd grown up. She'd always considered it her own. The fact that she had been born in Paris was not significant, as far as she was concerned.

Yes, her mother had been French, according to her birth certificate and her dad. She still had French relatives somewhere. Possibly in Paris itself. There was also that faded photograph with an address scrawled on the back. Her grandmother's old address? She had not yet felt brave enough to pursue that lead. And now she couldn't, because that old photo had been in her rucksack, which would have been dumped somewhere, with anything valuable taken out... Just the thought of it made her want to weep.

But her father had been British. And she'd barely spent any time in France. She'd left there while she was still a baby. It was insane to suggest she was no longer British.

It had to be a mistake.

Meanwhile, she was stuck here in Paris without any money and being forced to accept charity from these lovely people who were basically strangers. Naturally enough, she was feeling horribly guilty. And Mr White had been right about one thing at least. She needed to pay them back in some way. And the only way possible was through her labour.

'I wouldn't dream of it,' Madame Rémy replied, tutting and wagging a finger at her. 'No, not at all. You are a guest here.'

Nonna, who was knitting, made some incoherent comment which Maeve guessed was her agreeing with her daughter.

'But I feel so... parasitic.'

Both women stared at her.

'*Pardon?*' Madame Rémy sounded baffled.

'Parasitic,' she repeated. 'It makes me feel parasitic to be just living here, leeching off you...' When they still turned blank faces in her direction, Maeve hesitated, and then mimed sucking blood, along with sound effects. Now they looked horrified. 'Erm, like a bug... You know, a mosquito?' She pretended to suck on her arm. 'Mmm, lovely blood. Slurp, slurp.'

Nonna crossed herself.

'Is it the bang on your head?' Madame Rémy asked in a sympathetic tone, and now even Bernadette had turned from her gardening and was gazing at her, wide-eyed. 'Do you need a doctor?'

'No, no, I'm just trying to say... Oh, it doesn't matter. But please let me take a turn washing up, at least? Unless you have a dishwasher?'

'*I'm* the dishwasher,' Bernadette said darkly.

Nonna muttered something under her breath, and the other two women stared at her.

'Oh, Maman, I'm not sure about that.' Madame Rémy shifted in her seat.

'That's not a good idea,' Bernadette said more bluntly.

Maeve blinked. 'What... What did she say? Sorry, I missed that.'

There was a short silence, then Bernadette sighed. 'Nonna thinks you should sit for Leo. She says if you want to help out, that's the best way to do it.'

Maeve sucked in a breath, instantly on the alert for danger. 'Sit for *a portrait*, you mean?'

Instinctively, she distrusted that idea. It sounded like the kind of thing other people did, not her. She was far too dull and sensible to be an artist's model. Besides, it would mean spending hours alone with the man. And that was out of the question. She had no room in her life for ambiguities. And Leo Rémy was definitely... ambiguous.

Madame Rémy said hurriedly, 'You don't need to do it, Maeve. Please understand, my mother is obsessed with encouraging Leo back into painting, that's all.'

'*Back* into painting? I don't understand.'

Another short silence left Maeve worried that she had said something wrong.

'It's a sensitive topic,' Madame Rémy said quietly. 'You see, Leo hasn't produced any new paintings for some time. Since his older brother died, in fact.'

'I'm so sorry.' Maeve felt awful. 'I didn't even know his brother had died.'

'Oh, it was three years ago now. Poor Francis. They weren't close, of course. More like enemies than brothers. But his death meant Leo had to come home and take over running the family business.'

The family business.

It sounded thoroughly Godfather-esque. She saw in her mind's eye a dry, dusty landscape and Leo Rémy as Michael Corleone, ordering some violent assassination in a bored, laconic voice.

'What is the, erm, *family business*?'

'We have a vineyard in Bordeaux and sell our wines internationally.' Madame Rémy's prosaic answer was at odds with Maeve's ridiculous imaginings. 'You met Sophie and Marie at breakfast. Their father Henri is my other grandson, and he runs the vineyard. But it's very expensive, the wine business, and we've had a succession of difficult years, weatherwise.'

Madame Rémy swallowed, looking away. 'It's been a heavy burden for Leo to bear. I'm worried about him.'

Maeve frowned. 'I'm not sure I understand fully... Why didn't you inherit some of the business too, Bernadette? You're his sister.'

Bernadette flushed, and Maeve realised she had once more put her foot in it with this complicated family.

'Half-sister,' the young woman corrected her in an angry mutter. 'My mother...' Her mouth tightened and she abruptly changed trajectory. 'My real father wasn't a Rémy,' she finished awkwardly.

'I see.' Maeve didn't see at all. But what else could she say?

She bit her lip, wishing she was not so ready to blunder into other people's business. But it sounded as though Leo's mother had not conceived Bernadette by Leo's father. And she hadn't mentioned a second marriage for her mother, which rather suggested his mother had slept with some other man behind her husband's back. Goodness...

Not wanting to pursue that prickly subject, she asked hurriedly, 'So Leo doesn't paint anymore?'

Nana shook her head, evidently having understood that part in English at least, and tutted, her knitting needles clacking noisily.

'That's so sad.' Maeve sat forward, eager to

learn more. She recalled the gendarme's admiring recognition. 'I knew Leo was an artist, but... Is he really well-known?'

Madame Rémy smiled sadly. 'My dear, he was once one of France's most notorious young painters.'

'He still is,' Bernadette said pointedly, without looking round, having returned to her garden name. She was weeding now below the fig trees that grew against the sunny wall.

'But we no longer see so many stories about him in the press.' Madame Rémy clasped her hands together, staring down at them. 'We were all so proud of him, Maeve. Even Francis, in his own way, though he would never have admitted it. But that was all a long time ago. Now Leo is... *broken*.' A tear ran down her cheek. 'No, there's no other word for it. Leo is a broken man.'

'But what about Liselle? Nonna said...' Maeve tailed off, uncomfortably aware that she had only guessed Nonna's meaning when she spoke of Liselle being Leo's "Muse".

Perhaps she had misunderstood.

'Liselle was his model once,' Madame agreed. 'But she hasn't sat for him in ages.'

'So why does she still...?'

'Live here?' Madame Rémy gave an unhappy smile. 'Liselle is his manager now. She organises exhibitions of his work in France and around the world, and deals with sales of his paintings.'

She paused, her brows knitting together, her eyes troubled. 'But he has so few unsold paintings left, and nothing new to come. So she's had to, erm, *double up*, as you say in English.'

'*Double up?*' Maeve didn't understand.

Nonna shushed them, pointing with her knitting needles.

Loud footsteps behind them made Maeve turn her head. Liselle was headed their way out of the château, a tray in her hands. She was wearing an apron over a pale green summer frock and what looked like clogs on her feet. The slap of the heavy shoes on the stone was almost menacing.

'These days Liselle is our housekeeper,' Bernadette said, jumping up and dusting off her hands on navy blue culottes. 'Did you bring out the little cakes I made?'

'Of course,' Liselle replied in French, her voice disdainful. 'And a pot of coffee and some cold drinks, as Madame requested.' She slammed the tray down on the ironwork table beside Maeve, shooting her a resentful glare as all the glasses and cups rattled. 'I don't like people talking about me behind my back,' she snapped in English. 'Is that clear?'

'Crystal,' Maeve replied, sitting up very straight and returning her glare. She didn't know what Liselle's problem was with her. But she was not going to be cowed into submission. 'I'm sorry. I didn't know you could hear me.'

'*Evidemment.*' Liselle's lips were pursed, her eyes snapping.

'Now Liselle,' Madame Rémy said uneasily, 'please don't be impolite to our guest. I was the one who mentioned you first, not Miss Eden.'

Nonna grumbled something.

Maeve suspected it might've been, 'It was me, actually,' but she hadn't yet got a grasp on the old lady's gnomic utterances, so couldn't be sure.

'I know what you all think of me, Madame,' Liselle began angrily but then fell to silence as the door behind her opened.

Liselle turned her head to look at the newcomer, red-flame hair glinting in the sunlight, and a strange look came over her face. It was an expression of vulnerability, and it made Maeve feel bad, seeing that change. Liselle might come across as quite unpleasant at times but she wasn't as iron-plated as she appeared. No doubt her feelings had been hurt by what she'd overheard.

'Ah, Leo, Madame Rémy exclaimed nervously, sitting up and reaching for the tray, 'you're just in time. Liselle has made coffee. Or perhaps you'd prefer something cold. It is quite hot today, isn't it?'

Maeve felt the skin prickle on the back of her neck as she realised that the man himself had arrived in the courtyard garden.

'Yes, Paris is stifling today,' Leo agreed. 'And you really shouldn't gossip on such a hot day when all the windows are open,' he added, a distinct edge to his voice.

Tilting his head, he indicated the château above them. Maeve looked up along with the others, and realised guiltily that some windows were either ajar or fully open, with others shuttered but no doubt with the windows thrown wide behind them, meaning their voices would easily have carried in this still, sunny air to the upper storeys.

'Unless, that is, you want the subject of your gossip to hear everything you're saying,' he finished.

With a furious narrowing of her eyes, Liselle flounced back into the château. As much as anyone could flounce wearing clogs.

'Oh dear,' Maeve said.

'Oh dear, indeed,' Leo agreed, and looked down at her, one dark brow high and crooked.

'Coffee?' Madame Rémy asked her politely.

'Oh, em, yes please,' Maeve gushed, jumping up to accept a cup of coffee from her.

She didn't much like their strong, sludgy black coffee – which never came with milk except at breakfast time, it seemed – and had originally intended to drink something cool and refreshing. But it gave her an excuse to break free from the hypnotic stare of Leo Rémy without looking like a coward, as she suspected his grandmother had realised.

Goodness though, if there was ever an Olympic

staring contest, her host could successfully compete for France. And win gold!

'However,' Leo drawled in a voice like melted chocolate, so close to her ear that she jerked away, startled, and spilt her coffee into her saucer, 'I couldn't help overhearing Nonna's excellent suggestion.'

She had almost backed away into an urn of bright, tumbling geraniums. Their thick fragrance was intoxicating. 'You... You couldn't?' Maeve turned her gaze on the old lady, who at once bent her head industriously over her knitting, and then looked back at him warily. 'Which, erm, part?'

'It's true that I've been looking for a new model for the past year or so. Someone to sit for me... Liselle won't mind me saying this, I'm sure, but she no longer suits me as a sitter. If you always use the same model, your work becomes a bit... '

'Samey?'

His mouth twitched but he shrugged. 'All right, yes, we can say that if you like. *Samey.*' He helped himself to a tall glass of something citrus-smelling, a pale yellow drink poured over ice, with a sprinkle of tiny blue flowers bobbing about in it. 'I haven't been able to decide which new direction I want to take, artistically speaking. So I've been considering my options.' He threw an ironic look at his grandmother. 'No doubt the long delay has caused some to wrongly view me as… What was the word, Grandmère? Broken?'

'I didn't know you were listening,' Madame Rémy said, her brows drawn together, chagrin in her face.

'I am not broken.' He hesitated. 'Just… conflicted, perhaps.'

'Of course,' his grandmother agreed.

Leo sipped his drink and gazed at Maeve over the rim of his glass. 'When I saw you in the street yesterday – '

'You mean, when I was unconscious?' she demanded.

He blinked. 'Yes, but afterwards too.' He cleared his throat. 'When I saw you, it was a significant moment. I experienced a kind of…'

'Seizure?'

'Epiphany.'

'Isn't that a religious thing?'

'Maybe a little.' His smile was dry. 'I just mean I got some ideas about a potential new direction for my work.'

'Okay,' she said slowly, worried about where this was leading.

'Oh Leo!' Madame Rémy exclaimed, clapping her hands in obvious delight. 'How marvellous. I'm so glad.'

Even Bernadette was smiling. 'Good for you, brother,' she said in French, and raised her glass to him. '*Salut.*'

'*Salut*,' he murmured, and they both drank.

'I'm sorry, have I missed something?' Maeve was confused, looking at brother and sister. 'How is that significant?'

'My brother... has not had any... thoughts of this kind since Francis died,' Bernadette explained slowly in English. 'It is a... a big thing.'

'Very, very big,' Madame Rémy agreed.

'Well...' Leo said modestly, and the others all laughed.

Maeve, still wrestling with a feeling of uncertainty, felt his gaze on her face and blushed. 'No,' she said preemptively.

'No?'

'If you're about to ask me to be your model, it's a no.'

'I see.' Leo drank again, watching her contemplatively. 'You have a reason for saying no?'

'It's just not my kind of thing.' She raised her coffee to her lips, hoping it was cool enough to drink now.

'There would be no nudity.'

She spluttered coffee everywhere and had to reach for a napkin. 'I'm sorry, what?'

'Nudity. You perhaps think I want to paint you with no clothes on?'

'I certainly do not.' She dabbed at her mouth, her heart pounding wildly. 'I mean, that is... Do you?'

'*Non, non.*' He shook his head vehemently, and

then paused, looking her up and down before repeating firmly, '*Non.*'

She couldn't decide whether to be relieved or offended. '*Non?*'

'*Non.*'

'Okay, then.'

'So now that you feel safe in accepting an invitation to sit for me, will you do me the honour, Miss Eden?'

'Oh.' Maeve had assumed he'd given up. But evidently not. 'But why on earth would you want *me* as a model? Why not someone else? Bernadette, maybe?'

Bernadette choked on her drink.

'*Bah, non,*' Leo exclaimed, chuckling as he smacked his sister helpfully between the shoulder blades a few times. 'Bernadette is not... Ah, she does not... inspire.'

'*Merci,*' Bernadette said, baring sharp white teeth at him.

'*Je t'en prie,*' he replied easily.

'I know nothing about art,' Maeve told him frankly.

'You don't need to know anything.'

'I've never sat for an artist before.'

'There's nothing to it. The simplest thing in the world.'

'And what if my face gets itchy?'

'*Pardon?*' He was looking perplexed.

'What if my nose needs to be scratched, for

instance? How long do these sittings last? I don't think I could hold still for hours on end,' she said flatly. 'In fact, I'd ruin everything within ten minutes by forgetting to hold the pose or needing the toilet or something. You really don't want me.'

'But I do want you,' he said firmly, a gleam in his eye that unnerved her. 'And of course you can scratch your nose or take comfort breaks or move about, if you need to. It will make no difference to my work.'

'I don't want to do it,' she said desperately.

She felt a hand on her arm and turned to find Madame Rémy there, sympathy in her kind face. 'Nobody will force you to do this,' she insisted. 'Including Leo.' She threw a stern look at her grandson. 'Will you?'

'No, of course not,' he said heavily, and turned away, his head bent as though examining the tiny blue flowers in his drink.

'There,' Madame said, smiling. 'You can relax, Miss Eden. Please, sit down. Enjoy the garden.'

Maeve thanked her and sat down, but she felt awful.

She had asked specifically if there was some way she could repay the Rémy family's hospitality. And then, when a way was provided, she had refused pointblank to do it. And for what reason?

Because she was too shy to be a model? Because it all felt a bit too exciting and exotic? A bit too wild and bohemian, perhaps, for Miss Maeve Eden of North London? Because she wasn't that kind of girl?

'No nudity, you said?' she queried.

Leo stopped pacing and came back at once, his gaze fixed on her face. 'Absolutely not,' he told her gravely.

'And I can move about?'

'Within reason.'

Maeve took a deep breath, feeling as though she were about to plunge hundreds of feet into an icy ravine, which might have been a relief in this scorching heat, and said, 'All right, then. If you must.'

'You've changed your mind? You'll sit for me?' His voice was blank, carefully neutral.

'Better take the offer before it's withdrawn,' she warned him.

Leo smiled, and raised his glass to her. 'Can you start tomorrow morning?' When she gave some incoherent reply, not having thought it would be so soon, he went on, 'At this time of year, the light in my studio is usually best in the early hours of the morning. Shall we say, a five o'clock start?'

'Five o'clock?'

She must have sounded as horrified as she felt, because Leo grinned at her expression and said, 'Six, then.'

He threw himself down onto the bench next to his great-grandmother, who was beaming with pleasure at the two of them. Affectionately, he kissed her on her wrinkled cheek. 'I'm going to try painting again, Nonna,' he murmured in French, and took her hand gently in his. 'You were right. Thank you.'

Watching this, Maeve had a funny feeling in her tummy. She suddenly had no idea why she had agreed to sit for him. But it was too late to back out now. Or not without looking ungrateful and a bit mean.

You were right. Thank you.

What on earth had he meant by that, though?

Right about what?

CHAPTER EIGHT

Leo was close to losing his famous cool. He checked his phone. Two o'clock in the morning. A paintbrush clamped between his teeth, he turned back to the canvas in frustration. Rapidly, he scanned the figure he'd sketched out in pencil, ready for painting, and experienced a burst of fury that he can barely control.

It was wrong. All wrong. He couldn't get it right. No matter how hard he tried.

'Damn it to hell!' he yelled at the canvas, and then stood with his head bowed for a moment, breathing harshly.

He glanced at the bottle of cognac he'd brought up with him from supper.

But he never drank when he was painting.

He'd almost forgotten that private rule of his, it had been so long since he'd spent any time painting...

No, he wouldn't drink. That would only make things worse.

At last, he felt his breathing settle and calm return to his mind. Calm and logic.

'It's wrong, but it can be salvaged.' He took a

piece of erasing putty and set to work tidying the figure's outline and face. 'There... and there... and here.' He resketched the lines, this time more loosely, his hand more fluid, leaving plenty of room for the paint to interpret his vision.

Once he was ready, Leo removed the paintbrush from between his teeth and began painting. First, a pale wash of colour. Then, once that had almost dried, he came back with a palette of mixed paints and a narrow brush, and began tentatively to paint.

He had chosen watercolours after an initial flirtation with oils... Oils would be too bold and definitive for something he saw as vague and dreamlike.

Too dreamlike, perhaps. As he worked, he saw it was nothing like the painting he'd originally envisaged. It was a poor shadow. Yet it was all he had. And at least he was painting again.

For the past few years, he had not been able to stand in front of a canvas and just paint. It had been hard enough coming into the studio and looking at the empty easel and the scarcity of canvases stacked against the wall, where once there might've been dozens waiting to be sold or touched up and completed.

At least he had a paintbrush in his hands tonight and some idea of where he might be going, rather than none. And a canvas taking shape under his brushstrokes rather than a blank space.

Hours later, he sighed and took two or three steps back to see what he had achieved, and cried out again in fury. The colours were wrong, the lines were clumsy, it was a mess.

'No, no, no, no, no...' Driven to despair by his frustration, he kicked out at the easel, and the canvas went spinning across the floor.

Leo tossed aside the paintbrush and strode away, grasping his hair in his hands and battling an urge to throw himself off the balcony.

A soft knock at the door made him stiffen and turn, wondering how much noise he'd been making. He glanced at the shutters, drawn back to keep the room cool, the window ajar. It was still dark outside, but long past the middle of the night. Almost dawn, perhaps.

What time had he told Maeve to come for her first session?

Six o'clock.

He lunged for his phone and checked the time, bleary eyed.

Five-thirty in the morning.

It couldn't be her yet, surely? Unless she had changed her mind about getting up so early.

But if it wasn't Maeve, this visit meant he had been making such a racket, he had actually woken someone. Possibly his grandmother.

Guiltily, he stumbled to the door, unlocked it

and flung it open to reveal… Liselle.

His glamorous ex was wearing her favourite green silk dressing gown, knotted at the waist, her long hair fanning down over her shoulders, the colour of a sunset. Her feet were bare, her pale-skinned cleavage plunging between high breasts that pressed against the silk in a seductive manner. As always, she smelt of perfume and feminine allure. Her large dramatic eyes surveyed him almost hungrily.

She came pacing barefoot into the room and he recoiled, not wanting her to touch him.

'What… What are you doing here, Liselle?' he demanded thickly, and ran a hand across his face. God, he was tired. Dropping with fatigue. What had he been thinking to stay up all night like this? Especially before his very first session with Maeve…

Madness, pure madness. He was thirty-one, not twenty-one. But he had felt like a man possessed when he came up to the studio. It had been so long since he'd felt the urge to paint anything. He had come up here at, what, eleven o'clock, midnight last night? And with this wild vision in his head…

But it hadn't worked out.

His vision had fallen apart even as he tried to paint it, to make it *real*.

Liselle stood over the fallen canvas, and then turned back to him, sympathy in her beautiful face. 'I had to come,' she told him. 'I didn't mean to interrupt your work. I didn't even realise you *were* working. I heard shouting, you see.'

'I'm sorry if I woke you.'

'You don't need to apologise. Not to me.' Liselle sounded surprised. 'You're an artist, Leo. Of course you feel passion, and of course you must express it. That passion is part of who you are and I welcome it.' She turned, heading towards him. He shifted backwards automatically, but she kept coming. He backed all the way up against the wall of the studio, until he couldn't retreat any further. She placed a hand on his chest, her big eyes gazing into his. 'You're painting again. That is all I care about. It's... miraculous.'

'Hardly. I can't seem to get it right,' he muttered.

'You will,' she said simply. 'I have faith in you.'

His lip curled. 'Fine talking. I wish you'd lend me some of that faith. Because I have none left.'

'Willingly,' she whispered.

Alarm bells rang in his head at that look in her eyes. He looked down at the hand on his chest.

'Listen to me, Liselle... I'm not interested. How many times do I have to tell you?' Leo inhaled sharply, struggling to push away the inner demons that had been crowding him for hours. This was Liselle... Beautiful, wild, unpredictable Liselle. He needed to pick his words with care. 'You being my manager, that works. We're a good team. But we can't go back to how things once were between us.' He tried to make her see sense.

'I'm no good for you. I don't love you. This thing... It's toxic.'

'Only because you won't let me in. You need someone, Leo. You can't do this alone. Why not let it be me?' She stretched on tiptoe to kiss him and he grabbed hold of her shoulders, holding her back as gently as he could. Her eyes flashed with anger. 'Let me go!'

'Not if you plan to kiss me.'

'You can't possibly prefer that English idiot to me. She's barely female.'

'Don't be offensive,' he growled.

'Have you seen her figure? If she even has one under those mannish clothes she wears.' She shuddered.

'Those are Bernadette's clothes. Of course they don't fit her very well. Bernadette has a much larger physique.'

Liselle stared. 'Why on earth is she wearing your sister's clothes?'

'She lost her luggage. I asked Bernadette to lend her something.' He grimaced, aware that his sister's spite towards their guest had extended to lending her the drabbest, least appealing clothes she could unearth from her drawers.

'Oh, well... If the little fool can't even keep hold of a suitcase... Leo, darling, you can't be serious about wanting to paint her.'

'Watch me.'

Her lips tightened. 'I love that you're painting

again. It's so exciting… But why ask *her* to sit for you? What quality can she bring to your canvas? Dullness? Ordinariness? A sensible little librarian type who looks like she's never even had a lover.' She paused in her tirade, her gaze devouring him with sudden fury. 'Is that what you like about her? Her *innocence*?' She took a step back at last, her hands dropping away, a knowing look on her face as she finished softly, 'I can do innocence if you like. We can role-play. There doesn't have to be all this drama between us.'

Leo's gaze narrowed on her face. 'I thought we'd agreed that you'd only be my manager from now on. I thought we were over this.' He was perplexed and more than a little irritated. 'What's changed?'

She pouted. 'Oh yes, I've been so happy, trailing about in your shadow, waiting for you to start painting again, so I can make some money as your manager and sell your work.'

'I'm sorry if I've had a dry patch lately… '

'Dry?' Her laughter was cruel. 'Any drier and it would be the Sahara.'

His jaw hardened but he said nothing. She was merely baiting him, trying to drag emotion into the argument, so she could unbalance his calm.

When he stayed silent, she went on unsteadily, 'But that was before she turned up. Quite out of the blue, wasn't it? And all that business about getting knocked down in the street… I don't believe a word of it. You must've known her before yesterday. None of this makes sense otherwise. A complete stranger, walking in here, turning your life upside down, inspiring you to start *painting again* with one look from her very boring eyes?'

When he failed to answer this clearly rhetorical question, Liselle shook back her long Titian hair, a curtain of shimmering flame. 'No, I don't believe it! You were lying. She is lying. But I tell you this, Leo, she will hurt you. Because she doesn't understand you.' She tapped her chest, her chin thrust proudly in the air. 'I, Liselle, understand you. I will always put you and your art first. Now, leave this little English thing and come back to me.'

'Liselle, please,' he began wearily, his head throbbing from lack of sleep and possibly the start of a migraine, but she interrupted him with a violent gesture.

'No, I am done talking. It is time for you to *paint*. So I have come to you.'

Her eyes fixed on his, Liselle unfastened the belt of her dressing gown, exposing her nude body beneath.

As he caught his breath in protest, she shrugged the green silk from her shoulders and stepped away from it, standing naked in the middle of his studio, straight-backed and defiant.

'Paint *me*, Leo,' she ordered him. 'You know you want to.'

'Put that back on,' he rapped out, averting his gaze. 'I told you, I'm not interested.'

She came towards him, smiling sweetly, her eyes shining with mischief and excitement.

'But Leo, look at me... No, look at my body. Not my face. Don't you want to paint *this*?' Her voice dropped, low and husky. 'Don't you desire *this*?'

'Now you're just embarrassing yourself,' he said coldly, knowing the words were cruel but needing to shock her out of this madness. 'And me.'

Her confidence faltered at last. The big eyes searched his face and her smile became fixed. 'You... You don't mean that, my darling.'

'Oh, don't I?' Leo bent to retrieve her dressing gown and was just straightening, the green silk bunched in his fist, when he caught a blur of movement out of the corner of his eye, and staggered backwards, arm raised to shield himself. Liselle had launched herself at him, fingers stretched wide, swiping at his cheek as though hoping to shred his skin with her painted talons.

He grabbed for her wrists but missed, and they tumbled together onto the floor, mere inches from his fallen canvas.

'Dammit, Liselle,' he growled, lying on his back and struggling to hold her at bay, her dressing gown somehow tangled between their bodies. She was almost demented, her bare breasts bouncing in his face, strong thighs gripping his middle…

A sudden noise alerted him to the horrifying realisation that they were not alone anymore.

A voice exclaimed in English, and he stared over Liselle's shoulder at the door to the studio, which had creaked open.

Maeve stood frozen on the threshold, dressed in another of Bernadette's shapeless garments. Her face was blank with shock, her gaze fixed on the two of them wrestling on the floor – and Liselle's nudity.

He swore under his breath.

Turning her head, Liselle gave a wild burst of laughter. 'Oh dear,' she said in English, her tone mocking. 'Oh dear, oh dear. Poor Maeve.'

Maeve did not even seem to have heard her. Her gaze was fixed on his face. He saw vulnerability there, and hurt accusation. A shudder seemed to run through her. Then she turned and fled.

'Get off me, Liselle, for God's sake,' he snapped and lifted her off him while she was still cackling. This time Liselle didn't resist but lay on her back on the studio floor, limp with laughter, while he scrambled back to his feet.

'Here.' Leo chucked at the silk dressing gown over her. 'Cover yourself up and get back to bed. We can talk about this later.'

Without waiting for a response, he strode after Maeve.

She was nowhere to be seen. He stood a moment

in indecision, unsure whether he should chase her back to her bedroom, or whether that would make matters worse.

In his mind's eye, he was replaying what had just happened... Liselle pitching herself at him, stark naked and vicious as a polecat, his struggles to dislodge her as gently as he could, and Maeve's horrified expression as she opened the door.

He ran a furious hand through his hair, wishing he felt fresher and hadn't spent all night slaving pointlessly over that ruined canvas...

Maybe then he might have spotted earlier what Liselle intended when she turned up at the studio door at such an early hour. Because he saw now that the whole thing had been engineered by his former lover, an incident designed to embarrass and warn off Maeve before she could sit for him. Liselle had known when Maeve was due to arrive at the studio, after all. She'd always been on the cold and calculating side, but this was extreme even by her depraved standards.

By contrast, Maeve was an innocent, not part of the unholy circus that revolved around their artistic community, especially in certain areas of Paris. That lack of sophistication was precisely what had transfixed him and made his growing urge to paint her irresistible, despite not having put paint to canvas in years...

He took a few determined steps towards the stairs leading up to the attic rooms, and then forced himself to stop. Perhaps this was not the best moment to talk to Maeve about what she'd seen. Besides, he felt odd and off-balance. And not just through lost sleep.

What was this sinking feeling, so heavy in the pit of his stomach?

Shame.

His breath caught in his throat. Was he... Could he be *ashamed* of himself?

The realisation struck him like a blow and he turned on his heel, swearing ferociously as he headed to his own bedroom instead, deciding to sleep it off.

What the hell? He'd never felt like this before. Shame simply wasn't in his range of emotions. And it hadn't even been his fault, but Liselle's.

Though if you had cut Liselle loose years ago, it wouldn't have happened.

That sharp little voice in his head left him angry with himself. Because it was true. He could have insisted that Liselle return to the South of France and never see him again. But she'd proved too useful as a manager, always there by his side, always devoted to his cause, and if she had sometimes read more into his approving smiles than was really there, he had ignored those danger signs and let the situation slide.

This was the result.

Now Maeve would refuse to sit for him, no doubt disgusted by what she'd just witnessed in the studio. Perhaps she even thought he had done it deliberately, hoping she might join in the orgy...

He gave a dry bark of laughter, mostly aimed at himself. If only she knew... He had barely looked at a woman in years, and not just in artistic terms.

Still, what did it matter if the Englishwoman refused to sit for him? He could still paint Maeve from memory, though he knew it would never be as good as having her there in person, to see how her skin responded to light, and to capture her essence.

No, it didn't really matter.

Except that he didn't want Maeve to think badly of him, he realised with a jolt. A woman he had only just met.

What was that about?

CHAPTER NINE

Someone was knocking at his bedroom door. Loudly and insistently. With a groan, Leo rolled over in bed, gathering the sheets about his lower half, and said thickly, 'Come in.'

He had half-expected to see an angry Liselle at his door. But it opened to reveal Bernadette, carrying a steaming cup of coffee.

He raised his brows. 'That for me? Very kind of you. What have I done wrong?' As if he didn't know...

But it seemed that news of his naked wrestling bout with Liselle had not yet hit the grapevine. For his sister merely handed him the coffee.

'Uncle Henri says he needs a video call with you sooner rather than later. I told him you were still in bed. But he says it's urgent. He's been calling your phone all morning.' She glanced at the empty bedside table. 'Where is it?'

Leo frowned. 'I must have left it in my studio.' He checked his watch. 'Damn, it's barely eleven.'

'I call that late.'

'Yeah, well.' He ran a hand through tousled hair, wondering how much to tell her. What time had he tumbled into bed? Long after six o'clock, for sure. 'I only got to bed a few hours ago.'

'Sounds like you had a good night.'

'Hardly.'

'Come on, what have you been up to?' Bernadette perched on the side of his bed, her eyes lively with curiosity. 'I thought you were meant to be painting Maeve today. Did you forget?'

He sighed. 'Okay, you might as well know... There was a hiccup.' He told his sister the basics of what had happened, leaving out some of the juicier details, and saw her eyes widen. He'd expected her to be annoyed, because he knew she liked Liselle. But she laughed instead.

'Liselle doesn't mess about, does she?' She shook her head at him. 'I have no idea what she sees in you. You've been ignoring her for years. But there's no accounting for taste, is there?'

Luckily, this seemed to be a rhetorical question, so he merely shrugged.

Bernadette gave up prying and got up. 'Talking of love rivals,' she added cheekily, ignoring his exasperated look, 'I've just seen Maeve downstairs. She didn't seem very happy though. Scurried away as soon as she saw me coming,'

'I'd better get up and apologise to her properly. I should have done it at the time but didn't want to chase after her. She might've thought it inappropriate for me to turn up at her bedroom door after what she'd just witnessed. Or in bad taste.'

Bernadette chuckled. 'Oh, to be a fly on the wall during that conversation.'

'Shoo,' he said briefly, but added as she walked away, 'Thanks for the coffee, by the way. I desperately need the caffeine.'

At the door, she shot him an odd look. 'Leo?'

'Yes?'

'You're not drinking again, are you?'

His jaw hardened. 'Give me a little credit for common sense, would you? I may have the odd drink occasionally, but I gave up my drunken nights when Francis died. As you know well.'

'Yes, it's just that… You've been having a hard time of it lately. All the stress over the family business. And now this thing with Liselle.' She paused, studying him thoughtfully. 'And Maeve.'

'Maeve?' He took a sip of his coffee, which was still scalding hot, and grimaced. 'I barely know the woman. I just thought she would make a good model. Plus, she wanted to help out, so why wouldn't I accept? There's nothing between us, so don't build it up into some grand affair.'

'Of course not, brother dear,' Bernadette said sweetly. 'I wouldn't dream of it. Enjoy your coffee.'

He glared at the closed door for some time after she'd gone. Why did everyone in his family insist on creating dramas for him where there were none?

It was ludicrous. Though not, perhaps, as ludicrous as that scene with Liselle this morning. He took another sip of his coffee and realised, guiltily, that he was remembering his former girlfriend's naked body bouncing against his. The strange thing was, the memory didn't arouse him. Once upon a time, he might have been tempted to accept her offer of sex. But this morning, he'd been more interested in getting her clothes back on and pushing her out of the door before Maeve arrived.

He had barely thought about that side of life for months, even years. At one point, he'd given up on it, sure his libido had died. All the stress of the family business, Bernadette had said. And she wasn't far wrong. Stress could kill a man's libido, couldn't it?

But the truth was, his libido had been alive and kicking this morning. But not for naked Liselle. No, he had been entirely focused on Maeve instead. Thinking about her, waiting for her, anxious about how things would go...

What had Liselle said about her? That she was dull? Ordinary? And *innocent*? She was neither dull nor ordinary, and he didn't know that she was *sexually* innocent either, which would be unlikely at her age. But she was certainly unsophisticated and inexperienced, because everything about her shouted that. She was like someone from another age. Or in this case, another country. So maybe it was just her Englishness that intrigued him.

Though he suspected her body was also fairly intriguing. Because he'd started to wonder, almost as soon as he'd seen her, what her lips would taste like and how she would look after making love...

So that put paid to the dead libido theory.

Somewhat heartened by this, Leo finished his coffee as quickly as was humanly possible, given its extreme temperature, and stumbled into the shower to wash off the night's endeavours. Dried paint was streaked across his hands and forearms, even one cheek. He was surprised that Bernadette hadn't commented on it. But he'd noticed her looking at him strangely.

No doubt his sister was trying to be discreet. They all hoped he would start painting again, after all, but he'd snapped at them so often when they enquired about his artwork that she was probably afraid to raise the subject.

He had to stop doing that. Snapping at people. He had to become a better person. It had been three years since Francis died, and it was time he stopped complaining about the responsibility he'd felt unable to evade. A responsibility he had never wanted and didn't particularly enjoy – apart from the wine-tasting, which had its moments. But his life was what it was, and he needed to grow up and stop pining for a past he could never hope to retrieve.

In time, he might even become dull and sensible, like Maeve.

Leo threw back his head and laughed as the water cascaded over him. Dull and sensible? Him? Never in a thousand years...

Returning his coffee cup to the kitchen later, he was taken aback to find Maeve sweeping the tiled floor, an apron about her waist, her hair hidden under a blue head scarf that he vaguely recognised as belonging to his sister.

A sudden vision flashed through his head, leaving him transfixed... A portrait of her in apron, headscarf and kitchen clogs, going about some homely task, maybe with a toddler tugging on her skirts.

He was shocked by the way his imagination was leading him. His portraits had always been of women in wild, provocative poses or making political statements. He'd never been interested in what some people called 'kitchen sink' portraiture, considering that old-fashioned and disrespectful to modern women.

As for painting Maeve in an apron, cooking or cleaning, with a child in tow...

Talk about *regressive* imagery.

If she could read his mind right now, he thought grimly, she'd probably hit him with that broom, and quite blamelessly.

'Good morning.'

She jumped at his soft greeting, jerking around to stare at him. Light from the kitchen window illuminated the turn of her cheek, a few strands of blonde hair peeping out from under her headscarf.

Hurriedly, to cover his growing fascination with her, he asked rather brusquely, 'What are you doing? That's not your job. You don't have a job, in fact. You're a guest.' He took the broom away from her, just in case she was moved to use it as a weapon later on. 'If the floor needs sweeping, I'll sweep it myself.'

As the words left his mouth, he cast a swift glance about the place, hoping not to find it did indeed need sweeping.

But it was spotless, as usual.

She did not protest but looked back at him with her chin raised, folding her arms. 'I told you yesterday, I want to help out around the château in return for board and lodging. It's not right simply to lounge about, enjoying your hospitality for the next couple of weeks.' A slight colour came into her cheeks as she added in a stilted voice, 'Besides, it looks as though the painting thing isn't going to happen. Not after what I saw this morning.'

He gripped the broom handle tightly. 'That wasn't my fault. She threw herself at me.'

Now she swung her head to stare at him,

incredulous laughter in her face. 'She threw herself at you? In the nude, no less? My goodness, you must be a regular Tom Jones.'

'Sorry?'

'Tom Jones, the Welsh singer? You must have heard of him.'

'Vaguely.'

'Women used to throw their knickers at him when he was performing on stage.'

He blinked, and started some incoherent sentence that petered out long before he'd worked out what he wanted to say.

There was a scathing smile on her lips as she went on, 'Although it looked as though Liselle had skipped the knicker-throwing part and moved straight to what comes after.'

'It was a mistake. Liselle thought… '

She raised her eyebrows when another sentence foundered hopelessly on the rocks. 'Yes? What did she think?'

'It was a misunderstanding, okay? Not that it's any of your business,' he finished defensively.

'In general, I'd say yes. But when I've been asked to be in a certain place at a certain time, and turn up to find you rolling on the floor with a naked woman, then it absolutely is my business.'

Leo winced inwardly; he could hardly argue with that.

Carefully, he put the broom aside. 'All right, yes, that's fair. And I apologise, even though I wasn't to blame. I shall ask Liselle to apologise as well.'

'Oh, please don't! Not on my account.' She grabbed a damp cloth and began wiping down the kitchen surfaces in a furious manner.

'There are things about Liselle and me that you don't know... And I can't elaborate.'

'I didn't ask you to.'

He had no idea why he still felt this burning need to paint her. If he could simply walk off and forget... But he couldn't. And it had been so long since he'd felt anything akin to this urge, he couldn't let the chance slip away.

'Let me make it up to you,' he said, leaning against a kitchen cabinet, watching while she worked. Though there wasn't much for her to do. Bernadette was a conscientious worker and kept the place immaculate. 'I still want to paint you, Maeve.'

'Sorry, bit busy right now.'

'I didn't mean immediately. I have a call to make, anyway.' He frowned, battling frustration. Why wouldn't she even look at him? Surely it couldn't be Liselle's nudity that was still making her blank him? 'Ordinary' she might be, compared to the wilder elements of the Parisian artistic community, but she didn't strike him as that much of a prude. 'Please stop cleaning.'

'I like cleaning. It keeps me fit.'

He sighed. 'Okay, next time I'll come and fetch you to the studio myself. If that makes you feel more comfortable.'

Maeve paused in her hurried, overly dramatic wiping and turned to glare at him, her eyebrows arched. 'No thanks. Not if I'm expected to take all my clothes off and engage in... in *floor exercises* with you.'

Now she was mocking him. He gritted his teeth, managing a smile in return. 'Ha ha. You know that's not what was happening this morning.'

'Oh, I know.' She snorted, returning to her task. 'Trust me, I know.'

'Let me take you out to dinner,' he said suddenly, and grabbed her by the apron strings while she was still turned away from him. She protested, clearly outraged that he'd dared touch her, but he unfastened her apron with ease, throwing the damn thing onto the counter. 'No more cleaning. You're our guest,' he reiterated firmly. 'Besides, there are some things I'd like to talk to you about which I can't discuss under this roof.'

'What kind of things?' she demanded, her face flushed.

'Come to dinner with me and find out. My cousin Jean runs a café at the end of this street. We can eat there.'

Maeve kept her back firmly turned away while she washed and dried her hands. 'I'm not sure that's a good idea, Monsieur Rémy.'

'Oh, we're back to Monsieur Rémy, are we?' He sucked in a breath, thrusting his hands into his pockets. 'Dinner. Eight o'clock tonight. I'll come and find you. My treat.'

'Well, it can hardly be my treat. I haven't got any money.'

He frowned, surprised. 'I thought your bank was going to transfer funds to you here in Paris?'

'Yes, but the thing is...' She shuffled, looking uncomfortable. 'I don't actually have much in my bank account at the moment. This trip to Paris wiped out my savings and I'm not paid again until the end of the month. They agreed to send me a few hundred, and I'll probably collect that at some point. But I'm worried about going too far overdrawn.'

'I see.' He felt sorry for her. What an appalling situation to be in. No wonder she was unhappy about accepting what she saw as charity from them. 'In that case, could I lend you some money? Just so you're not completely without funds.'

She looked appalled, her eyes flying to his face. 'No, thank you,' she said in strangled tones. 'I wasn't begging when I said that about my bank account... I was just trying to explain.' She stumbled over the words, her expression mortified. 'Oh, I wish I'd never come to Paris. This whole thing has been excruciating.'

'I'm sorry you feel that way,' he said deeply, and meant it. 'Because if you hadn't come, I would never have met you, and never felt this incredible urge to paint again.' He paused, very aware of her watching him, surprise in her face. He couldn't say much more. It would be too humiliating. But he felt something extra was required. 'As my grandmother was no doubt eager to tell you yesterday, it's been rather a long time since I picked up a paintbrush. But I can tell you more about that at dinner. If you'll come?'

She hesitated, and then said reluctantly, 'All right, yes. I would like to hear more about your painting difficulties.' Her eyes widened and she clapped a hand to her mouth. 'Sorry, that came out all wrong. I meant, I'd like to hear more about your work in general. I love art,' she added shyly. 'Though I can't paint for toffee.'

'*Toffee?*'

She laughed open. 'It's just an English expression... It means I can't paint at all. I don't have an artistic bone in my body. But I do love looking at paintings.'

He studied her, wishing he knew why this sensible, unshowy Englishwoman was so intriguing to him. Or how he could get her to relax enough to come back to the studio.

I do love looking at paintings.

Perhaps that would be a place to start... Talking about art, finding common ground, assuming they had any.

'Eight o'clock,' he repeated, and went in search of his mobile.

CHAPTER TEN

His uncle Henri was a jovial man in his late fifties, huge and bearded, and the father of nine children. Sophie and Marie, the twins, were his youngest children at seventeen. His wife Beatrice was also jovial and matronly, and when they sometimes got together as a family at Christmas, Henri and Beatrice would bustle about the Christmas tree with presents and eggnog and special delicacies for Noel, so like Father Christmas and Mrs Santa that it had become customary in the family to refer to them by those names. Speaking to Henri on the phone now, Leo was reminded of his Santa-like persona, listening to Henri's deep, booming voice as they exchanged pleasantries at the beginning of the call.

'Yes, uncle, I'm very well, thank you. I'm sorry I mislaid my phone earlier. Bernadette tells me you needed to speak to me urgently.' Leo sat down in a quiet corner of the courtyard and stretched out his feet, carefully positioned in the shade to avoid the early afternoon sun. He was hungry, but he had no time for a meal. He had wasted enough of the day as it was, sleeping off his idiotic all-nighter. 'What's the matter, Uncle Henri?'

'Well, Leo...' Henri's voice had lost its usual sparkling humour. He cleared his throat. 'The thing is, I'm afraid there's been an unfortunate incident here at the Cave Rémy warehouse.'

The warehouse was where they stored and sold wine, and held public wine tasting events, situated on the side of the road just outside their vineyard in the heart of Bordeaux territory. Compared to the modern house where that branch of the Rémy family lived, the warehouse and wine-tasting cellar was a lovely, old-fashioned space, wood-lined and redolent of vintage wines. The walls there were covered with huge, blown up photographs from days gone by: the harvest being brought in on wagons, or people in vats, grinning as they stomped the grapes down with their bare feet, and a large picture of his father alongside Henri, standing proudly outside the gates to the Rémy vineyard, both raising a glass of their own ruby-red wine.

Then there were the stores of barrels and bottles of wine, mostly housed in cool cellars deep beneath the public wine-tasting space.

Seriously alarmed by the thought that something cataclysmic might have happened, Leo sat forward, frowning. 'What kind of incident? Is it serious? Have the wine cellars been affected?'

'The wine is safe, thank goodness, but I'm afraid

it's not great news, Leo. I'm very sorry to say there was a fire last night. The sprinklers kicked in and we managed to put it out. But not before some damage had occurred. The pictures on the wall and most of the furnishings will need to be replaced. It could take weeks to put the place straight.'

'*Mon Dieu.*' Leo closed his eyes against the dazzle of sunlight on windows. If only he felt less exhausted. He wasn't thinking straight. But he was smitten with guilt that because of his reckless behaviour, he had missed this opportunity to advise his uncle earlier. 'That's terrible news. And in the summer season too.' He ran a hand through his hair, feeling grim. 'I'm sorry I'm only just catching up on this news. Have you spoken to the insurers?'

'That's the first thing I did. They'll cover the damage, but the excess on the policy is pretty steep. It's going to put us back several thousand euros.'

Leo tried not to groan out loud, aware of his grandmother crossing the courtyard. He didn't want to worry her unduly. 'Yes, I see. How did the fire start?'

'We're still not sure. They're sending somebody from the insurance company to examine the scene. But my theory is it was electrical. There's no other explanation, really. We had some new equipment brought in a few weeks ago. It may be that something was faulty. Bad wiring, you know.'

'Do you need me to come down there?' He glanced at his watch, making hurried calculations in his head. 'I could pack a bag and jump on a train. Be there later tonight.'

'That's very good of you, Leo, but there's no need. We've got it in hand.'

'All the same, it might be a good idea.'

'Well, if you get the time… Just let me know and we'll sort out a room for you.'

'No, I'll book into one of the local hotels. No need to cause extra work for Beatrice.'

'Don't be ridiculous. Besides, Bea won't do the work herself. Some of the children will help. You know I have a whole tribe here. Might as well take advantage of their free labour.' His uncle gave a deep rumble of laughter. 'Talking of my tribe, how are those young rascals Sophie and Marie getting along there? Not misbehaving, I hope?'

'I believe Grandmère and Bernadette have been taking it in turns to show them around the famous sights of Paris. Yes, and take them to art galleries and museums, as you requested. All very educational, and with no excursions after dark. They did ask but Nonna shook her head. And when Nonna says no, nobody dares disobey her.'

Again, he heard the rumble of his uncle's laughter.

He rang off, assuring his uncle that he would try

to visit Bordeaux, so they could discuss the fire in more detail and how the repairs were going.

It was a financial headache, all right. But at least the premises had been insured. Otherwise it could have been disastrous. Even so, having the Cave out of order at the height of the summer season would make a serious dent in their profits for that year. And they'd already been struggling financially after a series of problematic harvests, along with the recent hike in the cost of living. The fire was bad news, for sure. It might mean having to extend their bank loan.

As he checked the balances on their business accounts in his banking app, a shadow fell across him and Leo looked up, narrowing his eyes against the sun.

'We need to talk.'

It was Liselle, wearing a one-piece black and gold swimsuit that clung to her curves and a diaphanous housecoat over the top, carrying a bottle of sun oil and a thick white towel draped over one arm. She was wearing dark sunglasses so that he couldn't read her expression. But he could read her body language and it wasn't friendly.

'Talk?' Putting down his phone, he leant back slowly. 'What about?'

'For God's sake, Leo. Don't pretend you don't know.'

'I honestly have no idea what this is about. Unless it was our embarrassing tussle this morning... If you've come to say sorry, I would be happy to accept your apology.'

'Apologise?' she almost spat the words at him, fury in the tightening of her lips. 'Oh, I got the message this morning. You're determined to amuse yourself with that girl... Fine! You do that.' She gave a careless shrug that didn't fool him. 'But we need to talk business.'

'What kind of business?'

'Sascha rang.'

She gave a satisfied smile when he stared in disbelief. Sascha was a well-known impresario on the art scene in Paris, who was their go-to man when it came to setting up art exhibitions. But he hadn't had any conversations with Leo for some time. No paintings, no exhibitions. It was that simple.

'He had a minor exhibition fall through at the last minute,' she went on airily. 'It was set for three weeks' time and everyone seems to have left Paris for the holidays, so he's been struggling to fill the gap in his schedule. As your manager, I said you might be available.'

He jumped up, glaring at her, his heart thumping. 'You did *what*?'

'Calm down... It'll be good for your profile. It's only a small gallery space but in a prominent location. And it's only for a week. A flash exhibition. There and gone.' She played with her hair, watching him with a cat-like smile. 'I agreed to have drinks with him tomorrow, thrash out the details.'

'Have you gone mad? I don't have anything to exhibit.'

'Regardless, you can't miss this opportunity. A summer exhibition, Leo, with all the tourists here in Paris. Think of the sales you could make.'

'You're not hearing me.' Leo felt like grinding his teeth in frustration. Why wasn't she listening to him? 'I have no pictures to exhibit, let alone sell.'

'But you might have,' she said delicately, eyeing him sideways. 'You're still planning to paint *her*, aren't you?'

'*Her*? You mean Maeve?' He felt winded at the mention of her name, caught off guard as he remembered their recent conversation. 'She's changed her mind,' he said flatly. 'Doesn't want to go anywhere near my studio. Not after that stunt you pulled this morning.'

'Ah...' She pushed her sunglasses up and met his eyes. 'Okay, you wanted an apology. Well, here it is. *I'm sorry.* I was jealous. I didn't understand.'

Leo thrust his hands in his pockets. He wasn't sure he could trust her sincerity, but he'd agreed to accept her apology if she made one. 'Thank you,' he said grudgingly. 'But it doesn't change anything.'

'It won't happen again, believe me. I can tell her that myself, if you like.'

'No,' he said quickly, horrified.

'Fine, whatever. Then I'll leave it to you to lure her back to your studio.' With a shrug, Liselle slipped her sunglasses back on. 'Paint her, Leo,' she told him. 'Paint her as quickly and often as you can. In every conceivable position.' Her mocking laughter echoed about the courtyard. 'Then you'll have plenty of new paintings to exhibit, won't you?'

'In three weeks? Impossible.'

His former girlfriend sauntered on towards the sun loungers, slipping her see-through wrap off golden, sun-kissed shoulders. 'I have faith in you, Leo,' she threw back at him. 'And don't tell me it's impossible. I know exactly what you get like when you're *inspired*, remember?'

CHAPTER ELEVEN

The bar-café at the end of the street, now simply called *Chez Jean*, had belonged to the Rémy family for decades. His father had taken a hand in managing the bar at one time, but his love of alcohol had made it a dangerous place for him, and Leo's grandfather had soon replaced him. Leo himself had grown up there, threading through the tight-spaced tables on the pavement with lunch plates or fresh carafes of water. He had watched football games on the television inside the bar and, as he got older, had played cards with the pot washers between shifts, until his grandfather had found out and forbidden him entry for a few years. Francis had also briefly managed the place, but having always been groomed for the top position in the family, the café at the end of the street had been more of a side hustle then a position of prestige. So Cousin Jean had been parachuted in to look after it in the years before Francis's death, while Leo was still living in the South of France, painting by night and sleeping all day, like an artistic vampire.

When he'd taken over the family business in Francis's stead, Leo had left Jean in his managerial position at the café. His cousin was eccentric, to say the least, and occasionally annoying, but he had a sound mind for business and enjoyed turning a profit. In these difficult times, profit was hard to come by. So Jean remained at the café and Leo ate there once or twice a week, less to keep an eye on the place and more to escape the claustrophobic atmosphere of the château.

He loved his grandmother and his Nonna deeply, and held Bernadette in great affection, of course. But with Liselle at home too, he often had the sensation of walking on eggshells, trying not to provoke a scene. She could be difficult and unpredictable, though sometimes sunny and generous too, and then abruptly vile.

The plain truth was, Liselle was a complicated and contrary person, and his life felt calmer when she wasn't around.

He and Maeve wandered along to Jean's bar after eight o'clock. He had half suspected she might back out. That would have been frustrating. Ever since last night, he'd become increasingly obsessed with the idea of painting her, and he knew he wouldn't feel easy until he'd made a proper attempt to get something down on canvas.

As they approached the café, Maeve gasped, 'Oh,

it's lovely… How beautiful.'

Jean, with one of his eccentric touches, had placed large tubs of foliage outside the café, and set up strings of coloured lights among the leaves, so that it was permanent Christmas for the customers, the red, white and blue lights flashing merrily away as they drank and dined. Inside, the wall was also an aquarium, where fish darted and shimmered among thick green weeds and miniature shipwrecks.

Leo opened the door for her, 'I usually eat inside in the evenings. Unless you'd prefer an outside table?'

She rubbed her arms, glancing about at the busy outdoor tables. The evening was cool, and she was wearing a sleeveless summer dress that Bernadette had lent her. 'No, inside is perfect.'

'You can borrow my jacket if you're cold.'

She smiled at that but shook her head. 'Thank you, I'm fine.'

Jean emerged from the back of the café on seeing them, his smile broad. He was wearing a white, open-necked shirt with a black velvet choker about his throat, a large fake pearl dangling from it. More eccentric dressing, Leo guessed. But it seemed to draw the customers.

'Wonderful, wonderful,' Jean cried softly, kissing them both several times on each cheek, while other customers turned to stare at them. 'I'm so glad you could make it, Mademoiselle.

I've arranged a corner alcove table for you and Leo. *Maximum* privacy.' And he gave Leo an exaggerated wink, who bristled.

What the hell was his cousin trying to insinuate? He wanted Maeve to think of this as a business arrangement, not a seduction. But at least Jean seemed to catch his frown, for his smile disappeared, as did he a few seconds later, muttering, 'I'll fetch the menus, shall I?'

Leo waited while Maeve slid into the booth, and then followed her. 'I apologise for my cousin. He's not very sensible.'

'I think Jean's rather sweet. Funny, you know.'

'No, I don't know.' He grimaced, realising he must sound like a jerk, and added diplomatically, 'Don't get me wrong. I like Jean. And he runs this place extremely well. But he's not a subtle person.'

'Maybe I'm not, either,' Maeve said tartly.

He studied her thoughtfully for a moment. 'Actually, I'd say the opposite. You're not brash, at any rate.'

She had been gazing about the noisy café with interest, but now frowned round at him, leaning forward to ask above the hubbub, 'Sorry... what? Did you say I have *a rash*?'

'No, I said you weren't *brash*.' He frowned, instantly wondering if he'd mispronounced the word. He spoke English fluently but it had been a long while since he'd spoken it regularly with anyone.

'Oh, I see. No, I'm not brash. And I don't have a rash either.' Maeve raised her brows but sat back again. She seemed distracted, looking down, apparently fascinated by the pattern on her summer dress.

Was she *nervous*?

Did she too think this was a 'date,' perhaps?

Leo was about to dismiss the idea as ludicrous when he realised she might have a point. He could have spoken to her anywhere, after all. Instead, he had chosen to take her out to this intimate little bar where they played soft jazz and the lighting was kept permanently low...

Maybe it was a date.

Maybe he was the one who was behaving unpredictably this time.

Frustration churned inside him.

He still couldn't understand why this mousy little Englishwoman attracted him so much. Because Liselle had been unkind but unerringly correct in her assessment of Maeve, who was indeed quite ordinary-looking.

Leo studied her covertly. Her hair was the darker side of fair rather than blonde, the colour of old straw. She wore it in a neat bob too, well-regimented strands dropping to just above her shoulders and rather too perfectly framing her face, which was also not striking in any way. It was the kind of no-nonsense style he associated with schoolteachers from his youth, and indeed she had told them she was a teacher, as he recalled. Her eyes were blue, but not an electric or deep blue, more like the soft, generic blue on a faded willow-pattern plate.

And she wore no make-up to highlight her eyes or lips. Her mouth was on the generous side though, and his gaze did keep dropping to it. She had a habit of licking her lips when nervous, and he was uncomfortably aware that he found that sexually provocative.

Other than that tiny detail, she was not his type. If he even had a type anymore, which was doubtful.

Maybe once upon a time, he might have had a 'type' of woman he routinely fell for... And that would have been someone like Liselle, he suspected. Bold, vibrant, showy, and yes, hard work...

In the past, and especially in his late teens and early twenties, he'd routinely become obsessed with difficult women, the type who baffled and intrigued him, and who always behaved unpredictably. A psychologist would probably have said that was the result of losing his mother so young. He preferred to think of it as a fervent desire to avoid commitment, the sort of women who attracted him tending to be those with zero interest in settling down and starting a family.

But endless work and grief over his brother's death had all but driven women from his mind in recent years, much to Liselle's frustration.

Suddenly, he was interested again. Yet couldn't grasp his motivation. Maeve was no pushover, it was true. But neither was she a firebrand.

At that moment, she stopped staring down into her lap and shifted to study the massive fish tank instead, situated immediately behind their alcove.

He caught his breath, his gaze narrowing on her profile.

Again, a vision struck him.

Maeve sitting beside an open fire in a darkened room, her face turned away, light glinting in her hair, perhaps a half-smile on her lips...

'What are you thinking?' he asked abruptly, and she turned back, a startled look on her face. 'Just then, looking at the aquarium... What were you thinking about?'

'I was thinking how strange it must be,' she said slowly, 'to be a fish.'

Leo threw back his head and laughed at the unexpected absurdity. 'A fish?'

'Well, you did ask.'

'And let that be a lesson to me.'

She gave a little chuckle herself, seeming to relax. Though he had the impression she was never really relaxed, even when smiling. That she was always waiting for something bad to happen. That she feared making a mistake, perhaps.

'Would you call yourself a perfectionist?' he

asked, and saw surprise widen her eyes.

'I don't think it's possible to be perfect,' she muttered.

'But you *try* to be perfect.'

It hadn't been a question. He was starting to understand her.

Maeve hesitated. 'I try not to get things wrong, I suppose,' she said, sitting very straight, her back stiff. Jean came back with the menus and she gave him a dazzling smile. The kind of smile she had never given Leo. 'Merci, Jean.'

Jean grinned at her, and then encountered another hard stare from Leo. Hurrying away, he said, 'I'll fetch you both an aperitif. On the house.'

They perused the menu in silence, and when Jean came back with the drinks, they gave him their orders. His cousin seemed to have taken a liking to Maeve, he noted, Jean even going so far as to put a hand on her shoulder while he was laughing and explaining the intricacies of one of their signature dishes.

Leo glared at that hand until it was withdrawn.

Once Jean had disappeared again, Maeve sipped at her aperitif and choked on the strong alcohol. 'What on earth is this?' she enquired, peering at the milky pink substance in her glass.

'I have no idea,' he admitted. 'I don't take much interest in this place. Jean designs all the food menus and invents his own speciality drinks. Though this,' he said, indicating what he was drinking, 'is my usual when I come through. A non-alcoholic aperitif. Ruby Fruit, he calls it. Mainly orange and pineapple juice, with a kick.' He bit into one of the cherries bobbing about at the top of his glass, and caught Maeve's curious glance. 'What's the matter? You don't approve of non-alcoholic drinks?'

'I thought that you...' She bit her lip. 'That is, I assumed...'

'I used to have a problem with drinking,' he said bluntly. 'Which is why I try to avoid it these days. I'm okay most of the time. But when things get stressful, I like to drink and I can take it too far, if you see what I mean. So it's best avoided altogether.'

'I understand,' she said earnestly, leaning forward again with her gaze on his face.

'Do you? Do you really?' He saw her wary expression and pulled a face. 'Sorry, that wasn't fair. I didn't mean...'

He stopped himself and grimaced. How was it possible to keep sticking his foot in his mouth every five minutes? She seemed to bring out the idiot in him. Or maybe she made him nervous, which was a novel thought.

'Look, I brought you here to escape my crazy household,' he said in a more level tone. 'So we could relax and enjoy each other's company. Perhaps we should just concentrate on doing that.'

Her brow wrinkled. 'I thought you bought me here to tell me why you stopped painting.'

Leo had forgotten that promise, so focused on getting her alone. He stared back at her, winded, unable to say a thing.

She seemed to sense his horror.

'Of course, if you'd rather not... But since we're here and nobody else is listening...'

At that moment, Jean arrived with their order, both of them having ordered a light one-course supper, perfect fare for a bar meal.

'A carafe of water for you both. Moules frites for mademoiselle, steak frites for you, Leo.' He set the plates before them with a flourish as though serving the finest cordon bleu. 'Mustard? Mayonnaise?' He directed these queries at Maeve, already aware that Leo never took any bottled sauce with his steak, though he had been known to enjoy the occasional aioli.

'Do you have tomato ketchup?' Maeve asked.

A shudder ran through Jean but he maintained his professional smile. 'But of course... All the American and British tourists, they ask for ketchup. So we always keep ketchup.' He whisked away, returning briefly with a dish of tomato ketchup which he placed before her, bowing. The long silver earring he habitually wore jiggled and caught the light. *'Bon appétit!'*

When Jean had gone back to the kitchen, Maeve chewed cautiously on the mussel, and then smiled.

'That tastes good, I take it?' he asked her.

'Delicious,' she enthused. 'I'd never had moules-frites before coming to Paris, can you believe it? But I love them now. In fact, this is my third time of ordering them.'

'Not very adventurous, are you?'

'I'm working on it,' she said defensively. 'How's your steak?'

'Bloody.'

She shuddered. 'How awful. Better send it back.'

He shook his head. 'Bloody is exactly how I like it,' he explained. 'Whenever I come to Chez Jean, I nearly always order their steak-frites, so the chef knows how to prepare it for me.'

Her brows rose. 'Oh, so you always order the same meal when you come here? Not very adventurous, are you?'

He grinned. 'Touché.' Reaching for the carafe of water, he pouring them both a large glass. '*Santé.*'

'*Santé*,' she echoed, taking a sip of her aperitif instead, which she had barely touched, he noticed. Too strong, perhaps.

'Would you like something else to drink? A glass of wine?'

'This is fine.' She set down the aperitif and began to eat again, demonstrating a healthy appetite. But five minutes later, just as he was starting to relax and enjoy his meal, she caught him off guard him by saying, 'You've done a fine job of distracting me. But it's no use, Leo. I haven't forgotten.'

He stared, taken aback. 'Sorry?'

'You were going to tell me why you don't paint anymore.' She popped a crispy golden chip into her mouth, raising her calm gaze to his face. 'I'm still waiting.'

She was a determined creature, wasn't she? Almost to the point of making his teeth grind.

'Fine, all right, I'll tell you.' Finishing a last mouthful in a leisurely way, he picked up his plate and slipped out of the booth, leaving her staring. 'But I need to check something first, if you'll excuse me for just a few minutes.'

With a smile, Leo carried his empty plate through the double swing doors into the kitchen to speak to the chef, Pierre, and sous chef, Anton.

Whenever he came to Chez Jean, he always took a few minutes to touch base with the kitchen and waiting staff, and make sure everyone was happy and working productively.

It was a bore.

But it was also a key part of his duty as head of the family business to make sure things were running smoothly.

Before he'd taken over, he had never thought much about the people preparing his meals or serving him drinks at the bar, or considered the business side whenever he paid a bill. His only world had been painting. He had been a blinkered, self-obsessed idiot.

Now things had swung too far the other way though, and he was lucky if he could spare a few minutes to think about art occasionally. And it was turning his world grey.

With noisy greetings above the sounds of a busy kitchen, they all shook hands and discussed how business was going, while Pierre continued to dress plates for customers and Anton chopped fish heads, whistling as he prepared a spicy bouillabaisse for tomorrow's Plat Du Jour.

On his way back to the table, he encountered Jean, a wiping cloth over one shoulder, juggling dirty plates from a table he'd been clearing.

'That was a good meal,' he told his cousin, 'thank you. I don't think we'll bother with dessert though. We'll just have coffee and head back to the château.'

Jean frowned. 'Must you leave so soon? You see how busy we are, and that's largely down to you being here.'

'Me?'

'You're still a big name in Paris, Leo. You bring in the custom. Especially when you have such a lovely young lady with you.' He glanced towards Maeve. 'It's got everyone's tongues wagging, wondering who she is.'

'Oh, come on, Jean. I doubt anyone's interested in who's having dinner with me.'

'Don't be naïve. Look around.'

Nettled, Leo glanced about the bar, and realised with a shock that his cousin was correct. People were indeed looking round at him and Maeve. The curiosity in the air was palpable.

'I hear Liselle is setting you up with Sascha for a new exhibition soon,' Jean went on, also watching him avidly. 'I didn't know you were painting again. Congratulations.'

Leo's gaze arrowed back to his cousin's face. 'You know perfectly well I haven't been painting. It's a mistake on Liselle's part even to have spoken to Sascha without checking with me first. I don't have any new work to exhibit and she knows it.'

'Is that so? But if the little Englishwoman will sit for you...' Jean winked.

Leo felt a surge of annoyance. 'Keep your nose out of my business,' he said flatly. 'Is that clear?'

'Whatever you say, *boss*,' his cousin replied, his tone surly as he pushed through the swing doors.

Wishing that people would stop interfering in his life, Leo made his way back to the table.

'Come on then... You still haven't told me why you haven't been painting,' Maeve said impatiently as he sat down opposite. 'I'm beginning to think you brought me here on false pretenses.'

She was tenacious, he had to give her that.

But Leo felt cornered, staring at her as he struggled to respond without letting anything too personal slip. Was that even possible though?

Thankfully, he was saved by the coffee arriving, courtesy of a young waitress he didn't know. But he knew he couldn't put this off forever.

'Give me a minute,' he muttered.

She pushed his cup of coffee towards him. 'Maybe this will help.'

'Thanks.' He took a sip and grimaced. 'After my brother died,' he began slowly, 'my inspiration died with him. Francis despised art and painting. You would think it would have been a liberation. But I was forced to take over the family business and that became my life. There was no more time for painting. A few months ago, I set up a studio at the château and decided to produce some new work.' He stared at nothing, remembering. 'But I ended up just standing there, paintbrush in hand, staring at a blank canvas.'

Tentatively, she placed her hand on top of his, and he jerked at the unexpected contact. 'I'm sorry,' she said. 'I had no idea.'

'That's because nobody outside the family knows. They still think of me as Leo Rémy, famous artist,' he said bitterly. 'People stop me in the street and ask when my next exhibition will be.'

'But you said… You want to paint *me*?'

His heart thumped uncomfortably. 'Yes.'

'How strange.' She removed her hand, frowning. 'Though I suppose it wouldn't hurt for you to try again. And I've got nothing better to do at the moment.'

Unexpected joy swept through him as he realised she was agreeing to let him paint her. 'You're serious?' His eye caught by a gleam of light, he spotted Jean on the other side of the bar, staring in their direction and lowering his phone. His brows contracted. 'Excuse me a moment again, would you?'

Getting up, he strode across the bar, grabbing Jean's arm before he could escape. 'What the hell are you up to? Were you taking a photograph of us?'

Jean looked at him in astonishment. 'I don't know what you're talking about. I was just checking something on my phone.' Wresting his arm free, he headed back into the kitchen.

Leo stared after his cousin, suspicious and conflicted. He didn't trust Jean. But he couldn't make a scene here in the bar. People were already staring.

He went back and sat down.

'What's the matter?' Maeve asked, frowning.

'Nothing.' But he was now keen to get out of there, restless and impatient. 'Shall we head back? They can put the bill on my tab.' He saw her surprise and added brusquely, 'I can't wait to paint you.'

'Paint me?' Her eyes stretched wide. 'You mean... Right now? *Tonight*?'

'Why not?'

CHAPTER TWELVE

Maeve stood embarrassed and uncertain in the middle of Leo's studio. Why on earth had she agreed to do this?

Last time she'd set foot in this room, she'd been greeted by the sight of Leo rolling about with a naked woman, and she didn't want to be the next woman to shed her clothes for him. Or roll about on the floor with him, for that matter. Not that she had any qualms about her body. Although nothing special, her body was perfectly functional. But it was one thing to strip off in the gym showers without worrying too much about lumps and bumps, and quite another to pose nude under the cool, discerning eye of Leo Rémy.

She hugged herself, looking about. 'I... I'm keeping my clothes on,' she told him, and winced at the high-pitched, prudish note in her voice.

He laughed, going about the high-ceilinged room and flinging open the windows to the sounds of distant traffic and beeping horns, with sudden flurries of music behind those.

'Naturally.'

She was relieved by that reassurance. No nudity. Though on a scale of one to ten, her relief was still only about a four. The other six points were screaming at her to get out while she could...

'Where do you want me?' she asked stoutly.

His head whipped around and he stared at her. 'Do I *want* you?' he repeated in astounded tones.

'No – God, no!' She also stared. 'I said... *Where.*' She huffed out a breath, her heart thudding. '*Where* do you want me?'

'Oh.' Leo blinked and ran a hand through sleek hair. Why did he have to have such magnificent hair? She wished he was in his seventies with a head of woolly grey. Or younger than her, perhaps, with dreadlocks down to his waist and a cheeky grin that meant she didn't have to take him seriously. As it was... 'Sorry. I must've misheard.'

Dragging a stool forward, he pointed to it. 'Sit. No, facing me. One hand here,' he ordered her brusquely, positioning her as though she were a mannequin. 'And one there, in your lap. Yes, that's it.' He stared at her intently, then stalked around the stool, examining her from every angle. He did something to her hair from behind, while she sat still and alert, staring at the far wall. 'A few inches this way?' She shifted obligingly, and he stopped her, a warm hand on her shoulder in the sleeveless dress that Bernadette had lent her. 'That's enough... Perfect. Now, don't move.'

'You said I wouldn't have to hold still,' she grumbled.

'Did I?' He bent to a wooden chest, gathering pencils and sketchpad. His bottom was rather magnificent too, she thought, and realised she had been staring fixedly at it. When she didn't respond, he glanced at her over his shoulder and she hurriedly averted her eyes, pretending to be fascinated by a particular spot on the floor. 'Yes, my apologies. That was a lie.'

Abruptly losing interest in the floor, her gaze shot to his face again. Not his bottom, she told herself firmly. Never his bottom.

'*What*?'

'Well, not entirely a lie. You can move later, once I've got the basic outline down,' he elaborated with a grin. He returned to what he'd been doing and unknowingly her gaze drifted back down to his nether regions. Goodness, he looked very... fit. 'Until then, you need to keep still, okay?'

'Hmm.'

Leo shrugged out of his jacket, slinging it carelessly over the back of a chair. Flipping open the sketchpad to a fresh page, he started sketching her with swift, fluid pencil strokes. His dark gaze switched between her and the sketchpad every few seconds, penetrating and yet impersonal at the same time.

Maeve sat as still as she could. It felt unnatural. And her nose was itchy. She could feel it demanding that she lift a finger and give it a good old scratch. But he had told her not to move. She resisted. It got itchier. It became maddening. She bore it for a few more seconds, aware of her face twitching, and then demanded, 'How long before I can –'

'Hush.'

'Move?' she finished.

He didn't respond but bared his teeth, making a low noise under his breath as he sketched.

'What was that?' She stared, incredulous. 'Did you just growl at me?'

'Hush… I'm… working…' Thrusting his pencil between his teeth, Leo groped for a piece of putty on his cluttered work desk. 'Didn't quite get your… arm… right.' Frowning with concentration, he used the putty to erase something on the paper before tossing it back onto his desk. The eraser bounced, landing with a clatter in an open box of paint tubes. He didn't even glance in that direction, focused on the sketchpad. 'Can't have you… looking like…' He began sketching again without completing his sentence.

Still fighting the desire to scratch her nose, Maeve frowned. 'Like what?'

'Stop frowning.'

'But like what?' she repeated, trying not to

frown.

'Hmm?'

'You said... You can't have me *looking like*... Only you didn't finish what you were going to say.'

'Sorry?' He narrowed his eyes on her, then kept working. 'Oh, yes... I didn't want you looking like you have three arms. Or one arm twice the width of the other one, perhaps.'

Now she was incensed. '*What*?'

'Sit still, please. Just a little longer.'

She glared at him. 'You do know what you're doing, I take it?'

At that, his gaze rose to her face and fixed there. His look was arrested. Had he finally heard what she was saying? 'Yes, yes,' he hissed.

'Yes, you know what you're doing?' Her nose was itching intolerably. 'Or yes, something else?'

'Whatever you're thinking right now,' he muttered. 'That angry glare. Hold it, would you?'

'Are you serious?'

Leo grimaced. 'No!' The cry was anguished and from the heart, alarming her.

'You're *not* serious?'

'No... You changed expression. Weren't you listening to me? I said, don't move. I said, keep glaring at me.' He dashed furious lines across the paper. 'Whatever you were thinking before, think it again. Think it *harder*.'

'But I don't know what I was thinking.'

He swore in French, baring his teeth again. She

recognised the swear word and it was not a very pleasant one.

'Excuse me?' She fixed him with a cold stare.

'Yes, yes. That's perfect.' His eyes lit up with excitement and he began sketching almost violently. 'This time, hold it. Keep hating me... Yes! More hate! I love it!'

She exhaled crossly. 'You are a very strange person, Monsieur Rémy.'

'No talking. Just glaring, thank you.'

'Oh, for goodness sake...' But she lapsed into silence. Was the man crazy?

Maybe this was what all artists were like though when they were working, she thought, watching him with reluctant fascination. Shouty, sweary and a bit weird. She'd often wondered about that, being utterly uncreative herself and therefore entranced by the idea of someone being an artist, able to make art out of nothing. Dabbing paint onto a blank canvas or creating something out of a heap of odds and ends.

Lost in that thought, she raised a hand at last and absentmindedly scratched the maddening itch on her nose.

'Argh!' Leo threw down his sketchpad and tore at his hair.

'Oops.'

It was long past midnight when Leo finally allowed her to move. By then, Maeve had grown so stiff and wooden that he had to help her get up. She walked about the room like someone who'd been riding a horse for hours, bow-legged and slow, and stretched her back out cautiously while he examined the sketches he'd made.

She was exhausted. But at least the studio was warm. She could imagine what it must feel like to sit completely still in here for hours in the dead of winter.

He had a kettle in the room and got up to make chamomile tea for them both. They sat sipping it, with Maeve still on her stool and him sitting cowboy-style against a chair back, also looking every bit as exhausted as she felt.

'Perhaps we could pick this up again in the morning?' she suggested, and found her throat dry. She hadn't realised how dehydrated she was until she tried to speak. 'Goodness, it's almost one o'clock in the morning. Past my bedtime.'

His brows soared. 'Past your bedtime? Why? You don't have work in the morning.' He studied her. 'Do you never relax?'

She felt heat creep into her cheeks. 'Of course I relax,' she said defensively. 'Maybe being a schoolteacher has made me a little institutionalized, it's true. But there's nothing wrong in preferring to get an early night whenever possible. I'm still recovering from the other night when I was up until goodness knows what time,' she reminded him. 'Wandering the streets of Paris and wondering what was going to happen to me.'

He nodded, his intent gaze on her face. 'What would you have done if we hadn't been able to offer you somewhere to stay?'

The question threw her. Though she'd already thought about it and been thankful that she hadn't been left in that awful position. It would have been a disaster.

'I... I'm not sure,' she admitted. 'I don't know anyone in Paris. At least, not really.'

His brows drew together now. 'What does "not really" mean?'

'Oh, only that I have a grandmother here.'

He lowered his cup, his stare astonished. 'I didn't know you had any family living in Paris.'

'I didn't know either,' she said with a shrug, 'or not until recently. I lost my father not so long ago, but while he was still alive, he talked to me about some old photographs that he said belonged to my mother. One of them was of a woman in Paris holding a baby. My father said that was my grandmother and that the baby was my mother. But my mother left us when I was still a very young child myself, and we've never been back in touch. So for all I know my grandmother could have passed away by now.' She gazed dismally into her cup of chamomile tea. 'And I never knew her.'

There was a lump in her throat as she looked

away, feeling ridiculous. She didn't know why she was getting so emotional over an old lady she'd never met and probably never would now.

'What's her name, this grandmother of yours?'

'I don't actually know. And I only have her address.' Regret gnawed at her. 'Or rather, *had*, past tense. Because I don't even have that anymore. It was written on the back of the photograph which was –'

'In your rucksack,' he finished for her.

'Yes.' She sighed. 'It was in a zipped side pocket. So whoever took my rucksack has the photograph now.'

'And you can't remember the address?' He tipped his head to one side, regarding her in mild surprise. No doubt he thought her a prize idiot. 'Didn't you even write it down somewhere else?'

'I suppose it might be in my search history. But that's on my phone too. In my stolen rucksack.' She found herself wiping away a tear. It was tiredness, that was all. She'd had a very busy day and it was late. 'Perhaps I should go to bed.'

'Drink your chamomile tea. I want to take a few more sketches of you in a different position. Do you mind?' He got up and fetched his sketchbook without waiting for a response.

'Yes, actually, I do mind.'

'Hmm... Ten more minutes. I promise. Maybe fifteen.'

She glared at him resentfully. But what could

she do? He had made the point himself just minutes ago. She would have been sleeping on the streets that first night alone in Paris if he hadn't offered her a bed at Château Rémy. Or if his grandmother hadn't offered her a place to stay, more accurately. No doubt he would have had no qualms about her wandering the streets. But she felt infinitely safer at the château, especially given how few funds she had available.

She had savings, yes, but they were locked up in a special deposit account that was strictly reserved for putting down a deposit on a house one day. Whenever she'd saved enough to make a mortgage affordable rather than crippling... Surely she could put up with a few more days' hardship rather than break into her precious savings?

'That's it. Perfect. There's that hatred again...' His smile was almost feral as he dashed off a few strokes of his pencil, and then moved her about like she was a rag doll. 'Tilt your head slightly that way? That's it, stop.' He continued sketching. 'Maybe twenty minutes. Then you can go to bed, I promise.'

She gave him a fulminating look and his smile widened.

It wasn't hatred though. She wasn't sure of much when it came to Leo Rémy. But one thing was for certain. She didn't hate him.

Half an hour later, there was a tentative knock at the door. Leo's head shot around and it was his turn to glare now. 'Come in.'

It was his sister.

'Sorry to disturb you,' Bernadette said, hesitating on the threshold with uncharacteristic shyness.

'I doubt that you're sorry.' Leo frowned, addressing his sister in rapid French, 'And why are you disturbing us? Can't you see that I'm busy?' He glanced at his watch. 'Good God, is that the time?'

'It hasn't escaped my notice that you're working again,' Bernadette replied in the same language, 'but this is urgent.'

Leo lowered the sketch pad, instantly alert. 'What is it? What's happened?'

From behind her back, Bernadette produced Maeve's rucksack. 'The police dropped this off earlier. But I've only just tracked Maeve down. She wasn't in her bedroom… How was I to know she'd been in here with you *in the middle of the night*?' Her smile was almost malicious.

With a shriek of joy, Maeve dashed forward and was rewarded with her beloved rucksack. Well, not *beloved*. Nobody loves their rucksack. But in that moment, she loved it, and even hugged it to her chest, because it meant she was saved.

Then she weighed it in her hand.

'But... it... it's empty.'

'Yes, I'm afraid the thieves cleared it out. Apart from a few personal effects that they didn't bother taking,' Bernadette told her in careful, slow English mixed with a few French phrases when she couldn't recall the correct word. 'It was found behind some, erm, dustbins not far from where it was stolen. So the thieves probably emptied it and threw it away within minutes of stealing it. The police have left a number where you can talk to them, if you'd like. But, other than that, they say there's no news. Your passport is still missing, and although they found, erm, fingerprints on the bag, the prints don't match anything in their databank.'

Maeve unzipped the rucksack and peered inside. She had half-hoped to find her notebook inside, but it was gone. Her passport and mobile phone and all her notes on important phone numbers had been in that notebook.

Scrabbling about in the bottom of the rucksack, she found only pens and a few other odds and ends. A packet of gum. Hairbands.

She groaned, closing her eyes. 'They've taken everything of any value. I suppose I was lucky to get the bag back. Much good it will do me.'

'Have you checked *all* the compartments?' Leo asked, his voice a disturbing rumble in her ear. 'If they only had it a few minutes, they may not have been very thorough.'

She turned, surprised to find him standing so close to her, also peering into the empty rucksack. 'I don't imagine there'll be anything...' she muttered, but unzipped the small side pocket, and stilled, staring. 'Oh, there is something.' She produced the faded photograph of her grandmother. 'It's a miracle,' she breathed.

Bernadette came forward to peer over their shoulders at the photograph. 'A miracle?' She sounded puzzled, glancing at her brother. '*Je comprends pas*. Who's that in the photo? Why is it important?'

'My grandmother,' Maeve explained. 'It's the only picture I have of her, and I stupidly never made a copy. I thought it had been lost forever.'

'May I?' Leo took the photograph and studied it. 'That looks familiar. How do I know that street?' he mused, then turned over the photograph and read the address out loud. 'Ah, yes... I've taken Grandmère there a few times. In fact, I think that woman *may* be a friend of hers.'

Maeve's mouth fell open. She was probably gaping like a goldfish but didn't care. '*Your* grandmother knows *my* grandmother?' Astonishment made her voice lift to an almost childish pitch as she asked, 'You definitely know that street? Are you sure? You're not making this up, are you?'

'Why would I make it up?' He shook his head, handing her back the photograph. 'Grandmère will be asleep now. But I'll speak to her first thing in the morning.'

He touched his sister's arm. 'Thanks, Bernadette. You did the right thing, bringing the bag up tonight.'

'But I still don't understand,' she said in French. 'Are you saying Maeve's grandmother is French?'

'That's what my father told me.' Maeve spoke in French too, staring down at the lady in the faded photograph, who looked so like her. She had not expected to feel so much emotion on being reunited with this priceless piece of family memorabilia. 'Now I've got this back, maybe I'll be able to find out more.' She glanced hopefully at Leo, who nodded.

'Of course we must find out. I can see how much it means to you.' He bustled Bernadette out of the door, thanking her again with a wolfish grin. 'First though,' he said, reverting to English, 'would you mind just standing there with that photograph for a few minutes, while I take some sketches?'

'*What?* Are you kidding?' Maeve took a shaky breath, battling with outrage. 'You are beyond everything, Leo Rémy. I swear, I'm living through a nightmare here. I'm exhausted. I need to sleep and… and…'

'And spend time with your photograph?' Leo was already sketching her, ignoring her passionate outburst.

'Well, yes.'

'You can spend time with your photograph standing there,' he pointed out, 'while I draw you.'

She felt like stamping her foot. But she didn't want to come across like a spoilt schoolgirl. Not when he was so cool and controlled.

'You're incorrigible,' she muttered.

'Thank you,' he said seriously.

'It wasn't a compliment. And I'm going to bed.'

'Five more minutes.'

'*One* minute.'

He gave a hoarse laugh under his breath, still sketching her. 'Three minutes.'

She ground her teeth. 'You are the most annoying, persistent, infuriating man I've ever had the misfortune to meet.'

'Misfortune?'

With a jolt, she recalled everything he'd done for her since this nightmare began, and felt horribly guilty again. 'All right, I take that part back. You and your grandmother have been very kind. But you do seem quite arrogant,' she added, unable to stop herself, 'if you must know.'

'You're still here though, aren't you?'

Now she really did stamp her foot. Which made her feel ridiculous, especially when he glanced down at that offending foot with a flick of his dark brow.

'Only b-because I don't have much choice,' she spluttered. 'You... You'll probably throw me out on the streets if I don't say yes.'

'My grandmother would never allow that, as you know perfectly well. So I must assume you're here of your own volition, Mademoiselle Eden.'

'Why, you…'

'Look at the photograph,' he suggested pleasantly.

She swallowed the angry words boiling inside her and did indeed look down at the photograph. She'd said it was a miracle. And it was. The thief had not taken her grandmother's picture. Perhaps they hadn't even noticed that little zip compartment. Or they looked at the photograph and realised it was of no worth to them, so put it back and threw the bag away.

Whatever the reason, she was deeply grateful not to have lost this piece of her past. She ought to have taken a photo of it, and then it would have been preserved, for her photos were automatically uploaded to an internet folder. But she'd never imagined that she would have her bag stolen. As soon as she was able, she would find a way to make a copy. Just in case…

'Yes, that's it,' he said softly, nodding in approval. 'The expression on your face… I could paint you for hours.'

'Oh, you dare!'

CHAPTER THIRTEEN

It was almost two o'clock in the morning before Leo finally put down his sketchpad and allowed her to leave the studio. As she reached the stairs leading up to the attics, she staggered, so tired she could barely stand upright, her joints stiff.

He was there in an instant, an arm about her waist. 'Careful,' he murmured. 'Here, let me help you.'

'I can manage, thank you,' she said, but then almost missed the first step and tumbled sideways. Again, he saved her from bashing her face on the wooden banister. 'Oh, for goodness sake... Alright, maybe I do need your help. But only because you've kept me in that blasted studio for hours, barely moving.' She stretched, groaning. 'I think I've seized up. And that's your fault.'

'Absolutely,' he agreed, supporting her up the stairs. 'I'm a bad man.'

'You think you're so funny. But you're not,' she

said bitterly. 'You are, in fact, a *very* bad man.'

He chuckled, which made her grind her teeth even harder.

At last, they had almost reached her room. 'I need the bathroom first,' she said with dignity.

'I'll wait.'

'Oh no, you won't. I'll be fine from here.' And she stalked into the bathroom, as much as it was possible to stalk with aching legs.

Some ten minutes later, having done the necessary, brushed her teeth and washed her face, she groped her way out into the dimly lit corridor to find him waiting a few feet away.

'What on earth are you still doing here?' she hissed. 'I told you to go away.'

He had been studying his phone and looked up in a distracted way. 'Did you? Oh yes, you did. *Alors*, I ignored you.'

'I see that.'

'I was concerned for you,' he said, looking her over. 'You're right, I should never have kept you in the studio for so long. I'll go to bed now. I just wanted to check you were okay.'

'Of course I am,' she insisted, and somehow tripped over something in the gloom, falling to her knees.

He helped her up, frowning. '*Mon Dieu*, are you hurt?'

'Ouch... Maybe a little... I tripped over...' She peered behind herself accusingly but could see nothing. The corridor was clear of obstacles. 'I caught my foot on something, I'm sure.'

One brow rose, his expression skeptical. 'Of course.'

'Oh, forget it.' He was still holding her close, she realised, and felt a tiny frisson of electricity down her spine. She could smell his sharp citrus aftershave. A warning alarm went off in her brain… 'Please let me go.'

'Liselle said you were dull and ordinary,' he murmured, their faces mere inches apart in the gloomy corridor.

'Did she indeed? What a cheek!'

'She was wrong. Yes, you give a damn good impersonation of somebody sensible and uptight. But in fact…' He put a finger under her chin and raised her face to his, his gaze intent. 'I find you quite mesmerising.'

Then he kissed her.

Maeve knew she should not be allowing Leo Rémy to kiss her. She barely knew the man. And what she did know about him was not particularly complimentary. Yes, he was an artist. And yes, she admired artists. They were a breed apart as far as she was concerned. Magical, otherworldly creatures capable of weaving spells and bewildering the senses. At least, it seemed he must be capable of that. Because she didn't push him away or say no or make any kind of protest at all. She simply stood there, and enjoyed the unusual sensation of being kissed.

Unusual, but not novel. She had dated men in the past. But she'd never let those dates go beyond a certain point. She had no moral misgivings about becoming intimate with a man she was dating. She simply hadn't felt strongly enough about anyone to allow them to go much beyond kissing and cuddling. But the kissing and cuddling part was surely how a woman decided whether she enjoyed kissing and cuddling with that particular man.

And she never had.

Part of her had thought she must be less interested in sex than other women her age. Not quite wired up to enjoy frisky behaviour as her peers seemed to be, judging by what her colleagues at school occasionally revealed about their love lives, winking and smirking as they did so. And she would laugh back while wishing she was like them. But she wasn't.

She was boring and uptight, some might say. Liselle, for instance, from what Leo had just revealed. Or perhaps she'd simply never met the right man.

Until now, she thought with a sudden moment of exhilaration, as his arms tightened about her, cradling her close, and his kiss deepened.

Because she liked this.

This was nothing like the horrid, wet, sloppy kisses she had endured from boyfriends past.

This was rather splendid.

And yes, sexually exciting. Because what else could all these warm, funny, tingling sensations she was experiencing mean? Unless she was getting a water infection...

Time to throw caution to the wind, she thought wildly.

Extraordinarily for her, Maeve raised both arms, linked them about his neck, and actually *kissed him back*.

He made a noise against her mouth, a soft, heartfelt groan which she felt like echoing.

And suddenly they were pressing together in the gloom, and she could feel every inch of him. *Every. Incredible. Inch.* And there were quite a few inches down there, she felt sure. And that was spectacular too.

Goodness me, she thought, hot-cheeked, her heart hammering away like a piston. And when, a few seconds later, he slipped his tongue playfully into her mouth, she almost shrieked out loud, her whole body electrified and trembling.

Perhaps sensing the powerful charge running through her, Leo drew back, gazing down into her face. His dark eyes were heavy-lidded, a strange intensity in his gaze.

'You okay?' he asked softly.

'I... erm... I...' She groped for suitable words to fit the occasion. But even her extensive vocabulary failed her, alas.

Instead, she gripped his silky black hair between her fingers and tugged his head back to hers. Their mouths met again and she gave a sigh of contentment, only belatedly aware that he had gently manoeuvred her against the wall of the corridor, and was pressing against her urgently. And she didn't even mind. In fact, she welcomed it, and was just beginning to wonder if they should segue into the bedroom, or if that would break the spell, when suddenly it was over.

A strange wailing sound broke them apart.

'What… What on earth is that?' she exclaimed, pulling back in alarm.

Leo seemed less surprised, though clearly frustrated. 'Damn.' Glancing down to his right, he muttered, 'Duchess! What are you doing here?' The words were in French but she was fairly certain she'd interpreted them correctly.

A 'duchess'? Wailing in the dark hallway?

Well, maybe the old château was haunted. It certainly looked haunted from the outside.

She held her breath, half-expecting to see an eerie feminine ghost as Leo released her and took an unsteady step back.

But the wailer was no ghost.

Instead, sitting behind him in the corridor, a long, fluffy tail wrapped elegantly around its front paws, was a large white cat with glowing eyes.

'You have a cat,' she said blankly, staring down

at the wraith-like apparition. 'I didn't know you had a cat. Where on earth did it come from?'

'Duchess is my grandmother's cat. Named for the cat in the Disney cartoon *The Aristocats*, if you know it. She's quite elderly now, so rarely ventures out of my grandmother's apartments. I'm sorry if she startled you. No doubt that's what you fell over. She has a tendency to lurk in the shadows...' Running a hand through dishevelled hair, Leo shot her a wry glance. 'Perhaps just as well she came along to interrupt us. There's a certain chemistry between an artist and his model, especially after a sitting like that. At least, I've always thought so. But it would be a mistake to take it too literally. To act on it...'

Without finishing that thought, he bent abruptly, scooped the fluffy white cat into his arms, gave her a brief nod, and said, 'I'll let you get to bed. We can talk in the morning. I'd better take Duchess back to my grandmother's rooms so she doesn't worry.' He paused. 'Good night, Maeve. Thank you for sitting for me tonight. Next time will be easier.'

She watched him go, then staggered into her bedroom and shut the door. She threw herself on the bed without even bothering to undress.

Next time?

She wasn't sure how safe that would be. Or sensible. And right now, safe and sensible might be boring but it seemed like the best way to go if she wanted to retain her sanity.

There's a certain chemistry between an artist and his model.

Understatement of the century. She had kissed him. What an idiot. He had kissed her and she had kissed him back, instead of politely declining to be seduced. They had practically done it in the corridor. Good grief…

Dull, sensible old Maeve, kissing an artist in a French château after sitting for a portrait. Everything about that scenario was unprecedented and topsy-turvy. At any moment, the sky might fall on her head. Or the world erupt into flames around her. It was on that level.

But it would be a mistake to take it too literally. To act on it…

He was absolutely right.

No more of that nonsense, thank you very much, she thought as she drifted off to sleep. It would be strictly platonic 'sitting' from now on. If she even set foot inside his far too cosy and beguiling artist's studio again, which was doubtful.

Goodness though, but he was a marvellous kisser.

Mentally, she thanked the lurking white cat for having saved her from herself.

Leo couldn't believe he had given in to temptation and kissed her. In fact, he didn't even know why he'd been tempted in the first place. A bizarre impulse had come upon him, no doubt generated by a night spent staring at her intriguing face and body, and frantically trying to get them down on paper before the creative urge disappeared. He knew that kind of intensity could become erotic. But, other than with Liselle, he had never experienced it so *strongly*. And even with Liselle, it had been pure sexual desire. Liselle was a very attractive woman and it would be hard for any man to resist her once she'd made up her mind to seduce him.

Maeve, on the other hand, showed no interest in him as a man. She seemed interested in him as an artist. But that was completely different. She was certainly not behaving like a woman who wanted to be seduced. Quite the opposite, in fact.

And yet, it had been quite irresistible, catching her in his arms and becoming fixated by her mouth, and wanting to put his mouth against hers, and find out what she tasted of.

Herbal tea, as it turned out.

But something else too.

She tasted of Maeve. And that had suddenly become the most exciting flavour he could imagine. It was as if she'd bewitched him...

Despite clearly being under a spell, he threw himself into bed and slept soundly until late morning, when a knock at his door made him stir and sit up, yawning muzzily.

'Leo?'

He knew that voice.

Astonished, he jumped up in alarm and swiftly pulled on a dressing gown before opening the door. It was his grandmother. 'Grandmère? Is something wrong? Was I supposed to be taking you somewhere?' He checked his watch and blinked. It was nearly lunchtime. 'I'm sorry, I was up very late again last night.'

'No, I've come about something else.' Briskly, she looked him up and down. 'I think you should get dressed and then come downstairs for a chat.' And she went away again, leaving him staring after her.

A chat?

He showered rapidly, pulled on jeans and a T-shirt, and hurried downstairs to find his grandmother in one of the cool sitting rooms that overlooked the courtyard garden. As he walked in, Bernadette was placing a tray of powerful-smelling coffee and flaky croissants on a small table in front of their grandmother.

His sister looked round as Leo approached. 'You did manage to get some sleep then, last night?' Her voice was mocking, letting her know she suspected him of getting it on with Maeve.

She wasn't far wrong. But he had no intention of kissing and telling.

'I had enough to function.' He dropped onto the sofa beside his grandmother and snatched up a croissant. It smelt delicious and he was ravenous.

'You were painting Maeve last night, Bernadette told me.' His grandmother studied him. He couldn't tell if she was happy or disapproving. 'I hope you didn't keep our *guest* up too late.'

Definitely disapproving.

'Of course not.' When his grandmother turned, fluffing the large cushion at her back, he mouthed an ironic, 'Thank you so much,' to his sister for telling tales on him. 'And I brought Duchess back to your rooms. I found her wandering the house.'

His grandmother groaned. 'Poor old thing… I wondered why she was so sleepy this morning. But if she had an adventure last night, that would explain it. She's getting ancient, like me. Sometimes she forgets she's too frail to have the run of the château anymore and manages to slip out when someone leaves the door open to my suite.' She smiled at him. 'Thank you for returning her to me, dear boy.'

'Boy?' His sister sounded skeptical.

'At my age, nearly all males seem like boys to me,' their grandmother said regretfully. 'Once, I thought I might even try remarrying… But all the men I used to like are either dead or soon will be.'

His sister snorted.

Leo took another bite of croissant, directing a quelling glance at Bernadette.

'I'll be in the kitchen,' Bernadette murmured, and whisked herself out of the room.

Traitor, he thought, watching her vanish.

'I was in the mood for painting last night,' he told his grandmother, trying to make light of it. 'I've taken some preliminary sketches, that's all. Who knows where they'll lead?'

'To an exhibition, I'm told.'

'I see my sister has been having quite a long conversation with you.' He ran a weary hand over his face. 'Yes, if Liselle has her way, and if I have enough paintings worth showing by then, there may be an exhibition soon. At least, she's trying to set one up.'

'And Maeve... Is she happy for you to paint her?'

He finished the soft, flaky, buttery, home-made croissant – one of Bernadette's finest skills – and poured coffee for them both. He was feeling strangely exhilarated after last night.

But was that the sketching or the kiss?

'She didn't say no.'

'And she's aware that these paintings may be put on show to the public?'

'She knows.' A memory struck him, and he sat upright. 'By the way, you had an arty friend once, didn't you, a long time ago? I used to take you to visit her. She lived somewhere near the Boulevard St Germain as I recall.' He handed her a milky coffee, which was how she preferred to take it these days. 'I think her first name was Agathe.'

His grandmother stared at him, taken aback. 'Yes, that's right. Agathe Saint-Yves. But what on earth makes you mention her all of a sudden? Such a difficult woman… Goodness, I haven't seen her in years.' She sipped her coffee remorsefully, her delicate brows drawing together. 'We had a falling out, I'm afraid.'

'A falling out? Was it serious? I mean, was it bad enough that you would never want to see her again?' He knew his grandmother sometimes flew into towering passions over some political thing or other, and cut people out of her life forever. That would be awkward if it were the case with Maeve's grandmother.

'No, nothing that bad. Why?'

Briefly, he explained about Maeve and her grandmother's photograph. 'I'll ask her to show it to you.'

'Please do.'

Abruptly, he realised he hadn't yet told her about Uncle Henri's call. 'I've some bad news, by the way. There was a fire at the premises at Cave Rémy.' When she exclaimed in horror, he held up a hand. 'It's okay, the damage wasn't too extensive and Henri's dealing with it. But I promised him I'd try to fit in a visit soon, so I can assess the situation with my own eyes.'

'Oh dear.' His grandmother hesitated, and he saw a shadow in her face. 'Leo, there's something else.'

'Go on.'

'I didn't just call you downstairs for a chat. The

thing is, I... I have some other rather difficult news for you too.'

He had raised his coffee cup partway to his lips, but put it down when she said that. 'What do you mean? What news?'

She indicated a newspaper lying folded on one of the chairs. 'Bernadette showed me that newspaper report this morning. One of her friends had seen it and brought it round. A horrible rag, but... We both thought you should be told. Especially since it seems likely we may have a visitation soon.'

'A visitation?' Puzzled, he got up to fetch the newspaper, but stopped dead, his eye instantly falling on the gossip column article ringed in red ink. And the photograph that accompanied it. 'Good God. This must be a joke.'

'I only wish it were.' His grandmother looked at him with sympathy in her large, dark eyes. 'I fear we must steel ourselves, Leo.'

He felt his stomach contract. He was looking at a photograph of his father.

Sébastien Louis Rémy.

He hadn't seen him in years. But he would have known him anywhere, his own father, even under the hat tilted at an angle to half conceal his face, his arm about the shoulders of a young woman smiling beatifically into the camera.

He shifted his gaze to study the woman. Dressed in an exotic print caftan, with long, blonde hair, heavily made-up and dripping with jewellery, she was holding up a slender hand to the photographer, showing off a diamond engagement ring and gold wedding band on her ring finger.

The caption beneath read, *Theatrical impresario Sébastien Rémy, 56, wed 23-year-old model Chanelle Plaget in St Tropez this weekend.*

His skin grew cold and he swallowed hard. 'What the hell?' he said thickly, rooted to the spot as he read aloud the scanty gossip column that followed the photograph. 'A whirlwind romance. Met at a rock star's party. Good God… It's widely believed Chanelle is *carrying Sébastien's child.*' His voice shook. 'Private wedding held at romantic getaway… Couple to honeymoon in Paris.'

He threw the newspaper down and turned away, running a hand through his hair. He swore under his breath, barely able to contain his fury and frustration, despite his grandmother's presence.

'I don't believe it. He's more than twice her age. What was my father thinking? And she's *pregnant*? Will the man never stop making a complete laughingstock of our family?'

His grandmother said nothing but sat with her hands in her lap. 'I regret everything my son has done to disgrace his family name. But this, perhaps, more than anything else. That poor girl. She can't have any idea what she's walking into.'

She gave a long, heartfelt sigh. 'But he will bring her here, that's for sure.'

'Why? He hasn't been to Château Rémy in years.'

'They're honeymooning in Paris,' she pointed out mildly. 'Of course he'll come here. We shall have to be polite.'

'I won't be polite,' Leo responded savagely, and then caught her barely concealed flinch, and dropped to his knees before her, catching her hand. 'Forgive me, Grandmère. I know this hurts you more than it hurts me.'

'Don't forget, if she's pregnant,' she said softly, meeting his eyes, 'that baby will be my grandchild too.'

He bit back another swear word at the horrifying realisation. 'I can't stop him, of course,' he said grudgingly, aware that she was right. 'This place is his. But I hope he's not expecting to walk back in here after all these years and take over. I've done what he asked when Francis died and run the business for him. At a profit too, even though it was never my forte. And he's lived handsomely off my skills. What my father knows about business management could be written on the back of a postage stamp.'

'I agree, and I doubt he would ever do that. I'm sure he just wants to show off his inheritance to this girl he's married, this Chanelle. And he's not all bad. Your father loved Francis very much, you know.' Her voice faltered as she saw his face close up. 'He loved you too, Leo. But Francis was always...'

'His favourite, yes,' Leo agreed heavily. 'That was never a secret.'

'I was very grateful when you agreed to take over from Francis. It was a selfless act. The alternative, that Sébastien would come back and try to run things himself, was too horrible to contemplate.'

He nodded. 'That was the only reason I agreed. To spare you that horror.' He ran a hand through his hair in frustration. 'But what a time to pick to roll up here and start interfering in the business.'

She searched his face. 'What do you mean?'

'With me painting again.' He stood up, uneasy under her scrutiny. 'I had intended to devote all my free time to producing new work for this exhibition. Now this...'

Leo turned, restless, and began pacing the room. He had planned to spend the afternoon making a start on preparing a canvas based on the sketches he'd taken last night. But his head was in a mess now.

His father had betrayed his mother. Not once but many times. He had wounded her deeply, and Leo could never forgive him for that.

Certainly his grandfather had never done so, throwing his son out of the house and warning him never to come back if he valued his looks. Sébastien had laughed in his father's face, pointing out that there was nothing he could do under French law, since it did not permit a child to be disinherited.

In the end, everything had been left jointly to Sébastien, Henri and his grandmother, though her frail health meant she was unable to do much beyond nominally sign off on the annual accounts and sit on the company board.

Then his father had left Paris with barely a glance in young Leo's direction.

His mother had never recovered from the failure of her marriage. A short-lived affair had left her with Bernadette, but a new baby had only seemed to exacerbate her depression. Before Bernadette was even a year old, his mother had lost her bloom and turned inwards.

His mother had killed herself in the winter Leo had turned eleven.

He paused before the window, staring out into the enclosed courtyard garden. Sun glinted off windows, half blinding him. He was breathing fast and shallow, his mood volatile...

Maeve was out there, seated on a lounger in the shade, flicking through a magazine. She was barefoot, wearing the same sleeveless summer dress from yesterday. One of Bernadette's loans, of course.

He flashed back to their impromptu kiss on the attic landing – though it had been more than just a kiss, given the urgency of his desire at the time –

and again battled a sense of disbelief that he could have done something so stupid and ill-advised.

She had kissed him back, though.

What did that mean?

He grimaced, pushing such pointless speculation aside. He desperately needed to outline his first painting today and get her back into the studio as soon as possible. And in daylight this time. It was all very well working under electric lighting when there was no other choice, but he wanted to capture the soft glow of summer on her face…

'When do you think they'll arrive?' he muttered.

His grandmother hesitated. 'Well, the newspaper says they were married last weekend in St Tropez, so it's likely they're in Paris already. Which means Sébastien could appear on the doorstep at any moment, bringing his new bride with him.' Her voice trembled. 'Today, perhaps? Or tomorrow.'

Leo's hands tightened into fists at his side. 'Then we'll have to be ready for them, won't we?'

CHAPTER FOURTEEN

'I need you to put these on, if you don't mind.' Leo deposited a pile of clothing in front of Maeve, a strange look in his face. 'Don't worry... I'll step outside while you change. I'll get us some coffee, how's that?'

'You don't happen to have tea, do you?' Maeve asked, verging on desperation after days of coffee drinking. 'With a dash of milk?'

Leo pulled a face. 'I think we *probably* have tea somewhere in the house. And milk. But I can't guarantee that it will taste anything like what you think of as "tea".'

'As close as you can get it would be fantastic, thank you,' Maeve said, aware of a ridiculous desire to fall on her knees and *beg* for tea. 'Addiction is a funny thing, isn't it?'

'Hilarious.'

'Am I being intolerably British?'

'Not at all,' he said politely. 'Get changed. I'll do my best to produce some drinkable tea.'

Once he'd gone, Maeve's troubled gaze dropped to the clothes he'd left in front of her. They were very, um, colourful. She picked them up and examined them at arms' length. The material was flimsy, screaming orange and scarlet... Some kind of robe? Plus what appeared to be a matching headscarf or bandanna. And a pair of dangly earrings. Thankfully, they were clip-on, for although she wore studs in her ears, she didn't fancy sticking second-hand earrings in there.

It was like putting on clothes from a childhood fancy dress box. Or picking a bold new look and reinventing herself.

Why on earth did he want her to wear these? Presumably he had some vision in mind for his painting. But it wouldn't be a vision that matched up to her personality.

Well, she had agreed to help him out in return for bed and board, so it would be mean-spirited now to back out. Hurriedly, she pulled off the summer frock that Bernadette had so kindly lent her, which was tighter-fitting than all the other clothes in her meagre store. Then she cautiously wriggled and shrugged her way into the brightly-coloured robe that he wanted her to wear, all diaphanous, multi-layered folds, like a fairy costume or something out of a pantomime.

There was a full-length mirror on the wall. She did a twirl in the bright costume, arms wide, staring at herself, and was astounded by her reflection. She didn't look like Maeve anymore.

She wasn't entirely sure what she looked like instead, of course.

But not herself. Maeve had gone.

And in her place was this strange, exotic, floaty creature.

Feeling a bit out of her depth, she clipped on the dangly silver earrings and arranged the bandanna about her head. It was orange and blue, a truly violent combination.

But if this was what he wanted…

Now she looked odd. There was no other word for it. And something else… Yes, she looked daring. Pirate girl meets Kate Bush. As though she would do anything. Be anyone.

Apart from Maeve, that was.

How her colleagues at school would chuckle to see her in this outlandish outfit. They would point and make jokes. She heaved a sigh of relief, in fact, that they would never see her.

Then a terrible thought struck her.

Leo was going to exhibit his paintings, wasn't he? And those paintings would be of her.

Maeve Eden.

She shuddered at the realisation and had to suppress a frightened urge to pull all these clothes off and dash back to her attic bedroom. Though she would need to pull on her other clothes first. She had no intention of running amok in the nude through Château Rémy. She wasn't Liselle, she thought with a touch of acid.

As soon as Leo returned to the studio, carefully balancing a tray of hot drinks for them, she pounced on him. 'When these paintings go into the exhibition,' she demanded, folding her arms and glaring at him, 'will my name appear anywhere? Beside the paintings or in the brochure, if there is one.'

He set down the tray. 'I don't believe so. Many artists' models like to be named.' His gaze moved over her strange, colourful outfit, his face expressionless. 'But if you prefer to be anonymous, that's not a problem.'

'Yes, that's it, exactly. I want to be anonymous. No name anywhere associated with the exhibition. Otherwise I won't sit for you.'

He seemed amused rather than annoyed by her insistence. 'Fair enough.' He nodded to the dainty teacup. 'Bernadette and my grandmother put their heads together and found some tea leaves for you. Bernadette heated milk but Grandmère said you would prefer cold milk.' There was a small china jug of milk on the tray. 'Is that right? Cold milk for tea?'

'Absolutely.' Maeve knew a moment of horror at the thought of warm milk in her tea, and bent to examine the teacup, which was fairly brimming with black tea. It smelt fragrant. Picking it up, she added a dash of cold milk and took a sip.

He was watching her. 'Well?'

He was right. It didn't taste like tea back home. The milk was wrong. And the tea tasted... funny. But it wasn't coffee, and that would have to be enough for now.

'It's perfect,' she lied politely, and took another sip. 'Thank you.'

His gaze narrowed on her face, and she had the uncomfortable suspicion that he knew she was telling porkies. But what had he expected her to say? *This is grim*? Even with her not quite stable childhood, she had been raised better than that, or she hoped so.

'How do I look?' she asked shyly, hoping to distract him,

'You look like the woman I want to paint.'

She met his eyes, and shivered, even though the room was warm, the windows open on a hot sunny Paris. She had been suppressing her memory of that kiss. *Oh, that kiss*! But it came rushing back now, suffusing her with tingling sensations that had no business occurring in an artist's studio in the middle of the afternoon.

She thought he might be remembering too. His eyes had widened and he seemed to be breathing faster, as she was too.

Brusquely, he pointed to the stool she had occupied last night. 'Take a seat.' He turned away to grab up some equipment – a pallet with paints already mixed, a pot of brushes from which he withdrew a couple, sticking one brush behind his ear and wielding the other, and a paint-streaked cloth which he draped over one shoulder – and said gruffly, 'I've taken all the preliminary sketches of your face and outline I need... Now it's time to get something down on canvas.'

'You want me like this?' She attempted to adopt the same position again that she'd held for so many hours the previous night.

'Maybe a little more...' He adjusted her. 'And these sleeves... Let the material hang down like this... That's it.'

At last, he stepped behind the easel, which he'd set up with a large canvas, glanced towards her and then began to paint.

For a long while, there was silence in the suffocatingly warm studio. Every now and then, when he wasn't looking directly at her, Maeve dared reach for her teacup and take another quick sip, though it was rapidly growing cold. She noticed that he had knocked back his own coffee in a couple of gulps. His mouth must be lined with asbestos, she thought.

At last, when he stepped back to consider what he'd achieved so far, she asked tentatively, 'Did you speak to your grandmother about that photograph?'

His head turned towards her, his eyes narrowing on her face. 'Sorry?'

He was obviously in another world, far, far away...

'My grandmother's photograph, the one I showed you?'

'Of course. Yes, I showed it to her, and I was right. She does know your grandmother. They used to be friends but there was a falling out, she says. Though not such a serious one that she could never go back again.' He grinned at her expression. 'Don't worry, she's going to get back in touch with her. I don't know whether she'll say that you're here. Perhaps you should talk to her about it before she makes contact?'

'That's so marvellous, thank you.' Flushed, Maeve clasped her hands to her cheeks, her heart thumping. There was a chance she might meet her grandmother. It was such an incredible thought, she couldn't focus on anything else. 'So she's alive?'

'Well, I suppose she must be. We haven't heard anything to the contrary. And my grandmother keeps a close eye on the obituary columns in the newspaper.' He stepped back to the canvas, paintbrush in hand, and began working again, intent and frowning.

She didn't want to disturb him while he was painting. But he had given her so many questions and only a few answers. Threadbare answers, at that.

Eventually, she couldn't stand it anymore and blurted out, 'But what's her name?'

He didn't respond at first. Then he seemed to

grasp that she'd spoken to him, and gazed around at her, distracted. 'Pardon? Whose name?'

'My *grandmother's* name. I presume if your grandmother was once friends with her, she must know what her name is. They can't just have addressed each other, "Hey you!" or something.'

'I see what you mean.' He hesitated, brush poised above the canvas, then dabbed in some paint, apparently fascinated by whatever he was doing. 'Erm… Her name is Agathe Saint-Yves.'

'Agathe Saint-Yves,' she breathed.

It was a magical name. It sounded absolutely perfect for the woman in the photograph. Elegant, Parisian, yet also from another age. She looked out of the window, where she could just see higher buildings around the château, sun gleaming on the rooftops of Paris, and wondered what her grandmother would be like.

Would she want to meet Maeve though? Perhaps she had broken off contact with her daughter, Maeve's mother, and would refuse to see her. That was a possibility and one she had to face. But maybe she would be delighted. Her long-lost granddaughter. It might be a fairytale reunion. Or something in between those two extremes.

She couldn't wait to find out. And yet, she was also scared. It was the same fear that had prevented her from contacting her grandmother during those few days on the Paris coach tour. Because sometimes there wasn't a fairytale ending when people met up with long-lost relatives. She had seen enough family tree documentary shows on television to know that. Sometimes, they met up only to discover exactly *why* they were long-lost rather than still friendly with everyone.

Besides, right now, her grandmother was a wonderful image of kindly, wise perfection in her head. But once they'd met, the reality might be very different. She didn't want to be disillusioned by her grandmother and go back home to England disappointed.

Yet, if she didn't go and meet her, she would spend the rest of her life regretting it.

'Stop it,' Leo said sharply, and she realised that she'd been slumped on her stool for several minutes now, chewing on her lip and breathing gustily as she gazed out of the window.

'Sorry,' she muttered, and turned back to face him, sitting up straight in the designated position, the diaphanous folds of her strange outfit hanging exactly as he'd requested.

Goodness, he was a hard task master. Though she didn't really mind. She was rather fascinated by the dedication with which he worked.

Being a professional artist wasn't all dreamy creative moments and whimsical brushstrokes, she was discovering. It was about hard work and long hours, and she respected that, whilst secretly wishing she didn't have to put in the long hours too.

But she could see similarities between them now.

Leo Rémy was as focused on her portrait as she'd ever been on teaching a class or marking up a huge stack of schoolbooks.

As she watched though, she realised that the frantic brushstrokes were gradually slowing down. He seemed more hesitant now than in the beginning. Certainly, he was not working as swiftly and obsessively as he had been last night. But no doubt paint was a slower process, she decided. Less about inspiration, more about technical know-how.

Leo stopped and lowered his head. His brush hand dropped to his side. Closing his eyes, he gave an audible groan.

'Are you okay?' When he didn't answer, she felt unexpectedly anxious. 'Leo? What's wrong? Should I fetch someone?' She jumped off the stool, concerned.

But he raised his head and backed away as she came towards him, holding up the paintbrush as though to ward her off. 'No, no... I'm fine. Sorry, I had some bad news earlier. I'd hoped that by painting you today I'd be able to put it out of my mind. Forget about it for a few hours.' She saw a flicker of pain in his eyes. 'Who was I kidding?'

He threw down the paintbrush in disgust and strode towards the window. He stood there rigid for a moment, unspeaking. Then he shook his head. 'I'm not the man I was, that's the plain truth of it. I'm not Leo Rémy anymore. I've lost my way. And this...' He gestured behind him at the canvas. 'It's just a poor shadow of what I used to be capable of. I'm going to look like a fool at this exhibition. I need to tell Liselle to cancel the arrangement before they start to publicise it.'

She wanted to help him but didn't know how. Her gaze drifted curiously to the canvas, still turned away from her.

'May I see?' she asked tentatively.

'Absolutely not.' He spun around, gesturing her furiously back to the stool. 'It's no good. It's rubbish. But I'll finish it.' He picked up the paintbrush and returned to his place before the canvas. 'I've never left a painting unfinished in my life and I'm not starting now. Even if it's destined for the rubbish heap.'

'What makes you think it's rubbish?'

'Would you sit down again, please?'

'No.' She didn't move, ignoring his impatient gesture. 'Something has triggered this.'

'Spare me the psycho-babble,'

That dismissive attitude annoyed her. But she could see how defensive he was. Which meant she was close to the truth.

'Some of the kids I teach,' she said quietly,

'are excellent mathematicians. Then suddenly, one day, they decide they're no good at it. They just close themselves off from maths. And there's always a reason. A single bad test result, perhaps, or an issue at home that's knocked their confidence generally.' She studied his inverted profile. 'It's none of my business, I know. But if you want to talk about it...'

A muscle jerked in his jaw, then Leo gave another groan and muttered, 'If you must pry, it's my father.'

'Your *father*?" She was taken aback. Hadn't he told her that his father no longer had anything to do with the family?

'He got married again last weekend... Some young woman half his age. Apparently, he may be bringing her here to Château Rémy.'

'Goodness. When?'

'Today? Tomorrow? I've no idea. But I can't stop thinking about it.' He paused. 'That man tortured my mother. Oh, not literally. I mean, with his affairs... All the women.' He added bitterly, 'In the end, she killed herself.'

'Oh, Leo, I'm so sorry.' She put a hand to her mouth. 'I didn't know about that.'

'Why would you? It was a long time ago. But sometimes I think about my mother and...' He expelled a harsh breath. 'It doesn't matter. This thing with my father though. It shouldn't mean a damn thing to me, I know. But it does. Because it's brought it all back. And I don't think I can face him...' He grimaced. 'Or not without punching him.'

She was shocked. 'But he's your father, Leo... Whatever he's done, you can't *punch* him.'

'Then you'd better tie me up if he comes to the door.'

Tie me up.

Maeve said nothing. But the mental image he'd just conjured up wouldn't go away. Her lips tightened to stop her from smirking, and her eyebrows rose and fell, doing a quirky little dance above eyes that simply didn't know where to look...

'Okay, *now* what are you thinking?' he demanded, staring at her with his paintbrush poised above the canvas.

Oh my goodness, she thought, blushing. There was no way to answer that.

'Nothing. I'm just, erm, hungry,' she fibbed.

'Hungry?' He looked unconvinced but shrugged. 'Then I'll wrap this up quickly, so you can go and eat.'

She didn't like telling fibs. Though she was genuinely hungry, she realised with an internal shock, watching the Frenchman bend to his work again.

Just not for food...

CHAPTER FIFTEEN

After he'd released Maeve from the studio, sure that she must be heartily bored now of sitting for him, not to mention starving, Leo returned to stare at the painting he had been working on. It was not finished. But he'd made a good start. At least, he had felt good about it at first, painting like fury. Then, slowly, energy had drained out of him, and he knew it was partly the news about his father that was to blame.

Why the hell had he shared such private information with Maeve? It was none of her business. She wasn't one of the family. Yet, in that instant, it had felt like the right thing to do. The only thing to do, in fact.

Maeve was a sympathetic person. But not overly emotional, thankfully.

He couldn't have handled more emotion on top of the churning turmoil he already felt inside.

Telling Maeve about his father's marriage had made his own emotions easier to bear, at least for a short while. It had acted like a safety valve, releasing a little pressure before it could build to bursting point.

Leo stood in front of the painting for another half hour, fiddling with it, lightening areas that were too dark, shading areas that were too bright, and making the colour more subtle, especially around the face. He wanted a certain look, Maeve's lightness of being...

A knock at the door disturbed this intense work.

He felt aggrieved by the interruption. But he also knew he still had responsibilities. He couldn't simply shut out the world while he became a painter again.

'Come in.'

Liselle appeared in the doorway, glancing about the studio. 'Has she gone?' she asked, semi-ironic, flicking back her hair.

'As you see.'

He still wasn't sure how he felt about Liselle these days. On the one hand, she was a good manager, and he needed someone to take charge of his painting career. It would be stressful and a waste of his energy to find someone new. Someone trustworthy. And Liselle was trustworthy, he had to give her that. At least, she had been so far.

But her unpredictable nature and petty jealousies were becoming an issue. He had dismissed that side of her in the past, too intent on the family business to worry about such trivialities. But then, he hadn't shown any interest in other women during that time either. So Liselle's behaviour had remained within reasonable bounds. She had occasionally attempted to seduce him, and he had rebuffed her advances, and thus a state of uneasy tension had existed between them. But never outright war.

Now though, with Maeve sitting for him, Liselle was probably angry. No doubt she must be furious that her long patience had not paid off,

She probably also suspected that Maeve was his lover.

Maeve, in his bed...

Everything inside him tightened at the thought. He wanted the Englishwoman. But he also knew he couldn't have her. She might have kissed him back outside her room, but only because she'd been so tired and the kiss had taken her by surprise. She wasn't his type, he reminded himself again, irritated that he needed to drum that fact into his brain. Besides, Maeve would be going back to Britain soon and he would never see her again. He could do without that kind of emotional complication in his life. And if he acted on those urges, Liselle might lash out at Maeve, and that would be devastating too. He couldn't bear the thought of Maeve being hurt because of his stupidity.

'Are you sleeping with her?' Liselle demanded,

her gaze sharp on his face, flagging up that she knew what Leo had been thinking.

The woman was a human X-ray machine.

Balancing the paintbrush carefully on the palette, he thrust his hands into his pockets. 'Of course I'm not. I've only just met her. Besides, what kind of question is that?' He paused, frowning. 'Even if I were, it would be none of your business. You're my manager, Liselle, not my keeper.'

'A good manager keeps an eye on their clients' private lives as well as their work,' Liselle snapped back, and tilted her head to one side, a deliberate move that drew attention to the locks of glossy Titian hair tumbling over sun-kissed shoulders. She had bare feet and was wearing a tight white tank top coupled with minuscule shorts. He was aware of how sexy she looked. Yet it was strange how Maeve in some shapeless tent of a dress was a thousand times more desirable than Liselle in next to nothing...

'And I'm worried about you, Leo,' she went on, her voice coaxing now. A change of tack, no doubt designed to distract him from her true purpose in visiting the studio. Because he was sure she had some hidden agenda; it was in her eyes, the look of someone with a secret to share. 'You've not been yourself since that woman arrived.'

'I thought you'd be happy that I'm painting again.'

'I am,' she said hesitantly, and came in closing the door behind her. 'I just don't want you getting sidetracked.' Her gaze shifted to the canvas, which was not visible to her, but she didn't ask to see. She knew him better than that. 'Paint her, yes. Fall in love, no.'

'Fall in love?' he scoffed.

'You forget… I know what you're like, Leo, and how your heart works.' She paused. 'Maeve is vulnerable. She's lost and alone. She need someone to help her.' Her hungry eyes devoured him. 'That ticks all your boxes, doesn't it?'

There was enough truth behind that accusation to make him flush with annoyance. 'Was there something you wanted? Other than to disturb my work?'

'Actually, yes.' The malicious look in her eyes died away, replaced by something like wariness. 'I've got something to show you. You're not going to like it. But you need to be aware.'

'If it's about my father getting married and coming on honeymoon to Paris,' Leo drove back at her, 'you're too late. I already know.'

She blinked, looking taken aback. 'Your father *got married*?'

'Yes, to a woman half his age. Some young model called Chanelle, for God's sake.' He stared at her, perplexed, his brows tugging together. 'If that's not why you're here, then what are you talking about?'

Liselle messed with her already perfect hair, a sure sign that she was agitated. Then scrolled through some screens on her phone and thrust it towards him. 'I'm here about this.'

He didn't understand. She was showing him a report in some online magazine. He came closer, and stopped dead on seeing his own face there. And Maeve's too.

It was a photograph of them sitting close together in the booth at Chez Jean, their hands almost touching. The caption under the photograph read, *Popular artist Leo Rémy dines out with his new English girlfriend, Maeve Eden.*

Swearing, he seized the phone and read the rest of the scurrilous report. 'Pictured together at popular city bar Chez Jean... The couple enjoyed an intimate dinner before returning to Château Rémy, where Mademoiselle Eden is staying while in Paris.'

He tossed the phone back to her and stalked to the window, glaring out across the rooftops of Paris. 'I'm going to strangle Jean,' he said thickly. 'I saw him take that photograph. He swore he hadn't but clearly he lied. And this is the result.' Fury rocked him. 'How could he do this to me? *My own cousin.* Well, he can kiss goodbye to his job. Chez Jean is no more. It can be Chez Alfonse, for all I care.' He gave a hoarse crow of laughter. 'Or Chez Bernadette. Yes, my sister might do a good job.'

'Jean must have been desperate for cash, that's all I can think. Or desperate for publicity.'

Leo sucked in a breath, remembering that evening at the bar. Had he brought this situation on himself by not being sensitive enough to his cousin's problems?

'I'm going down there to see him.' He ushered her out of his studio and shut the door behind them. 'I can't simply let this go. I need to have this out with Jean right away.'

'Let me go with you,' Liselle said, following him along the corridor.

'No.'

'I'm your manager, Leo. Remember? This kind of publicity… It's good for you in some ways.' She ignored his furious protest, speaking over him. 'Look, I agree Jean should never have taken that photograph or released it to the press. But if this drums up public interest in the exhibition –'

He spun on his heel. 'Did you put him up to it?'

'No, God, no. But I do need to find out who else he's spoken to about you and Maeve, if anyone. So we can be forewarned.'

He wasn't sure he believed her. She loved publicity and he wouldn't have put it past her to coax Jean into sneaking a shot of him with Maeve… But he had no proof of that. Besides, as she'd pointed out, she was still his manager, so this business concerned her too.

'Fine, then come along,' he said reluctantly.

Chez Jean was half full. He found his duplicitous cousin laughing and chatting with customers as he served them dinner. Leo stood a few feet away, glaring at him, arms folded, until Jean caught sight of him and straightened, his look nervous.

'I want a word with you,' Leo said grimly.

Wishing the customers, *'Bon appétit!'* Jean hurried towards the kitchen, pushing through the double swing doors just as Leo strode after him, catching his arm.

'I... I can't talk now,' Jean insisted, trying to pull free. 'We're too busy. We're short-staffed today.'

'I don't care if you're running this place on your own,' Leo told him bluntly, 'you're going to sit down and talk to me right now.' He propelled him back towards an empty table and pressed his cousin into a seat. 'Wait there.'

Flagging down a passing waiter, he ordered three cognacs.

As he turned back, he found Liselle already seated beside Jean, whispering in his ear. Taking the seat opposite them, Leo tried to suppress his temper. What was she saying to him? Had she secretly organized that photo finding its way to the press?

He leant forward so he could keep his own voice discreetly low too. 'Liselle showed me the photograph you took. She says it's all over social media. Why did you do it, Jean?' His cousin flinched, glancing at Liselle. 'I understand your resentment towards me. That's always been obvious. But Maeve? She's a victim in all this. She's been stranded in Paris with no passport, no money, not even any clothes. I took out to dinner to make her feel better. And you've built that up into be some grand romantic gesture.' He shook his head. 'She's our guest. How could you behave so badly towards her?'

'I never said you and her were together… I sold the photograph to an online magazine, yes. And maybe a few other places too.'

'*What?*' Liselle exclaimed, looking annoyed.

'But I only gave them her name,' Jean finished hurriedly, seeing Leo's face harden. 'I didn't suggest that you and Maeve were an item. That's just the spin they put on it.'

'You're lucky I don't beat you to a pulp,' said Leo.

'Do it,' Liselle muttered.

'What, and give him another photo opportunity? He's trading on this situation, on my name, in order to promote himself. And why? Pure jealousy.'

'Me? Jealous of you?' Jean gave a bark of laughter, shaking his head. But there was a glint of temper in his eyes. 'You're talking rubbish, Leo. As usual.'

'Is that so?' Leo had himself back under control. He surveyed his cousin coolly. 'You think you're better than this place, don't you? You think you should be running the wine-tasting at the vineyard, not a corner bar in Paris. That's what this is all about.'

Jean didn't reply at first, but pulled a face, looking away. His earring caught the light. Then he exploded, 'All right, you're not wrong. I do think I'm better than manager of a café. I've taken Chez Jean as far as it can go. Is this it for me now? Am I going to be here for the rest of my life?' He slammed a hand down on the table, his lips drawn back to bare his teeth. Leo thought his cousin looked almost feral. 'You have everything, Leo. You have power and money and influence. But me? I have a few waiters to boss around, some kitchen staff to keep in line. It's not enough. I've got so much potential. You need to trust me more. Give me work that fits my abilities.'

'What he needs to do is kick your backside around this bar and out into the street,' Liselle snarled. 'You could have materially damaged Leo's public profile with that photo.'

'Don't be ridiculous!' Jean jerked back in his seat a little too violently. The chair fell backwards and his cousin disappeared below the tablecloth.

Leo half-rose and leant over, watching with a frown as Jean struggled to get back up. 'You okay there? You need a hand?'

'No, I'm fine.' Flushed with embarrassment, Jean set the seat upright and sat down again, though with marked care this time. 'The thing is, people have been talking about you, Leo. Saying you're washed up. That you haven't had a real exhibition in years.' He glanced angrily at Liselle. 'I did him a favour, selling that photo to the press. Now everyone's talking about him again. And that exhibition you've got lined up? You watch, it'll be a big success now.'

Leo regarded him coldly. He couldn't deny that what Jean said was true. Notoriety did publicise an artistic exhibition more than good behaviour. But his temper wasn't lessened. 'Maybe so. But Maeve didn't deserve what you've done to her. They put her name on that press report.'

Jean shrugged. 'So?'

'There may be people back home in the United Kingdom who'll see that. As you said, it's doing the rounds on social media. She works as a teacher. Did you never think that photo might be damaging to her career? Being seen with someone like me? I'm hardly respectable, am I?'

'Ha, nobody cares about that kind of thing anymore.' Jean dismissed his criticism with a rude gesture. 'She's more likely to be promoted.'

'Nonsense,' Leo said flatly. 'And what if she has a boyfriend back home? What's he going to think when he sees that?'

Jean lowered his gaze to the table. 'Okay, I get your point.' He hesitated. 'Though Maeve doesn't strike me as the kind of woman who has a boyfriend, if you see what I mean.'

'Actually, I don't.' There was a dangerous note in

Leo's voice.

The waiter arrived with their order. Liselle accepted her cognac from the waiter, her gaze fixed on Jean's averted face.

'The real point, Jean,' she said, 'is that you worked against the family by putting out that photograph and making it look as though Leo and Maeve are having a relationship. Not only against the family, but me too.' Fury flashed in her eyes. 'That wasn't very friendly, was it?'

Jean said nothing.

'Now we have to decide what to do about it,' Liselle went on.

'There's no *we*. I shall decide,' Leo told her.

Jean gave a burst of disbelieving laughter. 'You can't sack me, Leo. Your grandmother would never allow it.' His look was almost gloating, for it was true that Grandmère had a soft spot for Jean.

'My grandmother doesn't run the business,' Leo pointed out softly, 'I do. And while, yes, she may favour you as her brother's only son, that doesn't mean she'll be happy when she sees that photograph you took. You know how highly she prizes the Rémy family name. In fact,' he added deliberately, 'I'll be surprised if she ever wants to talk to you again after this.'

His cousin was looking troubled now. He shifted uncomfortably, taking a deep gulp of his cognac. 'All right, yeah, let's say it was a mistake. But you can't blame me. I was angry because you'd spoken to me so sharply. I... I wasn't thinking straight. But you can't sack me for it, Leo.' He leant forward, bitter desperation in his face, 'What would I do? How would I live?'

'You should have thought of that before you sold my private life to the press.'

There was a stir behind him. Leo saw people's heads turn towards the door. Liselle choked on her cognac. Jean stared over Leo's shoulder, his eyes widening, a look of sudden trepidation on his face.

Before he could turn to see what was happening, a familiar voice called across the bar café, 'Leo, my son!' It was his father's voice, deep and authoritative. 'Just the man I came to see. Come, let me shake the hand of one of Paris's most infamous artists... How long has it been, eh?'

CHAPTER SIXTEEN

Jerking to his feet, his skin cold, heart thudding violently, Leo spun to glare at his father. He had intended to say something cold and cutting, to put his long-absent father back in his place. But a hand had already reached out to grab him, and he found himself being hugged and kissed ferociously.

Sébastien Rémy took a step back to study him, with a shout of amusement. 'I think you've grown, boy... My God, yes, you've grown. But what happened to the beard? I've been telling Chanelle here about this mad artist son of mine with his long hair and beard and his Bohemian ways... And now look at you. You could be any idiot in an office job.' He shook his head in mock disapproval. 'Where's my wild, handsome Leo gone, eh? What have you done with him?'

Without waiting for an answer, which was just as well, as Leo had been knocked speechless by this extravagant entrance, his father squeezed him tight again, still laughing, before moving to grip Jean's hand and kiss his cousin on the cheek too.

'Jean, my friend... You look well. And this is your place now? Ah now, that's a shrewd business move. I like it... ' He clapped Jean on the shoulder so violently that Jean staggered, spilling his drink. 'But not as much as I'd like some of what you're drinking. What is that you're throwing about the place? Cognac? Excellent choice, my boy. But let's open a bottle or two of champagne. We have something to celebrate... ' Sébastien Rémy turned, indicating the beautiful young woman who had trailed in behind him, wearing a tailored, open-necked white blouse with baggy green culottes and a gold sash knotted about her waist. 'This is my new wife, Chanelle. Isn't she the most gorgeous piece of ass you've ever seen?'

'For God's sake, Dad,' Leo ground out furiously, 'keep it down, would you?'

Everybody was staring eagerly at them, listening to every word. Some of the customers were even filming on their phones or taking photographs. None of that seemed to have deterred his father from making a public spectacle of himself.

To his surprise, Leo felt sorry for the young woman, who was smiling in a slick, professional way – she was a model, after all, and no doubt used to being the centre of attention – but with her hands clasped before her chest, indicating anxiety, perhaps? The gossip column piece had said she was carrying a child. That could also account for the strain he thought he could detect in her face, especially as Sébastien made a point of guiding her forward to be introduced to them.

'Leo, my son, I'd like you to meet your new stepmother.' Sébastien gave a chuckle, slipping a possessive arm around Chanelle's waist. 'Your stepmother! What a thought, *hein*? Why, you're not much older than her. You'll wonder at us two getting hooked, I imagine. An unconventional couple… But there's no accounting for love.'

Pulling her close, his father kissed the young woman on the lips, who stood mute and still under this very public show of affection.

'Dad, please,' Leo muttered, horrified now.

'Oh, stop fussing. My God, who put that stick up your backside? As if I need ask… Your grandmother is to blame for this new prudery, I have no doubt. She tried that nonsense with me, you know. Guilt tripping. But I wasn't interested in living like that, with my head in a damn yoke. That's why I left Paris, even if it meant not being there for you and Francis. And look what I caught… Come, Chanelle, don't be shy. Shake your *stepson*'s hand.' And again, he laughed.

'Congratulations on your wedding to my father.' Politely, Leo shook Chanelle's hand, and kissed her on the cheek as was expected.

'I've heard so much about you,' Chanelle was murmuring as she looked him up and down, her gaze sharpening with interest. Her voice was soft and breathy. Was she channelling Marilyn Monroe? 'Your father was right. You are *very* handsome.' She leant closer. Rather too close, in Leo's opinion, for a recently married woman. Her perfume was cloyingly sweet. 'And I'm glad you lost the beard.'

She had blue eyes. Like Maeve's.

And yet Chanelle's eyes had zero impact on his libido. The only thing he felt for her was pity. She was too young and, he felt sure, too inexperienced in love to understand what kind of man his father was. Once Sébastien Rémy had used this beautiful model for his own purposes, mostly embarrassing his family and getting himself back into the public eye, he would dump her as he had dumped his previous lovers, and no doubt leave her broken-hearted.

While Chanelle was shaking Jean's hand and kissing Liselle on the cheek, his father clapped him on the shoulder. 'But enough about us,' Sébastien said, grinning. 'I saw that cosy snap of you with the English girl. You sly thing... Where did you meet her, eh? Should we expect wedding bells soon?'

Leo met his eyes with cold dislike. 'There's nothing between us. It was just Jean making mischief.'

'Of course, of course.' His father winked, his smile knowing. 'And you have an exhibition soon. May we be permitted a sneak preview? Perhaps when we come to the château for lunch tomorrow?'

Leo stiffened. 'Tomorrow? Have you checked with Grandmère that it's convenient?'

'I rang her before coming here. She invited us to lunch.' Sébastien looked about the café-bar, his keen eyes taking in every detail. 'I knew you'd probably be here. Though I'm disappointed not to find the little English girl with you. I'd rather hoped to introduce myself.'

Over his dead body...

Leo was aware of a surge of aggression, and was surprised by his desire to protect their guest from his father's intrusive, over-the-top personality.

'You didn't come to Francis's funeral,' he said bluntly. 'Why not?'

His father looked taken aback by this direct demand. Shocked, even. Then, to Leo's amazement, his eyes welled with tears. 'Ah, my poor son. My dearest boy... ' He shook his head, a tear trickling down his rugged cheek. 'I couldn't be there, don't you see? It would have killed me too, being asked to stand at the graveside and watch as my darling son... No, the whole thing was *impossible*.'

He laid a heavy arm about Leo's shoulders, lowering his head to mutter in his ear, 'But I saw it on the internet afterwards. And it brought me to tears, what you said at… at the funeral.' His voice had broken to a barely audible croak. 'Thank you.'

Leo was not prepared for the wave of raw pain that hit him, listening to this. His brother's death was still a weight on his heart. Now this…

'Let's take this back to the château, shall we?' he said hoarsely, and turned without waiting for his father to follow. 'This place is too public.' His voice thickened with emotion as he strode from the bar, muttering, 'I need to get out of here.'

He didn't want his father and his new stepmother setting foot inside the château. But what could he do? Sébastien Rémy had every right to be there, as owner and *chef de famille*. And Chanelle was apparently pregnant. It would be extremely discourteous to turn either of them away. But there was no doubt in his mind that his father had come to make trouble and interfere in Leo's plans. No doubt he'd want Jean kept on as the café manager, for instance, and would insist on that, undermining Leo's authority.

Worse, judging by the phones that had been trained on their reunion, all this would be front page news tomorrow…

Maeve was downstairs in the labyrinthine kitchens at the base of the old château, a medieval-like maze of pantries, walkways, nooks and crannies, watching with interest as Bernadette demonstrated how to make croissants, when the distant jangle of the château bell sounded above them.

'It's rather late for a caller,' Bernadette said in surprise, reaching for a cloth to wipe her hands. 'But I'd better answer the door. Grandma usually goes up to her room for a nap before supper, and Nonna's too deaf to hear the doorbell. Though she always hears when I offer to make her *chocolat chaud*, funnily enough.' She began removing her apron. 'Why don't you stay here and try folding and rolling the dough yourself?'

The process of making home-made croissants had been so lengthy and involved, Maeve was too terrified to touch the dough herself. If she messed it up, she might ruin the whole batch. Bernadette had already explained how she'd made the dough yesterday, kneaded it and rolled it several times, then left the dough wrapped in plastic in the fridge overnight. Now slabs of butter had to be folded into it before another chilling and rolling session, after which they could finally make the special croissant shapes ready for baking.

Given how complicated the process was, Maeve had no idea how people who made croissants themselves instead of buying them from a boulangerie had any time left for actually *eating* them...

'Or I could answer the door,' she said hurriedly, 'if that's okay. I'm not sure what the croissants would look like if I tried folding the dough myself. Like an advanced yoga position, I expect.'

'I'd like to get back into yoga,' Bernadette said, grinning. 'I am so unfit.' They had been speaking an uncomfortable blend of English and French but Bernadette was using simple words and going as slowly as she could when using French, often repeating sentences so that Maeve could catch up. 'Still, I could do with rolling this batch for the last time before the dough dries out... Either that or I'll need to wrap it in plastic and put it back in the fridge to finish later.'

'I'll go,' Maeve said firmly.

'*Merci*. It may be Monsieur Duvalle with our weekly grocery order, though he usually comes earlier than this.' Bernadette looped the apron back over her head and reached for her rolling pin. 'Ask him to carry it down, would you?'

Maeve hurried up to the ground floor, the vast kitchen complex being situated below stairs. No doubt to keep the servants out of sight and out of mind in the olden days. Before the days of the French Revolution, that was, when the servants had risen up and done unspeakable things to their employers, guilty and innocent alike, unfortunately. Though presumably things had settled down again within a few generations, and servants and masters had come back into fashion. Rich people tended to prefer paying other people to light their fires and cook their dinners and wash their linen. When they were not getting their heads lopped off, of course.

As she reached the grand entrance hall, the doorbell jangled again, a more prolonged, noisy summons this time.

'All right, all right, I'm coming... Keep your string of onions on, Monsieur Duvalle,' she muttered under her breath.

But even as she reached the door, it was flung open by none other than Leo Rémy.

'Get away from me,' Leo was shouting, waving a hand, not looking at her as he plunged into the hall. 'Go on, get lost!'

Maeve stopped in her tracks. What on earth?

She half expected to see an irate French grocer come chasing after him into the hall, perhaps brandishing a baguette or a bag of radishes.

Instead, an absolute throng of people on the doorstep met her astonished gaze, all lifting phones and cameras and other equipment in her direction, a barrage of flashes going off to illuminate both her and the dim interior.

Others hurried after Leo into the château. One was Liselle, her brows tugged together with irritation, a flushed look on her face. Behind her was Leo's cousin, also rather flushed and out of breath. Had they been running? After them came a large man who looked so startlingly like Leo that it was impossible not to recognise who he was.

Leo's father, Sébastien Rémy. Leo had told her about him earlier, and she backed away instinctively, recalling how much animosity lay between them. On his arm was a pretty young blonde. His new wife, presumably. Maeve had forgotten her name, if Leo had even mentioned it, which she didn't think he had.

But who were all these other people? Sébastien Rémy's fan club?

If so, they were surprisingly demanding.

'How about just one picture of you with your father and his new bride?' One of the men was trying to get a foot in the door, despite Leo's struggle to close it. 'Or maybe a foursome... You and your girlfriend, Mademoiselle Eden, with the other two. How about it, Leo? Come on, the publicity would be great.' The man gave a grunt of pain as Leo attempted to amputate his foot with the door and he hurriedly withdrew it. 'Just you and your father, then?'

The door finally shut, and Leo sank his back against it, growling like a wild animal.

But not for long.

'This is all your fault, Jean. I hold you responsible for that baying mob outside our home,' Leo rattled off in French. 'You'll be lucky if you have a roof over your head by the end of today, let alone a job. What the hell were you thinking, letting the paparazzi loose on me and Maeve?'

CHAPTER SEVENTEEN

But there was no time for an answer to that excellent question. The baying mob who apparently wanted to photograph her with Leo, for no reason she could possibly fathom, would have to wait. Because Sébastien Rémy was already reaching for her hand and she turned to face him, unsure what to expect.

'Mademoiselle, how wonderful to make your acquaintance. I am Leo's papa, Sébastien, and you must be Maeve.' He took her hand and bowed over it, putting his lips to her skin. His English was very good but heavily accented. 'You are more beautiful than in your photograph, Miss Eden. It did you no justice... No justice at all. You are radiant in that very special way that English girls have.' When she stared at him blankly, he smiled. 'Simple. Understated. *Au naturel.*'

'Erm... Thank you, I think.'

Simple? Understated? Who was he trying to kid? And '*au naturel*' just meant she hadn't got any make-up on and her hair was probably an unholy mess, caught up in a hairband this morning, but with flyaway bits straggling here and there.

She glanced at Leo and saw a fulminating darkness in his face. Of course. He'd told her how much he didn't want his estranged father to visit them... And yet here the man was, filling the hall with his larger than life presence.

Sympathy sparked in her and she shook his father's hand coolly, adding, 'Nice to meet you too. I'm not sure I understand though. What photograph?' But as her gaze returned to Leo's face, she caught a sudden look of consternation there. Even dismay.

What was he hiding?

She was a teacher. She had seen enough teenagers concealing their phones under their desks not to know that expression.

'What's he talking about, Leo? I'd like a straight answer, please. And what on earth are all those people doing outside the door?' She drew a deep breath, fighting off confusion. 'Why did that man want a photograph of you and me?'

'It's complicated,' Leo ground out.

'I'm fairly intelligent, I can probably keep up.'

'They are the paparazzi,' his father told her, still holding her hand, smiling like one of the angels in heaven. He seemed oblivious to her discomfort. 'You have heard of the paps, yes?'

'Yes.'

'Good... So, you start a relationship with my son. My son is quite famous in Paris. Yes, and around France too. The newspapers, the media, they want "a piece of the action," as the Americans might say. So they try to take a photograph of you and my son. Because love, romance, passion... It's what makes the world go around. Especially in Paris.' To her horror, Sébastien Rémy winked at her. 'This is the city of love, never forget.'

'Start a relationship with your son?' she repeated slowly, and then pulled her hand free. 'Excuse me, Monsieur Rémy, but I have done no such thing.' Her back had stiffened and she'd automatically used her 'no-nonsense' teacher voice, noting how everyone's head turned towards her. The 'voice' wasn't loud, but it was authoritative and could cut through kids' chatter in a busy classroom. 'What even gave you that idea?'

Leo, having now locked the front door for good measure, came forward, shaking his head. There was a warning look in his face. 'My father is mistaken. And they...' He gestured over his shoulder. 'The paparazzi... They're mistaken too but it's not *my* fault.' He pointed at his cousin. 'Jean caused all this.'

Jean shrank back, shaking his head as he stared miserably at the ground. 'It was only *one* picture. I wasn't to know they'd come here. I... I just wanted the money.'

'And now they know my father is here too,' Leo said sharply. 'They were already in a feeding frenzy because of his marriage. Now this... Damn it, Jean, this is worse than when Francis died. They had people camped outside the château for weeks. We'll never get rid of them.'

The woman she recognised from that magazine photograph as the new Madame Rémy touched him on the shoulder. 'I know it seems bad, Leo, but they'll soon lose interest. Something else will happen and the paps will disappear.' To Maeve's astonishment, the slender blonde seemed almost flirtatious with her stepson. Though they were a great deal closer in age, she considered, than the three-decade gap between her and Sébastien. 'You'll see, *mon cher*.' These last words were said so lovingly that Maeve's gaze shot to Leo's face, but he seemed unmoved.

'Could someone please explain all this from the beginning?' Maeve heard her voice, breathless and a little shrill, and took a deep breath, trying to steady her nerves. There would be a simple explanation, she was sure. But all this nonsense about a photo and the paparazzi... She was beginning to panic. 'Leo?'

Leo thrust his hands into the back pockets of his jeans, and the fine white-T-shirt he was wearing strained, highlighting flat abs and a muscular chest. Maeve stared, and then noted the young blonde staring too. She forced her gaze to shift a few inches higher to his face and stay there.

'My cousin took a photograph of us when we were out to dinner together. I saw him do it and went over to investigate, but he claimed he'd just been looking at his phone. I should have taken the damn thing away and checked the photo history. Instead, I trusted him.' His jaw hardened. 'He sold the photo to the press. And now it's all over social media.'

'Good God. But... But why? Maybe I'm being thick, but what's so special about you and me *having dinner*, for goodness' sake?' Maeve was flabbergasted. She looked from Jean to Leo to Sébastien, and then back to Leo, her gaze drawn back to his face like a magnetic needle seeking north. 'Because, trust me, I haven't got a clue. Perhaps it's the language barrier. Or maybe I'm missing some important piece of information.'

'But how sweet she is!' the blonde exclaimed, tittering behind one raised hand, on which flashed a large diamond ring and wedding band.

Glancing her way in impatience, Maeve suspected the new Madame Rémy had made that gesture simply to draw attention to her ring finger.

'You don't need to be ashamed of your feelings for my son, mademoiselle,' Sébastien assured her. 'You certainly don't need to conceal them and pretend there's nothing between you.' Ignoring her stunned expression, he beamed at her and Leo. 'As soon as I saw that photograph, I knew the truth. It didn't need a caption to tell me you two were *in love*.'

Leo swore very rudely in French, and Maeve had to agree with him.

'In... In love?' she faltered, then gulped. 'So you're saying, because of this photograph, everyone in Paris now thinks that you and I... That we're... *an item*?'

Heat crept into her cheeks as everyone turned to look at her. It was hugely embarrassing. And, as a teacher, she was used to being stared at for hours on end, and by at least thirty curious and sometimes hostile pairs of eyes. But this was beyond even that scale. Because this was *personal*.

'Not just Paris,' Leo told her bitterly. 'Try the whole of France. All Europe, in fact.'

'The entire world,' Sébastien added softly, a smile still playing on his lips as he looked her up and down as though she were a juicy lambchop he'd like to sink his teeth into.

Maeve stiffened at that vaguely lecherous look, thinking, *you're not sinking your teeth into me, mate.*

'Well, that's just stupid and ridiculous,' she told them flatly, and marched to the front door. 'It will take all of ten seconds to disabuse that lot. Just watch me.'

And with that, she flung open the door and

faced a rabble of reporters on the doorstep, all of whom began to shout at once, falling over themselves as they reached for cameras and phones and microphones.

Behind her, there was a shout of horror.

Hands grabbed her back into the hall and tried slamming the door shut. But the same persistent photographer had yet again stuck his foot in it, so she was still able to shout through the closing gap.

'He's not my boyfriend. I only met him a few days ago. Print that, please,' she yelled, determined to be heard, despite being dragged away. 'He's just a friend. A friend, you understand? *Un ami.*'

Jean gave the reporter an almighty shove, warning him in voluble French to get his foot out of their door, and Leo wrestled the door shut again.

The blonde caught Maeve as she staggered backwards and helped her upright again. 'Oh dear, you really shouldn't talk to the paps,' she told Maeve with soft-voiced reproach, shaking her head. 'They print whatever you say.'

'Good. That's what I want.'

'Ah yes, but they always leave out anything that spoils their story.' Sébastien's wife twirled a lock of blonde hair around one dainty finger, gazing thoughtfully towards the door. 'You used the word, *ami.* Now they'll make it sound as though you were admitting to being his girlfriend, and claim it's a whirlwind romance, because you only met him a few days ago.'

Maeve peered round at her in dismay. 'Oh... You really think so?'

The blonde sighed. 'I know so. Best to say nothing. Let them make up the story on their own.' She rolled her eyes. 'They always do anyway, whatever you say.'

'Sorry, I don't think we've been introduced,' Maeve said awkwardly, sticking out her hand. 'I'm Maeve Eden, and I'm absolutely *not* Leo's girlfriend. I'm sorry about the misunderstanding but I am genuinely just his... *ami.* Well, more his acquaintance, really. We barely know each other, in fact.'

She was babbling, she realised, and stuttered to an embarrassed halt. *We barely know each other, in fact.* Feeling Leo's gaze on her face, she coloured hotly, recalling their kiss on the attic landing.

'I'm Chanelle Rémy, Leo's new stepmother,' the blonde said in return, and shook Maeve's hand gingerly, almost as though it were infected, using just the tips of her fingers. Her smile was perfunctory. *'Enchantée.'*

'Sébastien?' A faint cry came from the grand staircase behind them, and they all turned to see Madame Rémy – the original – standing on the stairs, clutching the newel post at the end of the banister, staring at her son.

'Mama,' breathed Sébastien in return and hurried to greet his mother, kissing her three times on the cheek, then embracing her with a great sigh. 'Mama, Mama... How I have missed you. How are you?' He released her, saying, 'My poor mama, it's been so long. And I wanted to come and see you. Oh, so often, so badly... But I didn't think I would be welcome at Château Rémy.'

His mother had closed her eyes, shaking her head as though she didn't believe a word he was saying. 'Not even when dear Francis died?'

'Don't!' Her son thumped his chest in a gesture so staged and melodramatic, Maeve almost looked around for an audience. 'You wound me. I loved Francis. My son, my first-born. How could I stay away from his funeral? Well, I didn't.'

Everyone stared at him.

'Yes,' he continued, nodding with obvious satisfaction as he saw he had everyone's attention, 'I was there. But in disguise. I came to pay my respects to my son, but not to speak to the family.'

'Why would you do that?' Madame Rémy demanded, her brows knitted together, staring at him with a perplexed frown.

'I didn't wish to cause a scene at my own son's funeral. And it would have caused a scene if you had known I was there.'

Maeve felt this might actually be true. But none

of the others appear to believe him, judging by their incredulous expressions. Except perhaps Chanelle, who sighed and looked with tearful sympathy at her new husband.

'*Mon Dieu*,' Bernadette muttered, emerging from the steps down to the kitchen. She had her hands on her hips and was staring at Sébastien Rémy. She had a streak of flour on her cheek and a light dusting in her hair, and was still wearing her cooking apron. 'You.'

Not a terribly friendly greeting. He was her stepfather, wasn't he?

Maeve wasn't quite sure about the tangled familial relations at Château Rémy. Nor did she dare ask.

'Bernadette,' Sébastien cried and opened his arms to his stepdaughter. '*Ma petite!*'

Bernadette didn't move, frozen where she stood.

Awkward, Maeve thought with a grimace, feeling very much in the way and attempting to retreat into the shadows.

That was when she felt Leo's gaze on her face. He was expressionless. Even so, she caught a wave of conflicted emotions rolling off him…

Anger, pain, grief, despair, yet also a hint of grim humour, as though the situation was so bad, it had become almost funny.

'Perhaps we should all sit down together for a chat,' Madame Rémy suggested, but her reluctance was obvious. 'Nonna is having a nap. She's at her best in the mornings but I could go and wake her. I'm sure she would like to see Sébastien.'

Flushed and unhappy, Bernadette turned and stamped back down into the kitchen without another word.

'Oh no,' Madame Rémy murmured, frowning.

Maeve hesitated, watching the younger woman disappear. She didn't know why Bernadette was so upset. But she probably ought to go after her.

Perhaps reading her mind, Leo touched her arm. He'd appeared at her side without even seeming to move, she realised. Maeve glanced down to assure herself that he wasn't on wheels. He wasn't.

His look was dark and forbidding. 'Would you please check on her, Maeve?' His voice was low in her ear. 'I'm sorry to ask you but I can't go myself. I don't want to leave my grandmother alone with… with *them*.'

Them.

He must mean his father and new stepmother, she guessed, and was shocked by the hostility in his voice. But no doubt he had his reasons.

'Of course,' she said automatically, and was rewarded with a smile.

Goodness, Leo's face lit up when he smiled. He looked like an altogether different person when he wasn't scowling or concentrating on a painting.

But as she slipped away towards the kitchen, Madame Rémy spotted her and her face lightened. 'Mademoiselle Eden,' she exclaimed, 'I didn't see you there. Please wait, I need to tell you something.'

Maeve halted, torn.

'I've been in contact with my old friend Agathe,' Madame Rémy went on, 'and she's asked us to coffee at her apartment tomorrow afternoon. I presume that will suit you?'

Maeve sucked in a breath, registering this amazing news with difficulty. Yet she managed a nod. 'Oh yes, thank you, Madame. That's wonderful.' As the words sank in a little more deeply, she added breathlessly, 'Really, thank you so much. Did you, erm, explain about me?'

'I did,' Madame Rémy admitted, looking guilty. 'Agathe was surprised to hear from me after such a long time. So I felt I had to warn her that you would be coming too, as my guest. I hope you don't mind?'

'No, it's better to be honest... She might not have wanted to see me once we arrived and that would have been difficult.'

'Exactly my thoughts. Agathe was hesitant at first, but she seemed pleased once I'd explained the situation... That you're stranded here in Paris for a few days and thought you'd try to look up your family. She said she was looking forward to meeting you.'

Maeve smiled, pleasure warring with trepidation inside her at the thought of meeting her maternal grandmother at last. What would she be like? Would the old lady truly be happy to see her once they came face-to-face? And would Maeve finally hear news of her absentee mother after all these years?

'I'm glad I could help you,' Madame Rémy said happily, though her smile faltered as she hesitated, glancing towards the newcomers. 'Have you met Sébastien, my son?'

Maeve felt her own smile freeze in place. 'Erm, yes.'

'We spoke before you came downstairs, mother,' Sébastien cut in. 'She's an angel, this sweet little English flower,' he added, his smile turning sly as he glanced from Maeve to Leo. It was clear their conversation about his mother's old friend had bored him rigid, probably because it wasn't about him. Now it seemed he was determined to be the centre of attention again. 'Though an angel with a naughty streak, I suspect.'

'I beg your pardon?' Maeve demanded, turning in outrage. What on earth had he meant by that?

'Oh, no offence intended... I just meant, posing for an artist of Leo's reputation was bold of you.' Sébastien Rémy gave his new bride a knowing wink. 'My son used to paint only nudes, *cherie*. Leo told me once that painting a woman with her clothes on was a waste of time, as she would take them off for him soon enough.' Leo's father threw back his head, roaring with laughter. His wife joined in, tittering behind her hand, apparently finding this anecdote hilarious too. 'Now Jean tells me you've been sitting for Leo. So, does that rule still stand, I wonder?'

'Father!' Leo ground out angrily.

Sébastien hesitated, looking round at his son, a little uncertain at last. The uneasy silence that followed didn't last long but felt awkward.

'Well,' he said eventually, 'I suppose we all grow up in the end. A man needs to settle down. Talking of which...' He held out a hand to Chanelle, who took it with a brilliant smile, bearing white teeth. Honestly, Maeve thought, with that smile, she could be stuck on a headland to warn ships not to run aground on the rocks... 'Mama, may I introduce my wife to you, Chanelle. Darling, this is my mother.'

As the two women smiled and kissed each other stiffly on the cheek, Maeve shook her head and hurried after Bernadette.

She couldn't wait to meet her grandmother Agathe and speak to her about the French side of the family. For all she knew, she might have cousins and aunts and uncles galore here in France. But she and Bernadette had started to warm to each other after an initial period of mistrust, and she didn't want to leave her new friend alone and unhappy. It was obvious Bernadette didn't much like the man who had presumably been her stepfather. And having met Sébastien for herself now, she could see why...

Though she still felt a little off-balance, mentally checking she had understood his French correctly.

My son used to paint only nudes. He once told me that painting a woman with her clothes on was a waste of time, as she would take them off for him soon enough.

No, even given the speed at which that anecdote had been delivered, there wasn't much ambiguity there. It was not just *that* though that was worrying her.

Leo had spoken out furiously, silencing his father at once.

But he hadn't denied saying that, had he?

Partway down the steep, winding steps to the kitchen, a hand on her arm stopped her dead. Sharp, scarlet claws dug into her skin. 'Stop,' Liselle hissed.

'Ouch!'

'Let me go after Bernadette. I want to check she's all right,' Liselle muttered, pushing past her down the steps. 'You can go back... Stay with the others. She's *my* friend, not yours.'

Rubbing her arm, Maeve stared after the woman in dismay, but didn't feel it worth tangling with Liselle just to prove a point. Instead, she headed slowly back up the stairs only to find the grand entrance hall empty, a distant echo of voices sounding from one of many winding passageways in the old château.

The Rémys had all vanished.

With a shrug, Maeve found her way back to her attic bedroom as discreetly as she could.

Perhaps it was just as well.

The Rémy family was wildly complicated, and their troubles were none of her business.

My son used to paint only nudes.

Artists ought to come with a warning label, Maeve considered. 'Fascinating but dangerous.' To her peace of mind, at any rate.

CHAPTER EIGHTEEN

'I still can't believe you did that,' Maeve said in a discreet hiss, then pursed her lips, her head tilted at a disapproving angle as she studied the vast, gilt-framed painting on the wall before them. 'He's your father. It was... Well, it was rude.' She glanced at Leo sideways. 'And forcing me to come with you today... That was rude too.'

Leo ran a frustrated hand through his hair, but turned on his heel, studying the framed paintings on the other side of the gallery.

They were at the Louvre, meandering slowly and without purpose through the vast network of art galleries. He had escaped the Château at the earliest possible opportunity that morning, after a horrifying evening spent dining with his father and Chanelle, making small talk to honour his grandmother's wishes, rather than exploding at his father's reappearance in their lives after all these years.

Not to have even attended his own son's

funeral... Nonna had said wisely at one point, it did no good to rake over the cold ashes of the past. But he had so many questions, and so much fury still boiling inside, it was hard to keep it all bottled up.

And now his father was back, in Paris, with a new bride who was almost the same age as Bernadette.

Why?

It had to be about money. What else could it be?

Sébastien must be hoping somehow to persuade him into parting with some cash or position within the family business. But he wouldn't do it. It would be going against his grandfather's wishes.

Besides, he knew his father would either quickly squander the money or make a mess of whatever job he was given.

'If I was rude, I had good reason for it,' he responded, more curtly than intended. 'You don't know the whole story. There's a difficult history between me and my father. But I'm sorry if you had other plans for this morning. I thought you enjoyed looking at art. I certainly didn't mean to make you uncomfortable.'

'I do enjoy looking at art. But you could try simply telling me the whole story.'

'I brought you here to look at art, not talk about my father. Besides, we're short on time,' he said practically. 'A quick look around the Louvre, then a river trip for lunch. We're due to meet my grandmother and Nonna at a café on the left bank at two o'clock, and we'll walk together to your grandmother's apartment, which isn't far. So there's not much time for lengthy explanations.'

It was a pathetic excuse and he knew it. But the past was so painful, he couldn't bring himself to discuss it. Not when his father had just turned up out of the blue and his wounds were still smarting and raw.

'Maybe we could talk over lunch on the river?' Maeve suggested.

He almost ground his teeth. He had brought her to the Louvre because art soothed him. Plus, coming here on his own would have drawn too much attention, not just from the paparazzi but his own family. He didn't want people saying he was upset by his father's arrival, even though he was. He might be an artist, but he'd outgrown the dramatic tendencies of his youth, increasingly now a private person.

In particular, he hated people poring over his every reaction and trying to second-guess what he was thinking and feeling.

This way, he could study the paintings and lose himself in the art, and nobody would question it, for he was here to introduce Maeve to the greatest treasures Paris had to show. Though she'd already admitted to having been here before, which rendered this visit almost obsolete.

'If you insist,' he said testily, not sure why he was agreeing to share intimate family details with a stranger, except that she had an excellent way of getting under his skin. 'First though, you asked me to teach you something about art. So let's look at the old Masters. Here, for instance,' he said, pointing up at the nearest painting, 'what you think of that?'

'Erm... a woman with her boobs out, surrounded by men with guns?' Maeve pulled a face. 'Yes, I know it's a famous painting. Delacroix's *Liberty Leading the People*. But honestly, why do men always feel this ridiculous urge to paint women topless? You're not going to tell me it's necessary.' She indicated the rest of the revolutionaries. 'None of those men are topless, are they? Only the *woman*.'

Leo suppressed a burst of wild laughter. It really wasn't funny. Delacroix had painted the goddess or personification of Liberty topless to indicate her uncompromising, revolutionary spirit, not simply to titillate the viewer. Or had he?

But she had a way of making him smile, this fussy, eccentric Englishwoman. And not merely smile but *think*. Yes, she challenged his way of seeing the world. And not just the world, but her too.

With a shock, Leo realised he was looking at her in a way he'd never looked at any other woman. He didn't know exactly what he meant by that.

Perhaps that when he looked at her, he saw more than a face and body, or a female mind with ulterior motives behind it, or the person he had to deal with in a business situation, or any of that.

With her, he saw the whole package. He saw *Maeve Eden*. Whole and complete. Fully rounded, as it were, with nothing missing.

Except how it would feel to hold her close and make love to her. To merge and become one with Maeve. And that was something he wanted. Not just for sexual satisfaction, but to *experience her*. To discover who Maeve was behind the neat bob and pursed lips and occasionally frivolous replies.

The epiphany of such an unfamiliar longing struck him dumb, and he stood staring at her, his mouth slightly open.

'I take it that was the wrong thing to say?' she demanded, again tilting her head to study him as though he were an alien specimen. He wasn't sure if it was amusement or irritation he read in her face. There were small rosy apples in each cheek, and her fair hair was slightly mussed, which was unusual for such a tidy, well-presented creature, and she had her arms tightly folded across her chest in a defensive posture.

'I...' Leo frowned, genuinely unsure what to say. Embarrassed, even flustered, he stuck his hands in his pockets and jerked his head towards the next gallery. 'Delacroix not your style, I take it? Okay, so let's see if we can get a glimpse of the Mona Lisa, shall we? It's not far... Besides, you said you weren't sure what you thought of da Vinci's masterpiece when you were here last time.' He crooked an eyebrow at her. 'Though you didn't have me with you when you saw the painting.'

'Oh, and having you with me will make all the difference?'

Now he really did laugh. 'I just mean you'll have someone to bounce ideas off. Someone who knows a thing or two about art, and about the Mona Lisa. I wrote a thesis on her in art school.'

'Goodness,' she said innocently. 'So art school wasn't just splashing paint around and building towers out of toilet roll inners?'

'Oh, we did all that as well,' he threw back at her, leading the way through the busy gallery towards the room where the Mona Lisa was housed. 'But now and then, our tutors expected us to write to actual words about art and come to a few conclusions. They didn't have to make sense, you understand. But I happen to enjoy looking at the Mona Lisa. There's more to that painting than a mysterious smile.'

They had to queue, of course. And they were not alone in jostling about in front of the painting, which was housed safely behind bulletproof glass. But soon they were standing in front of the Mona Lisa, and to his relief there was nobody forcing them to hurry past, despite the portrait's universal popularity. It was coming up to lunchtime and the crowds in front of the Mona Lisa had briefly thinned.

Side by side with Maeve, he gazed up at the portrait that had so obsessed him in his youth, and found himself smiling back at the woman smiling down at him.

If that was a smile on the Italian lady's beautiful face, which he sometimes doubted...

'So, what do you think?' he asked after a moment's silent contemplation.

'I think you're holding my hand,' Maeve told him softly.

His head jerked round and he stared at her, astonished. 'What?' Looking down, he realised with a jolt that she was correct.

Somehow, in some moment of unconscious craziness, he had taken her hand and was holding it close, their fingers interlaced. It had felt so natural he hadn't even noticed.

He released her at once, muttering in a wave of heat, 'I... I'm so sorry. I don't know why I did that.'

She was looking rattled too. 'It doesn't matter.'

Thrown, he stood rigid, arms by his sides, and stared fixedly up at the painting without seeing the long-dead woman depicted there.

What was happening to him?

Is this how da Vinci had felt, faced with his famous Muse? Dumbfounded, lightheaded, possessed by a strange urgency...

Maeve cleared her throat.

'I... I was in such a tearing hurry when I came through here on my first visit,' Maeve began to say, also gazing up at the painting, 'that I didn't even pay much attention to the history behind the painting. Too worried about falling behind schedule and missing my coach. Ironic, really, given what happened.' She took a deep breath. 'All right... I know this was painted by Leonardo da Vinci, of course. Everyone knows that. But I don't know who the "Mona Lisa" is. Or why she seems to be smiling. If she is smiling.' She frowned, glancing at him briefly as though for confirmation. 'Do you know?'

'Some background might be useful here.' With a roll of his tense shoulders, Leo tried to relax, casting his mind back to the thesis paper he had written about this painting when he was younger. 'The woman in the painting is generally considered to be Lisa Gheradini, who was married to a Florentine silk merchant called Francesco del Giocondo. Because of that, someone later nicknamed this portrait "La Gioconda" in Italian.' He saw her confusion and added, 'It's a pun on her married name. "Giaconda" also means a happy or smiling woman, you see. The "jocund" one, you might say in English. So the nickname of the portrait is La Joconde in French. Or "the laughing lady" as my grandmother calls her.'

He studied the painting, confidence surging

back as he warmed to his subject. 'You want to know if she's smiling? That's always been a vexed question. Some people think it depends on which part of the painting you look at. If you look at it from one angle, she does seem to be amused. But if you shift your eye to another area, she suddenly looks serious. Or ironic, perhaps. Certainly her smile, if it is a smile, is known to be *enigmatic*.'

'Is that why the painting is so famous? Because of her smile?'

'Yes, mostly.' He hesitated, studying the soft, delicate brushwork. 'But also because of Leonardo da Vinci's great skill in painting this. It's so realistic, it could almost be a photograph.' He pointed to the face of Lisa Gheradini. 'You see the way light and shade are used to suggest her cheekbones and the orbital ridges around the eyes? That technique is called *sfumato*. Here, it indicates that the artist understands more than the surface of what is looking at. In this case, we're seeing the skull beneath the Mona Lisa's skin.'

'That sounds macabre.'

Leo grinned. 'Maybe. But what it demonstrates is how skilled da Vinci was at observation. Don't forget this was painted in the Renaissance. That's five hundred-odd years ago. Back then, painting was still at quite an early stage in terms of *realism*. And there are other things about the painting too that make it special. The intricate way he's depicted the folds of her clothes, for example, and the way each lock of her hair is differentiated... So very realistic for its age.' He paused. 'Of course, there may have been other equally skilled painters alive at the same time. But because da Vinci had a powerful patron, he quickly became famous, and his paintings grew in fame too. I often wonder about lost paintings, lost painters... How much great art has been forgotten or destroyed over the centuries?'

She was frowning. 'What do you mean?'

He shrugged. 'It's so simple to destroy a painting, that's all. The work of a moment, really. To slash, burn, deface... It's a miracle we have any art left from the Renaissance at all, when you consider how fragile these paintings are.'

He saw her shiver, and was surprised by that reaction. She must be a sensitive creature if the mere suggestion of destroying works of art had the power to distress her. It distressed him too, of course. But he was an artist, so was always mindful of how ephemeral some art could be. Besides, it was also a fact of life in this business.

Art had to be preserved and protected, especially in their age of cultural terrorism. That was why the Mona Lisa was kept safely behind bulletproof glass. But not everyone could appreciate why it mattered so much to preserve art for future generations.

'Are you all right?' Leo asked softly, concerned

that he might have genuinely upset her.

'Oh, yes,' she said, but shakily, turning to face him. There were tears in her eyes. He was taken aback, wondering what on earth he had said to make her so unhappy, until she added quickly, 'No, honestly, I'm fine. I was just thinking about the last time I came here, that's all. That awful day... Getting my bag snatched by that fiend on the motorbike, being knocked out, missing the coach home, and my lost passport...' She bit her lip, a tear rolling down her cheek. 'It feels like such a long time ago. And yet everything has happened so quickly too. I suppose I'm just a little homesick and wishing I knew when I'll get back to England and start my life again.'

'Of course, it must be upsetting.' He noted that others behind them were waiting impatiently for their turn in front of the famous painting. 'Shall we move on?' He checked his watch. 'It's time to catch a river boat along the Seine, anyway, and grab a quick lunch on board.'

She was wiping away tears. 'Yes, thank you. I'm looking forward to that.'

Making their ways through the crowded, noisy galleries, they eventually reached the exit and emerged into bright sunshine. She was wearing Bernadette's sleeveless dress again. Today though, she had found a belt so that it didn't hang so loosely, and her narrow waist was emphasized where it cinched in, folds of material falling softly to her knees.

He stopped dead, fixated by her again, urgently wanting to paint her in that dress and that position. But of course they were far from the studio.

He dragged out his phone and said roughly, 'Hold still a moment, please.'

'Sorry?'

'Hush.' Hurriedly, he took a variety of photographs of her as she stared back at him, turned at an angle towards him, the sun slightly behind her, turning her gold hair into a halo, a burst of light that streamed past one cheek...

'You're very strange,' she said, not for the first time.

Putting away his phone, he grimaced, aware that he had behaved erratically. 'Sorry. It's an old habit. I often sketch from photographs. And just then you looked...' Leo stopped himself from saying something he would later regret. 'Well, I liked the way you looked.'

There was colour in her cheeks. She bent her head, tucking a few strands of hair behind her ear as though embarrassed by this.

'Lunch, you said?'

They waited on the quayside a short distance from the Pont de l'Alma. There was quite a crowd queuing for tickets in the midday heat. Maeve had not bought a hat, and was looking flushed.

Leo studied her with concern, and then slipped away to a stall he had seen further along the quay selling scarves, sunglasses and hats. Among the vast array of 'I Heart Paris' baseball caps he spotted a floppy-brimmed straw hat and bought it.

He took it back to her. 'Here, this will stop you getting sunburnt.' When she protested, he shook his head. 'No, I insist.'

'Thank you,' Maeve said shyly, putting on the oversized straw hat, her face instantly shaded.

He was deeply conscious of the fact that her funds were limited. Bernadette had taken her to a bank where she had been able to access a few hundred euros to tide her over this enforced stay in Paris. But that would hardly stretch to luxury items. To his mind though, a hat was an essential in this baking summer weather.

Besides, she looked strangely alluring in the straw hat, glancing up at him occasionally from under its floppy brim...

Having been brought up in Paris, Leo was thoroughly bored by the time they were able to board the lunch boat. Maeve seemed delighted though, and as they sat at a table inside, he pointed out landmarks along the river, while she exclaimed and took a keen interest in the tourist commentary being piped through speakers. It was only a quick lunch service, as they would be disembarking at Notre Dame on the boat's second pass around the Isle of France. But the boat went slowly enough and he enjoyed studying her profile as she gazed eagerly up and down the river.

She really was quite ordinary-looking. And yet...

The Mona Lisa was ordinary-looking too, when studied in detail. Yet hers was a face that had captured millions of imaginations, he considered.

For some reason, Maeve Eden had captured his artistic imagination. He had hoped that, in beginning to paint her, he would gradually work out the puzzle of his attraction. Yet all it had done was increase his desire to spend time with her. Which was disastrous, really. Soon she would get her passport back and be on her way home to England.

'Have you heard from the embassy yet?' he asked abruptly, just as she was chatting about the other people on her coach tour, who sounded to him like a bunch of very dull people.

She blinked. 'Oh, yes, I did... There was a phone call this morning. Just to let me know they're still working on it. There's still some complication over my place of birth. I don't understand it myself. The fact that I was born in Paris has never been a problem before. But then,' she mused, 'I've never left the country before.'

He was astonished. 'You've never left the United Kingdom before?'

'I suppose you think I'm terribly parochial. A real country bumpkin.'

They had been speaking in English, which he enjoyed practising. But this expression threw him. 'Country... *bumpkin?*'

'Yes, a bumpkin is a sort of peasant...' She gurgled with laughter at his shock, and her face was transformed. 'It's an awful expression. I'm sorry, I shouldn't have used it. I'm sure people who live in the country are every bit as clever and educated as people live in cities. I only meant... Oh, forget it. I'm just babbling.'

'I don't think my great-grandmother has ever left France,' he remarked mildly. 'She's still the wisest woman I know.'

'Your Nonna? Oh, I love her. When a marvellous woman.' She frowned. 'I hope she'll be all right, walking about this afternoon in this heat. She really didn't need to come too.'

'You'd have to tie her to a chair to stop her. My great-grandmother is a deeply curious woman. Though I think the best English word for her is... *nosy.*'

Maeve grinned. It lightened his heart, looking into her laughing eyes. 'I shall be just the same if I ever get to her age. Nosy and determined to keep up with everyone.'

Leo thought back to what she'd said about her Embassy call. 'So you'll be going back to England soon?'

Her laughter died. 'It does look that way, yes. They suggested I come back to the embassy in person in about three or four days. For another interview.' She frowned, biting on her lip. 'I hope it's just a formality. I find that place rather intimidating. I keep thinking they're going to arrest me and drag me off to the Bastille and I'll never be seen again.'

'The Bastille doesn't exist anymore. It was demolished.'

'Oh.'

The boat was juddering as it slowed, backing gracefully toward a wooden jetty where tourists could disembark for the Ile de la Cité and Notre Dame, although repairs to the great cathedral were still ongoing, following extensive fire damage, so no visits were yet being permitted.

'This is our stop, I believe,' he said. They had pre-paid for lunch as part of the boat ticket price, so it only took a moment for them to leave the restaurant area and climb up onto deck into the sunshine. The wind snatched at her dress and made his trouser legs flap. But at least it provided a little relief from the heat. 'If you were arrested, I would come and rescue you. Even if I had to blow the prison gates off.'

It was a silly joke, and yet he meant it. The realisation surprised him. He was becoming oddly protective of their English guest. What did that mean?

'Then you'd end up in prison too,' she pointed out.

'I wouldn't mind if I was in the same cell as you.' Another joke. Wasn't it?

'Do they have unisex prisons in Paris?' Her look was cool. She thought he was mocking her. And he probably was. That made the most sense, he decided.

'I'm sure if I bribed someone, it could happen. So I wouldn't go to prison. I would simply rescue you and we'd ride off into the sunset together, never to be seen again.'

'I can't ride.'

He loved how prosaic she always was. Or was irritated by her down-to-earth replies. He couldn't be sure which. 'Not a problem,' he insisted, and ran a smoothing hand through his hair as the wind ruffled it. 'I'll bring a large motorbike. You can ride pillion and hold onto me.'

'Oh well, in that case… I've always had a soft spot for a biker boy.'

He looked round at her with raised brows, but Maeve was already drifting away, threading her way between tourists planning to disembark, apparently keen to watch the boat's slow approach to the quayside.

He raised his head to the sun and closed his eyes as the gangplank was set in place, enjoying the heat.

He had been cooped up indoors for too

much recently, he thought, absorbed by family business, like Henri's fire disaster at the vineyard. Or just painting...

'Alight here, *mesdames et messieurs*' the crew member on the gangplank was announcing, 'for the cathedral of Notre Dame and the left bank...'

'Maeve?' She had disappeared into the crowd, he realised. 'Maeve? We have to go.'

At last, he spotted her leaning over the side of the riverboat a few metres along the open deck, just past the jetty, as though straining to see something in the murky waters below.

He hurried towards her, but the tourists blocked his way, shuffling towards the gangplank. She must have seen him coming though, because she pointed down into the river, her face animated.

'Oh, Leo, look... Is that a fish?' she asked, her voice muffled as she leant even further. 'I'm sure that's a – oh no!'

It was famously gusty along the Seine, summer and winter alike. Shorts or jeans were de rigueur on the river.

As he elbowed his way towards her, Maeve's over-large borrowed dress was caught by one of those sudden gusts and blown upwards, granting him – and everyone else in the vicinity – a view of pale rounded thighs and an equally rounded and delectable derrière.

Leo stopped dead, his eyes widening at the sight of her bottom in tight white underwear. He didn't mean to but couldn't help it.

'Mon Dieu...' he breathed.

Meanwhile, Maeve had gasped in consternation as the dress blew up, as well she might, given what was now on show. Releasing the floppy hat she'd been holding in place, the modest Englishwoman clamped both hands to the hem of her dress instead, swiftly dragging it down...

But the treacherous wind instantly snatched the unprotected hat from her head and dashed it into the river. Or would have done, if the protective bumpers fixed to the lower side of the boat hadn't got in the way, leaving the hat hooked close to the lapping water.

With a shriek of horror, Maeve made an automatic grab for it, leaning precariously over the rail as she cried out, 'My hat... Oh no, my lovely hat!'

'Maeve, no, leave it,' Leo warned her.

A startled crew member darted forward at the exact same time as Leo.

But neither of them could reach her in time to prevent the inevitable from happening.

Somehow majestic, Maeve tumbled over the railing, pale legs waving in the air, and disappeared with a splash and a despairing wail into the filthy waters below.

CHAPTER NINETEEN

Maeve could not quite believe the stupidity of what she'd done. One second, she'd been stretching on tiptoe for her hat, sure she could probably reach it with a little help... The next she'd been plunged headfirst into chill water in the shadow of the boat, the rapid change in temperature a heart-wrenching shock after the hot sunshine on deck.

Sinking rapidly, she'd kicked and flailed about wildly, struggling to return to the surface and much-needed oxygen. It wasn't easy. The Seine was surprisingly deep and choppy, almost like the open sea...

She emerged with a violent intake of breath that also included some river water. *E. coli,* she thought with horror. This disgusting, oily fluid she spat out at once, working her arms and legs to keep afloat as she put aside embarrassment and focused on survival.

Up above, she saw Leo staring down at her.

Oh God.

She heard her thought echoed in a deep voice from the deck. 'Mon Dieu,' one of the crew exclaimed, tossing an orange lifebuoy ring after her. '*Les anglaises!*'

The lifebuoy ring bobbed about a few feet away. Keeping her chin above the filthy water, mouth clamped shut, Maeve doggy-paddled towards it, conscious of the looming bulk of the boat like a sheer wall above her. The ring evaded her, skittering away on a bobbing crest as she approached, but with an almighty effort she grabbed it with one hand and dragged it towards her.

'Maeve?' Leo was leaning over the side, peering at her. She stared up in dismay, hoping he wouldn't make the same mistake she had. But of course he didn't. 'Are you all right?'

Am I all right?

Good grief.

'What… does it… *blearh*… look like?' she spluttered crossly.

'Hang on,' he told her. 'We're going to rescue you.'

'Don't *you* try climbing down!' she cried, fearful for his safety.

But she needn't have worried. 'Not a chance.' There was laughter in his voice, she was sure. 'I'll leave this one to the experts. Try to stay warm by treading water, okay?'

Tourists had also gathered to stare over the side of the boat, some even forgetting to disembark. There were more on the river bank behind her, she realised, risking a quick glance that way. More than a few were holding up cameras, no doubt taking pictures or actually filming her humiliation. She pretended not to have noticed them, but it was pretty hard. Especially when a crew member climbed over the side of the boat, attached to a rope looped about his middle, to rescue her, and a buzz went up among those watching.

Like feeding time at the zoo, she thought furiously.

It took some fifteen minutes before she was safely back on board and being tended by a paramedic, who had arrived on a motorbike with sirens and lights, drawing yet more attention.

Dripping wet and shivering, Maeve was taken into a small inner cabin, wrapped in a foil blanket for warmth, while a female crew member dabbed ineffectually at her sodden hair and clothes with a towel. Her face, neck, hands and arms had been thoroughly cleaned and disinfected, and advice given about possible E. coli infection, though apparently the risk was low.

The boat steward stood over her, arms folded, complaining in a voluble fashion about her 'reckless behaviour'. Apparently, some of the tourists had been asking for their money back due to the lengthy delay. He also asked if she needed the police to be called, which was apparently what they were supposed to do in the event of someone going overboard. An incident report was already being drawn up by a crew member, and it was clear they wanted her to admit full liability.

'Did you not see the safety notices?' the steward kept demanding. 'They are posted at intervals all along the railing in French and English. *Danger. No leaning over.*'

'I was trying to reach my hat,' she said in a small voice.

'Not even to reach a hat.' The steward made an angry noise under his breath, shaking his head. 'What did you think was going to happen, *hein?*'

'Go easy on her,' Leo exclaimed at one point in growling French, glaring at the steward from under taut brows. 'Can't you see she's in shock?'

Ridiculously, she felt annoyed by his protective stance. Though she was grateful for it as well. Especially when, to her relief, the steward backed off.

Eventually, once the paramedic had declared her unhurt and gone on his way, and Maeve had signed a waiver, foregoing her right to make any future complaint against the boat company for negligence, they were allowed to disembark.

In fact, they were *urged* to disembark, the steward practically pushing them both off the boat.

Those still waiting impatiently onboard applauded their departure, some even cheering when the gangplank was withdrawn and the boat finally pulled away from the jetty, back on course. One of the men watching had clearly recognised Leo, for he called out his name and, when Leo glanced his way, snapped a photo.

'*Merde*,' Leo muttered.

'I'm so sorry,' she told him. 'So much for us keeping a low profile. Did you see them all filming us when I got hauled out of the water?'

'Yes.'

He sounded terse, and small wonder.

Maeve stared after the boat with a glum expression. 'I'm such an idiot,' she said dejectedly, picking more river weed from her hair. 'I made a complete fool of myself, didn't I?'

'Maybe not a *complete* fool,' Leo said.

'Thanks.'

He sighed. 'Look, it's no big deal.'

'Seriously? Were you even watching? I fell into the Seine.' She pulled a tenacious piece of weed from her hair. '*Blearh*.'

She'd expected Leo to be stressed and impatient, rightly annoyed by her antics, not least because he'd been forced to text his grandmother during the rescue to let her know they'd been unavoidably delayed. Instead, looking down into her damp, unhappy face, he chuckled.

'I was watching, yes. And okay, yes, you did fall into the Seine. Here, allow me,' he murmured, gently extracting another strand of green weed from her hair. 'But you didn't *drown*,' he pointed out. 'They got you out. You're unhurt. And alive.'

'Yes, but I lost my lovely hat...' Adding insult to injury, the floppy straw hat had blown out of reach during the rescue attempt. She had groaned to herself, watching as it bobbed away on the dirty water, eventually sinking to a watery grave in the distance. 'You bought me that hat and I got to wear it for less than an hour.'

'True.' With surprising patience, Leo guided her up a steep flight of stone steps that led onto the left bank of the river. 'But it wasn't expensive. And I can always buy you another one.'

'That's kind, but no thank you,' she told him miserably. 'It would only blow away again and I'd probably fall off the... the Eiffel Tower or something, trying to get it back.'

'Then I won't take you to the Eiffel Tower.'

'Oh you... You're just trying to make me feel better, aren't you?'

His eyebrows rose. 'What gave it away?'

'I did something ludicrous and ruined everyone's day.' Her voice choked. 'What happened... That was the kind of thing *other people* do, not me... Not Maeve Eden. Everyone knows that I'm organised and reliable and trustworthy. I don't lose p-p-passports or fall off b-b-boats into rivers.' The stutter did nothing for her confidence, her cheeks burning with humiliation as she recalled all those onlookers filming her moment of supreme idiocy.

No doubt she was on social media somewhere now, gaining some influencer thousands of hits. She only hoped nobody could make out her face at that distance. Though given that someone had recognised Leo, it was a thin hope...

'You were trying to keep us out of the media,' she added miserably. 'Now I've made everything a hundred times worse. I don't deserve to feel better.'

To her embarrassment, her trainers were making loud sloshing noises with every step, no doubt still waterlogged. But at least they had stayed on her feet. At one stage, she had feared she might have to try removing them. But, only being cheap sports pumps, they had remained lightweight enough not to pull her under...

'If that's how you see yourself,' he said after a moment's contemplation, perhaps listening to the noisy slosh of every step, 'I understand now why you were so upset at losing your rucksack.' He studied her thoughtfully. 'You still blame yourself for what happened. Not the thief.'

'Well, if I hadn't taken my eye off my rucksack –'

'You were looking after my grandmother.'

'But I should have kept the bag on my back. Then I'd still have it.' She nursed that bitter thought for a moment, her heart flooding with unhappiness. 'I would never have lost my passport. I'd be back home in England right now, sitting on my sofa, having a nice cup of tea –'

'Yes, and you and I would never have encountered each other,' he interrupted. 'Or only for a few minutes on the street before I drove my grandmother to the hospital. You would never have seen the inside of Château Rémy or met Nonna and the rest of my family... Or allowed me the great privilege of painting you.' His dark eyes seemed to pierce to the back of her skull. 'Is that truly what you'd prefer? That we had never met?'

'N-No,' she stammered.

'Good.'

'Is it?'

'Of course.' He took her elbow. 'Because I don't regret having met you, even if it's been a mess at times. That photo Jean took, Liselle's moodiness and jealousy, having to watch my father drooling over you... Now this, knowing there'll be photos of us all over social media by now. *You* like this,' he nodded towards her sodden, clinging dress, 'and *me* having to stand by and watch while other men rescued you.'

'I'm glad you didn't risk your own neck,' she remonstrated.

'It's not in my nature though to sit idly by when the woman I...' Something flickered in that hard, handsome face, then Leo blinked and hurriedly shifted tack, finishing, 'When the woman I'm with falls into the river.'

A memory slammed into her and she stopped dead, groaning out loud.

His hand released her elbow. 'What is it?' Concern drew his brows together. 'Were you hurt, falling out of the boat? You told the paramedic you were okay.'

'No, I'm fine, I just remembered… I'm meant to be meeting my grandmother for the first time this afternoon.' Maeve struggled with her wet dress, its folds clamped to her thighs. 'I was so careful to try and look my best today as well… Now look at me.' She was usually good at staying calm under pressure, but the shock of her mishap had shaken her confidence and it was hard not to burst into self-pitying tears. 'What.. Whatever will she think?'

'I imagine she'll think you fell in the river,' Leo said, his mouth quirking with humour.

She glared up at him. 'That's not very helpful.'

'Maybe not. But there's nothing you can do about your dress. Or your hair.'

'Oh, my hair!' She ran her fingers through its tangled strands, but it seemed to be weed-free at last. Small mercies. It still felt damp and bedraggled though, slowly drying in the sunshine to a frizzy mess. 'Perhaps we should call it off. See her another day.'

'And if she changes her mind about meeting

you?'

He was right. Her grandmother might well consider it intolerably rude for her to cancel their meeting last minute. She clapped her hands over her face, despair almost swallowing her. 'This is just the most awful bad luck,' she wailed.

'True, but you can only work with the situation you're given. What would you prefer your grandmother to see when she opens the door to you?' he asked, gently pulling her hands away from her face and peering down at her. 'A young woman in a mess, laughing at her own foolishness? Or someone miserable, riddled with fear and uncertainty?'

'I am *not* riddled with fear and uncertainty,' she said stiffly.

'I'm glad.' He moved a damp strand of hair out of her eyes. 'In that case, why don't you try seeing the funny side of the situation?'

'Because there's nothing funny about this.'

He gave her sodden figure a quick up-and-down glance and his lips worked with amusement. 'Is that so?' Then he gave a shout of laughter. 'If you could see yourself…'

'You, Leo Rémy, are a complete brute.' She stamped on ahead, but the effect of wounded dignity was rather lost, given the loud squelching of her wet trainers.

He hurried after her. 'I'm sorry,' he said, and put an arm about her waist. She felt herself go rigid, her head jerking back, her wide gaze shooting to his in shock. 'It *is* funny,' he insisted. 'But I'm not laughing at you. I'm laughing at what happened. At the way they had to fish you out of the river... And as for the look on your face right now –'

'Yes?' she whispered when he stopped dead, her eyes on his face.

'I'm sorry,' he repeated in a low voice, 'but I'm going to kiss you again, even though I know I shouldn't.' His arm snagged her closer, his dark head bending towards hers, eclipsing the bright dazzle of sunlight along the Seine. 'Because you are completely irresistible.'

CHAPTER TWENTY

Maeve's head swam under his demanding kiss. She had been so tired and bewildered the last time they'd kissed, her brain had not properly processed the situation. Or so she'd told herself, confused that she had even allowed such inappropriate behaviour from a man she barely knew. Though she knew him rather better now, or felt she did. It was strange, she mused, how a few electrically charged days with one person could leave you knowing them better than people you'd known for months, even years...

Of course, this time she had fallen into a river first. She was soggy and shaken. But the unexpected dunking had left her alert and her brain was working just fine. So it was even more of a shock when she didn't instantly push him away as she probably ought to have done, but instead linked her arms about his neck and stood on tiptoe to deepen the kiss. Just like last time. Just as though she'd learnt nothing in the interim...

His mouth moved on her persuasively. Goodness, he smelt so good. Clean and male, his aftershave tangy with citrus. While she probably smelt of... No, best not to think of that. Besides, Maeve wanted more, and she *never* wanted more. That primal urge to go further left her stunned, so that when Leo pulled back to gaze down into her face, she found herself unable to speak. She merely gawped at him as though drunk.

'I apologise,' he murmured, still holding her far too close, which rather undermined the whole apology thing. 'I seem to be making a habit of this. Kissing you, I mean. Not saying sorry. I've never been one for apologising if I can avoid it. But in this instance, I probably should. You're our guest at Château Rémy. It's not right.'

'I, erm... Yes, I...'

To her relief, as she appeared to have temporarily lost access to the language centres in her brain, she heard a wail above the sound of the traffic, a high-pitched 'Coo-ee!'-style cry from across the busy road. Baffled, her gaze drifted that way and hooked onto the familiar sight of Madame Rémy and Nonna, seated together at a pavement café only a few hundred feet from the river bank, trying to catch their attention.

'Erm, your gran,' she whispered feebly, attempting to pull herself free.

'I'm... grand?' he repeated, frowning.

'*Grand*? Why would I say you were grand?' She shook her head, still reeling from his kiss. Her lips felt numb, her body tingling. 'I said, your gran.' And she pointed in the direction of his relatives. 'See? Gran.'

He glanced that way and swore under his breath. His arms fell to his sides, releasing her at once. Sunlight dazzled her once more, free of his shadow. 'Ah, yes... My gran. *Bien, d'accord.*' They began to walk towards the two ladies, who were now waving. 'I suppose it would be too much to hope she hadn't seen us kissing.'

Maeve considered that. 'I take it she wouldn't be very happy?'

'I'm more worried she'd be pleased,' he growled.

Squelching along beside him, Maeve shot a startled look at his face, unsure if she'd heard him correctly. 'Sorry... *Pleased*?'

'What you have to understand is that my grandmother is one of the biggest matchmakers in Paris. Apart from my great-grandmother, that is. When the two of them get together...' He shook his head in weary resignation. 'They have been disappointed for years that I've refused to settle down and present them with great-grandchildren. The moment I show any interest in a woman – apart from Liselle, whom they both dislike intensely – I think their brains spiral off into weddings and babies.'

Weddings and babies.

She was blushing, and couldn't seem to stop herself. But oh lordy-lord, That Kiss…

What had his Nonna said on first meeting her? That she would be his *Muse*? And now she had to face the two older ladies, who had no doubt spotted the two of them canoodling and might expect news of an engagement at any moment. And it wasn't like that at all between her and Leo. It had just been a kiss. Nothing special. Nothing to report.

They had almost reached the busy road between them and the café, cars zooming along with the usual mad disregard for safety or traffic rules.

'Wait, they don't like Liselle?' Her stupid brain had focused on that interesting nugget of information instead of all the rest, trying to work it out.

He gave a short bark of laughter. 'And that's putting it mildly.' His clever gaze narrowed on her face. 'You know, I half expected you to slap me for kissing you just then. Or to tell me exactly what you think of me at the very least. You weren't angry?'

'It was only a kiss. Goodness, of course not…' Guilt rose in her like a hot tide, aware that she was lying to herself as well as him. 'But we'd better not keep them waiting any longer,' she babbled. 'They must be so bored, poor things. We've been ages. And it's all my fault.'

Hurriedly, she squelched to the edge of the kerb,

and was poised to run across the road in front of oncoming traffic when he grabbed her arm.

'Hey, what do you think you are doing? This is Paris. These drivers take no prisoners. You'll be killed if you don't wait for the lights.'

'Oh, don't exaggerate.'

He raised his brows at her wild gesture. 'All right, you'll be seriously maimed if you run in front of those cars.'

As though to demonstrate the truth of that, the next few cars to pass them did so in a blur of speed, engines roaring.

Breathlessly, she peered down the road. 'There are traffic lights?'

Almost on cue, the cars coming towards them ground to a halt. Though she noticed the drivers still revved their engines impatiently at the lights, as though dying to mow someone down.

'Yes, we Parisians do occasionally allow pedestrians to cross the street without fear of death. But you have to hurry.' He ushered her across before the traffic could start moving again. Safely on the other side, he trod purposefully towards his grandmother's café table, kissing this elegant lady on the cheek and then bending to kiss Nonna too. 'I'm sorry we took so long,' he told them in French, 'but I'm afraid there was an accident... Maeve fell in the river.'

Madame Rémy, who had leant forward to embrace Maeve, as the French seemed to do at every possible opportunity, pulled back to study her in horror. '*Mon Dieu*... I wondered why your hair was wet. And Bernadette's lovely dress. Oh, and your shoes too.' She pointed to one of the empty wicker seats at their table. 'Please, join us. How did this happen?'

With an uncomfortable smile, Maeve sank damply onto the seat. Was she really going to be forced to relive that epic humiliation?

'It's quite a long story,' she begun reluctantly.

'Her hat blew over the side of the boat,' Leo told them succinctly, 'and she fell in the river trying to retrieve it.'

Okay, maybe not that long a story, Maeve thought, throwing him a strained look of gratitude.

'*Mais quelle horreur*! You need a hot chocolate after such an ordeal,' Madame Rémy said sympathetically, and turned to look for the waiter.

'Thank you, no, we don't have time,' Maeve told her, jumping to her feet again, far too wound-up and nervous to settle. 'If we don't leave now, we'll be horribly late arriving at my grandmother's place.' Maeve ran her fingers through damp, frizzy hair, and despaired. 'I don't suppose you have a hairbrush I could borrow, madame? Or maybe a comb?' she whispered to Madame Rémy. 'What a nightmare. I must look a complete mess.'

As Leo helped Nonna to her feet and took her

arm, supporting her along the street, Madame Rémy fished a comb out of her bag and handed it surreptitiously to Maeve. 'You don't look so bad,' she said politely. 'Perhaps just a bit… windswept.'

Following Leo and Nonna at the older lady's leisurely pace, they crossed a narrow side street and wove carefully between tourists past a range of bustling cafés, restaurants and shops.

Despairingly, Maeve dragged the comb through her hair, wishing she had a mirror. Her shoes were still squelching, though not as loudly, and her sodden dress still clung to her thighs in an embarrassing manner. But at least there didn't appear to be any more weed in her hair.

'Thank you for waiting,' she whispered to Leo's grandmother. 'I half expected you to have gone home by now.'

'We were perfectly comfortable, enjoying a drink beside the river. Anyway, Leo warned us you would be late, so I called Agathe and let her know we would be delayed. So you don't need to worry she'll be angry.'

Maeve sagged with relief, her breath going out in one long sigh. She had been worried about that, there was no point pretending otherwise. Indeed, it felt as though she'd been holding that breath tight in her chest for ages. And why on earth had she behaved so recklessly before, almost dashing across the embankment road in front of rushing traffic?

That wasn't like her at all.

She had always been a sensible pedestrian who waited at the crossing point for the lights to change, refusing to move before it was safe to do so.

Clearly, there must be something wrong with her brain at the moment. The signs were all there. Falling in the river. Kissing Leo *twice*. Trying to cross a road and forgetting to check she wasn't about to be squashed flat by speeding Parisian rally-drivers...

'Are you alright, my dear?' Madame Rémy asked quietly, her brows tugging together in concern.

'To be honest, I'm not entirely sure.' But Maeve forced a smile to her lips. It wasn't anyone's business but her own what was going on inside her wacky, messed-up brain. 'I suppose I'm just worried about this meeting,' she admitted, and that wasn't a complete lie, even though her fears were more amorphous than that. 'I didn't even know I had a grandmother before this trip. That is, I didn't realise she was still alive and living in Paris.' Shyly, she glanced at Madame Rémy. 'You said you used to be friends... What's Agathe like?'

The older lady thought about that for a moment. 'Agathe... Yes, we were friends. Though that's a long way back.' Her smile was guarded. 'She's a difficult woman.'

Maeve's heart sank. 'How so?'

'She's a very private person.' Madame Rémy

paused. 'She never married, you see.'

'Sorry?'

'My apologies,' she said hurriedly, looking embarrassed. 'It's none of my business. I really shouldn't have said anything.'

'No, please, I was the one who asked.' Maeve swallowed, startled by this unexpected new information about her family tree. 'So you mean, my mother was... illegitimate?'

Madame nodded slowly. 'These days, it's barely worth mentioning. So few young people care about the sanctity of marriage. But back in my day... Well, it was a serious problem for Agathe when she found herself pregnant. Not least because she couldn't carry on working and earning a living.'

Maeve frowned as a memory came back to her. 'My father once said that my grandmother had been an artist's model when she was younger. But I always assumed that was a family myth.' Maeve handed back the comb. 'Thank you.'

'You're welcome.' Madame Rémy returned it to her handbag, her expression distracted. 'Yes, Agathe was a model. Like me, in fact.'

'You?'

'Oh yes. That's how we knew each other, of course. We were both part of the same close-knit circle... Artists, models, critics, writers... We both sat for various artists. And not always wearing clothes.' She chuckled at Maeve's widening gaze.

'Oh, we lived rather wildly in those days. But when poor Agathe fell pregnant, she tried to go back home and her parents disowned her. They were strict Catholics, you see.' She shrugged. 'Things fell apart for her after that. She finally managed to share an apartment with a friend. But she never worked as a model again. It was such a pity because she really was very beautiful... The artists loved her.'

'But what about the baby's father? My grandfather? Why didn't he - ?'

'I'm afraid he couldn't help. You see, he was a married man. An artist she'd often sat for. And not French.' Madame Rémy sighed when she saw Maeve's horrified expression. 'I'm sorry. This must be hard to hear. And really, I should have let Agathe speak to you herself. It's not my story to tell.'

'No, I'm glad I know at least the basic facts. Thank you. It helps me feel more prepared. You say my grandfather wasn't French, though? Was he English, then?'

'No,' Madame Rémy said with a grimace. 'He was Russian.'

'Goodness.'

So her grandfather had been a Russian artist. And already a married man when her mother had been conceived. What a mess that must have been.

But that made her... What, a quarter Russian?

The thought was so alien, Maeve fell silent, feeling a little lost and bewildered. Then she realised that Nonna, walking very slowly with Leo just ahead of them, had stopped before a tall, stately apartment block that she recognised at once as the one from her mother's old photograph.

Again, she felt a sickening jolt of nerves and struggled to control them. Her chest tightened as she gazed up at the familiar balconies and rows of shuttered windows that she'd studied so often...

'Oh, I think we're here,' she whispered.

With a reassuring smile, Madame Rémy squeezed her shoulder and then rang the bell for Apartment One, clearly the ground floor flat.

A crackling female voice spoke over the intercom, asking who it was. Maeve got the shivers just listening...

Was that her grandmother?

'*C'est moi, mon amie*,' Leo's grandmother told the disembodied voice, and a second later the door buzzed open.

Maeve followed the others into a high, echoing hallway with a steep flight of stairs and a large set of postal lockers to one side. Its stone-tiled floor gleamed from a recent cleaning. The door to the ground floor apartment was to the left of the entrance, and as they approached, it was opened.

'*Bienvenue*,' a woman's voice said, low and guttural, but as Maeve stopped, anxious to see her grandmother for the first time, she saw a wheelchair in the doorway, a woman sitting in it, wrapped in a cardigan with a tortoiseshell cat curled up on her lap.

The woman had a shock of silvery hair, huge blue eyes – almost identical to Maeve's – and pale, powdery cheeks. Her bright eyes searched for Maeve and fixed eagerly on her face.

'Ah, it's you at last,' she cried in hoarse English, 'my granddaughter. Your name is Maeve, yes?' She beckoned her inside the apartment, hurriedly wheeling backwards. 'Come in, Maeve... Come in, please... I am delighted to meet you at last, *ma petite*.'

As Maeve hesitated in the hallway, now horribly nervous, her hands clasped tightly together, her pulse thundering in her ears, the others stood back, allowing her to enter first.

'After you,' Leo murmured when she didn't move, gesturing her inside.

She couldn't even look his way, too afraid to meet his eyes in case he was looking sympathetic and it made her break down. Oh, what had made her dream this would be a good idea? Her father had always said the French side of the family was trouble and best left well alone.

She supposed it was far too late to run away.

And where would she run to, anyway?

Maeve took a deep, unsteady breath, and followed her grandmother into the elegant old apartment from the photograph.

CHAPTER TWENTY-ONE

The apartment was crowded with quaint old furniture, shutters over the windows that had been partially opened to let in the sunshine, paintings on almost every available square inch of the wall, and every surface covered with dusty photograph frames, ornaments, bric-a-brac, vases stuffed with wilting flowers. The room smelled musty, and she suspected some of that came from the brightly coloured parrot, watching her from a cage beside the window. It squawked loudly and ruffled its feathers as they all piled into the room which, she imagined, must ordinarily be rather quiet.

Despite the crowding of the furniture, it was clear that Maeve's grandmother had a navigable route through the space, as she demonstrated by thrusting her chair furiously forward, before spinning it around so she could face her visitors.

'Please, sit down.' She indicated the sofa and a few uncomfortable-looking chairs. 'I made coffee.

I'm sure it's still warm. And there are cakes.' She pointed to the low table, and Madame Rémy, having seated her own mother on an upright chair, began pouring coffee for them all.

'Come here, girl, and kiss me.' Agathe beckoned her forward, turning her cheek for the anticipated kiss. Shyly, Maeve bent to kiss her. Meanwhile, her grandmother made strange smacking noises, as though to indicate a kiss of sorts had occurred on her part too. 'I thought you would be older. But maybe my memory...'

'Everyone under forty looks like a baby to me these days,' Madame Rémy said, handing her old friend a tiny cup of coffee on a dainty saucer. 'Do you still take it black, Agathe? Or should I add a dash of milk?' she asked in French.

'Black, of course,' Agatha said dismissively, her gaze still on Maeve's face. 'Dear child... I couldn't believe it when Virginie rang to tell me who was staying with her. But how is this possible? How do you know the Rémy family?' Her gaze narrowed sharply between Maeve's sudden embarrassment and Leo's hard profile. 'Has young Leo been painting you?' She smiled when Maeve bit her lip, embarrassed. 'After Virginie called me, I admit, I made a few enquiries. No need to look so surprised. I have a computer. And a phone. I am not a technophobe. I saw that photo of you and Leo at dinner. All very romantic, I thought. But then today I see another story where he denies it and says you are only a visitor. So I ask myself, what is the truth here?'

Taken aback by this question, Maeve found herself blinking and tongue-tied, grappling with the coffee cup that Madame Rémy had passed her. The coffee looked strong enough to strip wallpaper. But there was at least some milk in it. Maybe enough to fill a third of a thimble.

'Erm...I, um...' Her gaze swivelled to Leo, who looked abruptly away as though to say, *'You're on your own, kid.'* Fiercely, she stuck her chin out and blurted out, 'The Rémy family were very kind, taking me in when I lost my bag and passport. I owe them a great deal. So when Leo asked if I would sit for a painting...' She gulped and stopped, unsure where that sentence was going.

'Our guest will be going back to England as soon as the Embassy allows her to leave,' Leo said crisply. 'There's nothing between us, Madame. It was just a story my cousin Jean made up for the paparazzi so he could make some money out of us.'

Agathe didn't look convinced, but she pulled thoughtfully on her lower lip before shrugging. 'If there is money to be made, be sure someone will always try to make it.' She studied Maeve avidly. 'I am glad you're here now but it's been a long time. You were a baby last time I saw you. Why have you never written?'

'Because I didn't know you even existed?' Maeve

felt a little aggrieved at this accusation. She took a sip of her coffee to steady her. It was so strong, her eyes smarted and she was surprised she could even make coherent sounds afterwards. 'After my mum left, I had no contact with anyone from your side of family. Not even Mum. I had the photo… Of this place, I mean. But I didn't really know if you were still living here. Or even if you were actually my grandmother. Yes, the address was on the back of the photograph, but my father wasn't sure if the lady in the photograph was my grandmother. I'm sorry, if I'd known that you were alive and still living here, of course I would have written. But to be honest,' she finished in a sudden hot rush, 'I assumed nobody from my mother's side of the family was interested in me. After all, you never wrote *to me*.'

She half expected her grandmother to look offended by this forthright speech. But Agathe merely gave a sharp burst of laughter. The cat, shocked by this, jumped off her lap and ran away, while the parrot squawked as though taking enjoyment in its departure. *'Brava, my petite,'* she said. 'Quite right. I should have tried to contact you. I am as much at fault as anyone in this business. But my daughter… Your mother… She asked me never to contact you.'

Maeve sank down into the chair beside her grandmother's wheelchair. She felt like she was going mad. 'I don't understand. Mum told you not to contact me? But *why*?'

'If you want to know that, it's probably best if you ask her yourself.'

The cup shook in its saucer, Maeve was trembling so much. '*Ask her...myself*?' she echoed in a hollow voice.

She gazed about the small, overcrowded room, as though half expecting her long-gone mother to pop up from behind the sofa or jump out of the cupboard. Her astonished gaze met Leo's, then she looked at Nonna with her curious, bright-eyed stare and Madame Rémy, whose soaring brows showed she knew as little about this as Maeve.

'Sorry, but do you mean to say she's *here*? In Paris?' She was breathless. 'In this apartment?'

'Not right now,' her grandmother said flatly, dashing her hopes. She raised the dainty coffee cup to her lips and sipped noisily, followed by a series of appreciative lip-smacking noises, much like the ones she'd made when air-kissing Maeve's cheek. 'But she will be soon,' she added as she put down the cup. Her gaze wandered to the clock on the wall. 'I imagine Sylvie should be home from work within the hour. Unless she has some business to detain her.'

They had been speaking mostly in French and Maeve began to wonder if she had completely misunderstood everything that was being said.

Her mother, who had abandoned her as a young child, lived here? And would be home soon?

It couldn't be true, surely?

'I don't believe it,' she stammered.

'I don't tell lies, me,' Agathe insisted, raising thin pencil-drawn brows at her, and then made an odd noise like she was blowing a raspberry.

Maeve stared at her, and then at the others. Heat flooded her cheeks. 'But I have so much to ask. Why she left me, for instance? Why she never came back? Why she never bothered to keep in touch or ask how I was or *anything*.' She ran out of breath, adding with a gasp, 'Oh dear...'

And she burst into tears.

A firm hand took away her coffee before she could spill it, and she opened her eyes to find Leo kneeling beside her chair. His face swam. Or rather, her eyes were so shiny with tears, she could barely see him.

'It's okay, we're all here with you.' Leo squeezed her hand when she said nothing. 'If you'd rather leave now, we can do that too. If you like, we could bring you back another day, maybe when you're feeling more prepared.'

Maeve almost said yes to that suggestion. The idea of running away felt so appealing. But she knew it would be nothing but cowardice, and shook her head. 'No, I have to face her sometime. That is, I'll be thrilled to see my mother again. But there's so much hurt too, you know?' she whispered.

'Yes, I do know,' he agreed in a deep voice, his

gaze locked with hers.

Of course he knew, she thought. His family was almost as dysfunctional as hers. If that were possible.

'There are reasons why your mother was never in touch with you,' Agatha said into the silence that had fallen. 'But it's not for me to discuss those reasons. Come, let us eat cake. Your mother made that one.' She smiled at Maeve in what was obviously supposed to be a cheery way. 'Orange and chocolate. So decadent. Too rich for me though, I'm afraid. But your mother loves it. Try some.'

There are reasons why your mother was never in touch with you.

What reasons? What on earth did that mean?

Nonna reached for a piece of cake, her hand trembling, and Madame Rémy got up to help her.

'*Mmm, oui, le gateau,*' Nonna mumbled, her look eager.

The parrot squawked, and bobbed up and down on its perch, rolling its eyes.

Everyone laughed, except Maeve, who was feeling deeply confused and on edge. She wiped her damp cheek with the back of one hand, sniffing discreetly. Yes, her nerves were in tatters at the thought of being reunited with her mother after all these years. But she couldn't believe she'd just burst into tears in front of everyone. It was so horrifyingly non-British.

To her relief, Agathe and Madame Rémy began chatting about the old days when they had both been part of the thriving Parisian art scene, while Nonna chimed in with the occasional comment, usually something derogatory about male artists, her bosom and lap soon covered with cake crumbs.

She couldn't entirely follow their conversation; it was too rapid and colloquial, and punctuated by raucous laughter. But she was glad the awkward silence was over and she was no longer the centre of attention.

'Relax,' Leo told her quietly. 'Everything's going to be all right.'

He was still holding her hand, kneeling beside her chair. Almost as though he intended to propose marriage...

She stared down at him.

Why did this man care what happened to her? They had barely known each other a few days, for goodness' sake. Yet she welcomed his support, all the same. It genuinely made her feel less alone. And those 'few days' seemed to have occurred over an eternity, or that was how it felt.

But she summoned up a breezy smile and pulled her hand free. 'Thank you. Yes, I know.' She had been self-sufficient for so long, wholly independent and reliant on nobody for approval of how she lived her life, and though it was true she enjoyed having a network of friends and colleagues to fall back on when under stress, she was by no means helpless without them while here in Paris. 'I was just surprised, that's all.'

He got back to his feet. 'Of course.'

The sound of someone unlocking the front door to the flat and coming inside stopped the chatter and laughter dead.

Agathe stiffened, glancing at Maeve.

Maeve bit her lip. 'Oh my.'

There was a short, tense silence.

'In here, Sylvie,' her grandmother called in French. 'We have visitors.' She whispered to Maeve, 'I didn't tell her about you coming here. Just in case you didn't turn up.'

The door opened and a woman peered in, her face blank as she took in all the people gathered in the cramped space.

She was about Maeve's own height, immaculately made-up, with blue eyes and thinning blonde hair cut in a smart bob, dressed in a cream linen skirt and matching blouse, a green leather handbag hanging from one shoulder.

'*Maman?*' she queried, then her gaze drifted back to Maeve's face and stopped there, widening slowly.

Maeve stood up, all eyes on her. 'Hello,' she said in English, her voice faltering, her heart beating a mad tattoo under her ribs. 'I'm Maeve... Your daughter.'

CHAPTER TWENTY-TWO

It was cool in the shadow of the apartment block as Leo stood waiting for their taxi, watching as Maeve exchanged a few last words with her mother. They had both gone into another room in the apartment once Maeve had introduced herself, after the initial shock had passed, her mother clearly unable to believe her long-lost daughter had finally tracked her down. Once she understood who this English visitor was, Sylvie had embraced Maeve in a warm enough manner, but he could tell the woman had been shaken by her unexpected arrival.

He wished he knew what had gone on between the two women behind closed doors, especially given Maeve's pale and almost scared expression when they'd emerged over an hour later. But there had been no chance to ask her yet. Or not without being overheard.

Once his grandmother had run out of anecdotes about their wild younger days in bohemian Paris, he had waited patiently for her and Nonna to take their leave of Agathe and make their leisurely way out into the sunshine, and then had aided them into Bernadette's car, his half-sister having been called to collect the two older ladies.

'Shall I wait for you and Maeve?' Bernadette had asked, tapping the steering impatiently.

'No, we'll come back on the metro. Maeve is still speaking with her mother,' he had told her, and waved them off into busy afternoon traffic, not expecting to be held up much longer than another ten or fifteen minutes.

Yet here he was, still waiting outside… nearly an hour later.

At last, Sylvie raised a cool hand to him and disappeared back inside the apartment. He raised his brows to Maeve.

'Well?'

'Oh, not here… Not here,' she whispered, looking flushed and agitated. 'Where… Where's your mother? And Nonna?'

'Gone home. Bernadette came to collect them. I'll hail a taxi for us.'

'Okay, but not yet. Let's walk for a bit first.' Together, they began to walk briskly down the street. 'My goodness,' she muttered, glancing back once at the apartment building, bathed in the soft golden glow of afternoon sun, before setting her face forwards with a determined expression.

He was curious but waited until he'd hailed a

taxi and they were safely on the way home. Maeve folded her hands in her lap and stared out of the window at nothing, tight-lipped and still, but it was clear she was disturbed. Her usual composed demeanour seemed fractured…

As the taxi snaked its way through heavy traffic, he touched her hand. 'You can tell me what your mother said, if you like. I won't repeat it to anyone else.' He searched her averted face. 'You seem upset. Talking about it might help. Unless you can't?'

'I'm not sure that I'm allowed to tell you,' she said after a minute, shooting a quick glance at the taxi driver, who was listening to music and swaying about in the front, hopefully oblivious to their conversation, which after all was in English.

'Not allowed?' he repeated, mystified.

'I think the word is, *classified*.'

He couldn't tell if she was joking or not. 'Sorry, I don't understand.'

'My mother… She's…' Maeve gave an exasperated gasp. 'Oh, this is ridiculous.' She leant sideways and put her mouth to his ear, whispering, 'I think she's *a spy*.'

The warmth of her breath so close to his ear made him shiver. He was aware of a wave of urgent desire. Only what she had said stopped him from turning and kissing her mouth.

'What?'

'I know it sounds crazy. And she wasn't really

that clear about it. She didn't say that in so many words... But I understood what she meant. That is, she told me she works for the French government. But can't talk about it.' She was still close, speaking in a whisper, and he sat very still, breathing in the subtle scent of her perfume. 'It's all very complicated and hard to grasp. But she suggested that might be why I've had so much trouble at the British Embassy since losing my passport. Because of my connection to her.'

He frowned. '*Mon Dieu.*'

'Apparently, she's going to try and sort it out for me. I hope she can, but...' She shook her head. 'Oh, I don't know what to think.'

He quirked a brow. 'You're not alone in that.' He considered what she'd said, then asked delicately, 'And did she explain why she left England while you were still so young? And never got back in touch?'

'She said the French government had demanded her return. That she had no choice if she didn't want to fall foul of her bosses. So she asked my dad to live with her in Paris instead. Only he refused point-blank and said he'd fight for custody if she took me away.' Her voice wobbled. 'She claims Dad was worried it would be too dangerous for me, growing up with a mother like that... And that he was the one who told her not to keep in touch.' She bit her lip. 'Dad was probably right to try and protect me from all that. It does sound like a precarious existence. But knowing that doesn't make any of this easier to bear.'

'I'm so sorry.'

Maeve merely bowed her head, saying nothing more.

'What can I do to help?' he asked after a moment's silence, warring with the desire to take her in his arms. He knew she was unlikely to welcome that kind of attention, and besides, they were in a taxi, and everything just felt wrong. But he knew this thing he felt for her was more than just a passing attraction to a girl he wanted to paint. It wasn't like his relationship with Liselle, which had been tortured and yet oddly compulsive at the start, until it had finally burnt itself out some years ago. This was on a completely different level and he didn't know what to make of it.

Deep-down, he was a little unnerved by his growing interest in Maeve. If he was honest with himself, and he did prefer to be honest with himself, this feeling had him poised to run away. Yet something was stopping him from doing precisely that. In fact, everything seemed to be tugging him further towards her…

'Nothing,' she said simply, but there was a desolate look on her face. 'I met my mother at last. And my grandmother. It should be the happiest day of my life. And yet I feel like everything is falling apart. *Be careful what you wish for*, they say.' She gave a crack of laughter. 'Well, I wished for this. So that serves me right.'

'I want to paint you again,' he said on impulse, and saw her head turn towards him in amazement. Remorse swept through him. 'Sorry... Feel free to say no. Bad timing. I'm just being selfish.'

But she shook her head. 'No, it's okay,' she said. 'Actually, I'd like that. I expected to be bored, modelling for you. But there's something strangely calming about sitting still for hours. Your mind drifts away, and yet everything feels so centred.' She looked out of the window again, blinking, a curious half-smile on her lips that had him transfixed. Her Mona Lisa smile... 'That probably makes me sound a bit odd.'

But he understood perfectly, dismissing her suggestion with a gesture. 'As soon as we get back to the château,' he promised her, 'we'll grab something to eat and then go up to the studio. A longer session this time.' His gaze caressed her, already imagining her in that small space, posing for him, the brush gliding silkily across the canvas. 'Maybe you could wear something a little more revealing this time...' Again he realised how that sounded, and cleared his throat, straightening up. 'Unless that would make you feel uncomfortable?' he asked in a more professional tone.

She had knitted her hands together in her lap, and now sat still, staring fixedly down at them. 'No,' she said slowly, 'something more revealing would be fine. If you think that's necessary?'

Heat rose inside him and he struggled to suppress it. 'Oh, quite necessary,' he agreed, his voice unsteady.

'But not nude?' she queried, still not looking at him.

His brain spun.

Now he was on fire. Or one part of him was, at any rate.

Oh, for a fire extinguisher, he thought wildly.

'Nude?' He gulped at the thought of her in his studio without a stitch on her nicely rounded body, and then swallowed hard, carefully not looking at her either. The back of the driver's head was suddenly fascinating to him. 'Erm, no... Not this time. That won't be... *necessary*.'

'I see.'

Thankfully, the driver slewed to a halt near the château a moment later and he was able to focus on payment while she climbed out.

What on earth was wrong with him? He was behaving like a schoolboy with his first crush. He had painted beautiful women many times before, both clothed and in the nude, and thought nothing much of it, except to acknowledge the glory of the sitter. And, when it had been Liselle sitting nude for him, in the first flush of their toxic relationship, to take her to bed afterwards...

But this was Miss Maeve Eden, a sensible and well-behaved Englishwoman.

No, feeling anything beyond friendship for this woman was out of the question.

Nothing was ever simple, he found himself thinking shortly after their return to the château. Grabbing snacks for himself and Maeve in the kitchen, keen to get back to work, he had found Bernadette fuming and silent, bending over something bubbling on the stovetop, and got his head snapped off for asking what was wrong.

'As if you don't know,' his sister snarled.

'Sorry?'

'Him!' She waved a ladle expressively, gobbets of sauce flying everywhere. 'Him! Him!'

'My father, I take it you mean?' His half-sister had never acknowledged Sébastien Rémy as her 'father,' or even as her stepfather, despite him still being married to her mother when Bernadette was born, and his grudging financial support after their mother died. But that was because Sébastien had lost no opportunity while she was growing up to point out her illegitimacy and make her feel bad about it. 'I'm sorry he's come back and that he's being as difficult as ever. But the château belongs to him. I don't have the authority to make him leave.'

'Oh, I know that,' she spat, then bent to her

saucepan again. 'He says he's planning to stay indefinitely. Not just for his honeymoon.'

'My God...' He found himself grinding his teeth at the thought of his interfering father constantly underfoot. But while it was an inconvenience for him, Sébastien Rémy's presence was more painful for his sister. He supposed it was a reminder of how she had been sidelined all her childhood and youth as the illegitimate child, the girl who didn't quite fit... 'I'm genuinely sorry, Bernie. I know it must be driving you mad.' He touched her shoulder gently and she jumped, but didn't push him away. 'Look, do you want me to talk to him? Try to get him to modify his behaviour when he's around you?'

'Oh, what's the point?' But she hesitated, stealing a sideways look at him a moment later. 'Would you though? He might listen to you.'

He laughed, though it wasn't funny. 'Hardly.'

'You're his eldest son now,' she pointed out. 'Papa's only child.' He saw how she flinched at that inappropriate word, Papa. 'He'll pay attention to you far more readily than to me.'

He didn't like the idea but had to admit that was probably true. 'Well, I'll try then. But I can't guarantee anything will change.'

She moved away, seeming calmer, wiping her hands on her apron. 'How did it go? Maeve, I mean. Grandmère and Nonna wouldn't tell me anything about her grandmother. They said it was private.'

He shrugged, aware that he couldn't reveal what Maeve had told him. But it didn't seem indiscreet to admit a few bare facts. 'They seemed to get on well enough. But then her mother turned up.'

Bernadette stared round at him. 'Seriously? So she really does live in Paris too?'

'Erm, apparently so.' He pretended to take an interest in the bubbling stew, peering into the pan, disliking having to lie to his own sister. But he had promised Maeve not to reveal her secrets. 'I don't think she got on as well with her mother. But that's hardly surprising. Her mother left when Maeve was a baby.'

'How horrible... Why did she do that?' Bernadette sounded on edge, no doubt thinking of her own difficult childhood.

'She argued with Maeve's father, I believe, and he wouldn't let her bring Maeve back to France.'

'God, some parents!' Her voice shaking, Maeve reached for the ladle again, and he hurriedly backed away in case of more flying sauce gobbets...

But he was saved by Maeve's sudden arrival.

Her face was lit up, her whole being glowing, like a ball of light had just descended into the cavernous kitchens.

'What is it?' he asked at once. 'What's happened?'

'The British Embassy just rang the château

to say it's all been sorted out. I can collect an emergency passport whenever I like and go back home. Isn't that amazing? It's barely an hour since we left my mother, and she's already managed to get it sorted out as she promised.'

He was delighted for her, but his heart sank too.

'Yes, that's marvellous news.' He paused, willing his heart to stop thumping. 'So, when will you be leaving?'

'Oh,' she said, coming to a halt before him. She glanced at Bernadette, then said falteringly, 'I hadn't thought. I was just so pleased by the news that it's all over… But now I remember, you wanted to do another painting session.' Her hands clasped together tightly at her waist, as though she were fighting nerves. 'Of course, another night won't hurt. In fact, the man from the Embassy said there was no hurry. That I could enjoy Paris for as long as I like before going home.'

Bernadette was smiling. 'Congratulations… I'm glad for you.'

'Thank you.'

Leo felt oddly sick, but managed a smile too. 'Yes, I'm very pleased. But I have to admit I'll miss you. You've brightened up our lives.'

'Me?' Her voice was a squeak, her look incredulous. 'That doesn't sound like me. I'm more usually known for telling people off or dampening everyone's spirits.'

Bernadette laughed, returning to her stew. 'Not

in this house.'

'She's right,' Leo agreed, 'you haven't been like that here. Quite the opposite.'

'Oh, well,' she murmured, blushing.

He collected their snacks on a tray, his smile fixed, trying not to think of the future. Of the days stretching ahead when she wouldn't be there to be painted or to exchange barbs with or to escort around Paris... But he had work to do, so he wouldn't miss her that much, would he? He had been neglecting his duties since her unexpected arrival. Perhaps this was a good thing.

'Shall we go up to the studio while the light's still good?' he suggested lightly, and she followed him without a word.

But they had barely got up there when someone knocked at the studio door.

He glanced at Maeve, who had just changed into the diaphanous wrap she'd worn for their last session. 'Are you okay if I answer that?'

She looked uncertain but shrugged. 'It's probably just Bernadette. Maybe we left something in the kitchen.'

'Come in,' he called, for the sign on the studio door said DO NOT ENTER WITHOUT PERMISSION and most people stuck to that when they knew he was painting. Except Liselle, of course, who loved to barge in without knocking.

The door opened to reveal his father, dressed as though he were still in his twenties, in an awkwardly tight pair of white jeans and a tee-shirt that showed every bulge, large sunglasses on even though he was indoors. His hair seemed a darker shade than it had been yesterday, a few strands slicked oddly across his forehead to disguise a receding hairline.

'Oh, it's you,' Leo said in an unpromising way, his jaw hardening. This might be Sébastien's property but he still disliked his father wandering about, lording it over them all, when he spent most of his life doing absolutely nothing towards running the estate. 'Yes?'

Sébastien Rémy strolled in, smiling broadly, with his new bride on his arm as usual. Leo was beginning to wonder if they had been superglued together. 'Ah, I'm happy to see you're in here, working again. How wonderful. It's just like old times. And you're painting the English girl... Well, I suppose she has nice legs.' He turned to his wife, telling her in conspiratorial tones, 'My son will paint you next. Then you'll be able to see your own portrait in this big Paris exhibition he's got coming up.'

'Ooh, I'd love that,' Chanelle cooed.

'Excuse me?' Leo glared at his father. 'I don't think so. I choose who I paint and – no offense, Chanelle – but I'm not interested in painting you.'

His father frowned, removing his sunglasses as though to see Leo better. 'Nonsense. Is this your famous pride speaking, son? Because I won't stand for it. You'll paint my bride. Yes, and then you can paint us both together, and it had better be a good likeness.' He puffed out his chest in a ludicrous way. 'Chanelle is pregnant, you know.'

'I'm aware.'

His father blinked, clearly taken aback by that cool reply. 'The child she's carrying will be your little brother or sister. A portrait of us, perhaps showing just a hint of her pregnancy, would be ideal. Do you hear me, Leo?'

Leo counted silently to ten, then said as politely as he could manage, 'I don't think so. This isn't like hiring someone to paint your walls, Dad.' He met his father's smirking gaze. 'I'm an artist, not an interior decorator. And I choose who I paint.'

'But we're family.' His father paused significantly before adding, 'And I am your boss.'

Gritting his teeth at this implied threat, Leo replied, 'As far as the family business is concerned, yes, you're in charge. But not when it comes to my art.'

'Your *art*?' Sébastien made a derogatory sound. 'All artists accept commissions. Or they do if they want to eat. What's so different about this?'

Leo forced himself to take a deep breath and stay calm. Much as he disliked this situation, he was still talking to his father. 'Dad, I'm sorry. Maybe another time?' His smile was strained. 'Right now, my whole focus is on Maeve. I want her face to form the centrepiece of this upcoming exhibition. Anything else will destroy the integrity of my vision.'

His father stared at him blankly, before turning to study Maeve. His own barely polite smile turned to a sneer. 'You'd rather paint a complete stranger than your own stepmother?'

That was going too far. 'Stepmother?' Leo repeated, the word an explosion of contemptuous breath.

Legally, it might be true. But emotionally he refused to use that word. His whole being repelled against the idea that Chanelle, younger than him by some eight years, was now his stepmother.

'I am *technically* your stepmother,' Chanelle murmured, glancing around the studio with bored disinterest.

Leo decided to ignore her comment, since it was either naïve or deliberately inflammatory, and he refused to rise to anyone's bait. Also, he was conscious of her pregnancy and didn't want to drag her into the argument. This confrontation was between him and his father, nobody else.

'No,' he said firmly, keeping his eyes on his father.

'No?' Sébastien frowned. 'No to what?'

'No, you're wrong. Maeve isn't a stranger.'

'You said she wasn't your girlfriend,' Chanelle pointed out, her eyes abruptly narrowing on Maeve.

'Please don't argue over me,' Maeve interrupted,

strain in her voice.

'She isn't my girlfriend,' Leo ground out with difficulty, wishing she was. 'But she also isn't a stranger. Not anymore. And yes, I'd rather paint her than you and your wife.' He threw a not-terribly-apologetic glance at his *stepmother*. 'No offence, Chanelle.'

Chanelle pursed her lips and tossed back her hair, her expression defiant.

'*Not your girlfriend,*' his father repeated slowly, 'but also *not a stranger.*' He looked Maeve up and down with derision. 'In other words, she's your whore.'

Leo sucked in a breath at that outrageous insult, his vision clouding with a red haze of fury. Without thinking, he took three short strides forward and came bang up to his father, staring directly into his eyes, the two of them now a bare few inches away from each other.

'What the hell did you just say?'

CHAPTER TWENTY-THREE

His father blinked in surprise, hesitating as he scanned Leo's face, then said with deliberate provocation, 'You heard me.'

Leo's fists clenched by his side. 'If you weren't my father,' he began, his voice low and dangerous, but felt a hand tug his sleeve, and turned to look down into Maeve's face.

'Don't, it's not worth it,' she said quietly. 'Plus, he *is* your father, remember?'

As the red haze dissipated from his vision, common sense returned. Leo shook his head like someone coming out of water. 'You're right, he's not worth it. But *you* are, Maeve.' He turned back to his father, drawing himself up straight. He knew what he had to do. It was something he had been avoiding for years. But the time had come. 'I've had enough. I can't live like this any longer. You don't deserve me.'

His father gave a puff of laughter. 'What does that mean?' he demanded in his usual hectoring way, squaring his shoulders as Leo chose to retreat. No doubt his father felt he'd won that confrontation. But he was wrong.

'I'm leaving Château Rémy,' Leo said crisply. 'I'll pack my stuff tonight and be out of here tomorrow. I'll leave a breakdown of the current business for you to look over at your leisure. By the way, Henri wants the family to visit for Aunt Beatrice's birthday. And he needs help with the fire situation at the *cave*. Remember I told you about that?'

His voice was matter-of-fact, his anger having fallen away now that he had made his decision. And it was the right decision, he was sure of it. He already felt lighter, his burdens slipping away…

'You can't leave.' His father was staring at him, his expression incredulous. 'You're needed here.'

'I only took over when Francis died because I didn't want to leave my grandmother struggling on her own. I knew you wouldn't bother coming home to help her. Somebody had to look after her and Nonna. And Bernadette was still in college at the time. It wouldn't have been fair to ask her to step up. But she's older now and has a fair grasp of the family business. And you're here with Chanelle. So I'm no longer necessary.'

'You haven't got anywhere to go,' Sébastien pointed out cruelly.

'No, but I have friends. I'll sort something out.'

'And what will you do for money? Because you

won't get a penny from me.'

'You've never paid me a proper wage for running the business. It's time to collect on that debt.' He paused, adding softly, 'Even if I have to take you to court for what's due to me.'

'Take me to court?' his father echoed, looking astonished. 'I'll fight you. Anyway, you did it for love, you've just admitted as much yourself. And in return for bed and board here at the château.' His father threw up his hands. 'How many people get to live somewhere like this for free? You should count yourself lucky.'

Leo gave a humourless laugh. 'Oh yes, I'm so lucky...' He shook his head. 'I'm not staying, Dad, so you might as well face it. And I'll pot-wash if I must. At least I'd be independent at last. Though given how much I've learnt these past few years, running the business, I'm confident I'll find good work soon enough. And my art may even start to support me again, now that I've gone back to painting.'

He moved about the room, automatically collecting things he would need to take with him. He would have to arrange for some of his work to be put into storage, in case it got damaged, left here alone with his father and Chanelle. His father might not sabotage his work, but he didn't trust Chanelle and wouldn't put anything past her.

With a shock, he realised Liselle would have to

be told. She would have a meltdown when she heard that he was leaving. And Grandmère would be distraught. That hit him hard. But he couldn't live his life for other people anymore. He needed to get free of this place before it killed him.

'Are you okay?' he stopped to ask Maeve, still furious at the way his father had spoken about her.

To his relief, she nodded, seeming calm enough. If anyone had spoken like that to Liselle, she would have screamed and scratched their eyes out. Maeve was made of sterner stuff.

'You can't be serious,' his father stammered. 'You can't leave, Leo. I won't hear of it. I won't let you go. You can't expect me to run the business... I don't have the first clue what you've been doing since I've been away.' He took a deep breath. 'I *demand* that you stay.'

'I'm done, dad. It's over.'

'But I'm your father. I am *chef de famille*. You must obey me.'

'Not happening, sorry,' Leo said shortly, throwing open the studio door. 'I'll talk to you later about the business. Now I need to speak to Maeve alone.'

His father hesitated, then left, taking Chanelle with him. 'We'll talk later, yes. And I will expect an apology.'

With a derisive laugh, Leo closed the door after him, turning at once to Maeve. 'I'm sorry he spoke to you like that. If it had been any other man, I would have punched him for that. Please believe me.'

'I do,' she admitted, 'and that's what worries me. I don't want you punching anyone on my behalf. Let alone your dad.' Her gaze needled him. 'Thank you for your concern. But I don't need any man fighting my battles for me. Besides, it was just nonsense, what he was saying. So what's the point in getting irate about nonsense?'

He felt rebuffed and sucked in a breath. 'I get your point. I'm sorry. I felt embarrassed, that's all… That my own father could say something like that to a guest.'

Her smile looked almost sad. 'I'd better go and pack too. I'm not staying here if you're leaving.' Maeve got up and reached for her clothes, still wearing the diaphanous wrap she had donned for the painting session. 'It's true, your father's very rude,' she added thoughtfully, 'but are you ready to throw away your relationship with him over a silly argument? You could paint him and Chanelle in a few hours, surely?'

'Of course. But that's not the point. It's a matter of principle.' He knew she wouldn't understand though. She had never had to deal with the steady drip-drip-drip of unhappiness and repression that he'd experienced under his father's yoke. As she turned to the door, he caught her hand. 'A minute, please… My only real regret is the possibility that I might lose touch with you because of this.' He swallowed down a wave of yearning. This wasn't the time or place to be making romantic overtures to this woman. But he had to try. 'Will you still let me paint you? You won't go straight back to England now you're free to leave France, I hope?'

'Sorry, but yes, that was my intention.' She looked away. 'I've been away from home too long.'

'Then perhaps I could come to England.' He knew it was unlikely but he couldn't see any other way. 'Assuming you'd like to see me again?'

She said nothing, but there was a soft glow to her cheeks as she glanced back at him.

He added with difficulty, 'It can't be any time soon, unfortunately. I'll have to work from memory and photographs to complete the paintings from the exhibition. But it would be good to paint you one day in your natural habitat too.' He smiled at her look of confusion. 'England, I mean.'

But before Maeve could reply, Liselle slammed into the studio in a figure-hugging green silk jumpsuit, her face flushed, her eyes wide and furious.

Maeve tugged free and took two hurried steps backwards, almost as though afraid Liselle was about to attack her.

'What the hell is going on, Leo?' his manager demanded breathlessly, advancing on him with malevolent intent. She stopped barely a foot away, her hands dropping to her hips, her chin jutting dangerously. 'Your father's just told me you're leaving Château Rémy and that you don't plan to come back. And all because of *her*.' She flung out an arm in quivering accusation, pointing at Maeve. 'Is it true?'

CHAPTER TWENTY-FOUR

Maeve was just about able to follow that rapid, furious flow of French. Though even if she hadn't caught most of the words, the meaning behind Liselle's glare would have been unmistakable.

'Calm down.' Leo stepped swiftly between the two of them.

Maeve winced inwardly at this awkward choice of words; she could have told him that wasn't the best thing for a man to say to an angry woman. But he was about to discover that for himself, she suspected.

'*Calm down?*' Liselle repeated, staring across the room at him. The redhead looked almost feral, lips drawn back from her teeth in a snarl. 'You can't do this to me, Leo,' she snapped, the words tumbling out of her mouth at top speed. 'Your exhibition is coming up. Sascha called earlier to say it's all set up and there's a huge buzz about it. Don't you get it? This isn't just about *you* anymore. I've staked my reputation on this exhibition; you can't simply leave. I'll look like an idiot.'

'Trust me, I'll be there. With a good range of paintings, ready for the grand reveal.' Leo strode across and put a hand on her shoulder, his voice surprisingly calm now given the major upheaval he'd just been through. 'You always knew this would happen one day, Liselle. Well, things have finally come to a head between me and my father, so that day has come. I'm leaving Château Rémy.'

'But why *now*?'

'Because I couldn't stomach his behaviour anymore. The sly remarks, the demands, the insults...' He grimaced. 'Besides, you didn't hear what he said to me just now. Or how he spoke to Maeve.'

'Oh yes, Maeve...' Liselle's angry gaze shot to Maeve's face. 'I should have known this would be something to do with her. Ever since she arrived here, you've been all over her.' She shook her head with undisguised disapproval. 'You've changed, Leo. You're not the man you used to be.'

Leo's mouth quirked. 'Maybe not. But from my point of view, it's a change for the better.'

His manager drew a deep breath. 'Come downstairs with me. I've spoken to your father and he's not as angry as he was. I can make him see sense.'

Now Leo was frowning. 'What do you mean?'

'We've put together a plan. It's not ideal,

but it means you can stay here and keep painting. Please, come downstairs and hear his proposition.'

Leo looked indecisive.

Feeling very much in the way, Maeve collected her stuff and went to the door. 'This isn't anything to do with me,' she said lightly. 'I'm going to my room to pack. I... I'll speak to you again before I leave, Leo.'

Without glancing his way, she left before Leo could try to dissuade her. She didn't like getting in the way of a family argument, and she certainly didn't like Liselle's accusation that she had somehow caused this split between Leo and his father just by her presence at Château Rémy.

Up in her quaint attic room with its low, sloping ceiling, Maeve dragged out her rucksack, which the police had given back to her emptied of her belongings. But of course there wasn't much she could pack, unless she took Bernadette's clothes. She hesitated, and then changed into her own jeans and tee-shirt, the outfit she'd been wearing when she missed the coach. At least they were familiar and comfortable, even if they wouldn't suit every situation.

She was just looking tentatively through the meagre stack of Bernadette's clothes to see if there was anything she could ask to take with her and post back later, when a knock at the door disturbed her.

'Come in,' she said, jumping a little. She didn't feel strong enough to face Leo again right now. Things were so confused between the two of them.

But to her relief it was only Bernadette. 'Oh, so it's true,' she said on seeing Maeve's rucksack open on the bed, disappointment in her tone. 'You're packing.'

'I thought it was best that I leave. I've heard from the embassy that I can go back to England anytime I choose. And I feel that I've caused an argument between Leo and his father, quite without meaning to. So it's best if I go now.' Maeve bit her lip. 'Bernadette, would it be possible for me to take a few of your clothes with me? The ones you were so kind as to lend me? I'll send them straight back once I'm home, I promise.'

'Of course, take whatever you like. You don't need to return any of them though. I have plenty of clothes.' Bernadette paused, her bright eyes searching Maeve's face with puzzlement. 'I'm surprised though. I thought you and Leo... I mean, I thought there was something between you.'

Maeve swallowed, her stomach pitching. She felt suddenly vulnerable. 'I do like your brother,' she admitted. 'I like him a lot, in fact. But he already has a close relationship with Liselle, doesn't he? Besides, it's obvious his father doesn't approve of me. He was quite rude in the studio.' Her voice shook and she had to stop and clear her throat.

Why did someone being horrid to her like that make her *tremble*? It was ridiculous. She needed to harden up. She had faced the insult he'd thrown at her without reaction at the time, but now she felt herself processing it more deeply, her sense of self-worth genuinely wounded. Was that really how she came across? As someone who was only hanging around so that she could go to bed with Leo? That idea left a bad taste in her mouth.

'My... *stepfather*... is a nasty man,' Bernadette told her passionately. 'I hate even calling him that. He's more like my abuser. Please, forget him. He doesn't matter. But Leo... My brother deserves better than Liselle. He deserves someone like you. So please don't go. I've never seen him so happy as he's been this past week. And I think you two suit each other well.'

Hot-cheeked, Maeve began folding some of Bernadette's clothes very unevenly into her rucksack. 'Oh, I don't know about that.'

But that was a lie. She did know. And she secretly agreed. There was something between her and Leo, and it was both strong and surprising. She hadn't expected to come to Paris and meet someone who could potentially change her life. And yet here she was, and now they were going to be parted almost as soon as they'd found each other. It seemed so unfair.

Still, Leo hadn't said anything to indicate that he felt the same. She was just guessing at his feelings, beyond his clear desire to keep painting her. And she certainly wasn't going to make a fool of herself by declaring how she felt. Especially not given the uncomfortable argument she'd just witnessed.

'I left Leo downstairs with his father,' Bernadette told her, 'discussing the future of the business. I think they may be coming to some agreement that will allow Leo to keep running things here in Paris, but spend more time painting too. And for Sébastien not to live here. Though I can't believe he'll be happy to leave.'

Remembering how Sébastien Rémy had strutted about, lording it over all of them with insufferable rudeness, Maeve had to agree.

'And Leo? How does he feel about that?'

'I'm not sure but I imagine he'll be tempted. He loves Paris. And the château. He's put so much into the business too, he won't want to walk away now.' Bernadette studied her curiously. 'And how do you feel about Leo?'

Maeve didn't know how to respond. 'What does it matter what I think or feel? None of this is anything to do with me.

'Is that so?' Bernadette hugged her impulsively, and Maeve held her breath, astonished. 'You can't pretend, you know. I've seen how you look at my brother. And maybe you can help him.'

'Sorry?'

'Leo needs a clean break from Château Rémy. Somewhere he can clear his head. Madame Rémy suggested that he could accompany Sophie and Marie back to Bordeaux. The three of them will be taking the train down tomorrow, I believe.' She hesitated. 'Maybe you could go with them?'

Maeve felt like the breath had been knocked out of her. Go to Bordeaux? With Leo and his nieces? 'But I have to go home,' she said blankly.

'Are you sure? Even if it means never seeing Leo again?'

'I can't just stay in France indefinitely.'

'No, but the British Embassy... Did they insist you had to leave immediately?'

'No, they gave me a temporary passport, until the new one arrives, and said I could stay a little longer if I wanted, after all the upset of being mugged. But I think they meant, *stay in Paris.* Not go gallivanting about the French countryside with Leo Rémy.' Maeve put her hands to her cheeks and shook her head. 'Oh, I'm so confused. I... I don't know what to think anymore.'

'Then maybe we should talk about it,' came a deep voice from the doorway.

She turned guiltily to see Leo standing there, listening to them.

How long had he been there? What had he heard?

Bernadette gave an embarrassed chuckle and hurried away. 'Take all the clothes you want, Maeve. I'll see you later,' was all she said, discreetly closing the door behind her.

Leo stood unmoving, arms folded across his broad chest, his gaze on her face. There was a strange light about him.

'You heard, I take it?' he asked.

'Only that you've come to some kind of arrangement with your father.' She hovered by the bed, awkwardly folding and refolding one of Bernadette's dresses, not really aware of what she was doing. She only needed one alternative warmer outfit for her trip back to England, yet she seemed to be packing summer dresses instead. Was her subconscious trying to tell her something? 'I'm glad. I hated the idea that you'd argued with your father over me.'

'I'm still taking a break,' he said shortly. 'Though you already know that.' He hesitated. 'I couldn't help overhearing what you said to my sister. I hope you'll change your mind. I'd love you to come with me.'

'To the vineyard in Bordeaux?'

He came closer, his dark, intent gaze searching her face. 'It's a marvellous place, Cave Rémy. I spent many happy holidays there as a boy. I'd like you to see it.'

'I should g-go home,' she stammered.

'Why?'

The direct question threw her, and she had to stop and think. Which wasn't easy. Right now, any kind of rational thought felt like trying to force a watermelon through a colander. All that came out the other side was mush.

'Because...' She halted, conflicted.

'Because you should? Because you're worried what all this means?' He had taken away the cheerful yellow summer dress she'd folded very badly and was shaking it out. His voice was calm as he arranged its silky folds more carefully, every one of his movements graceful, almost ritual. 'I understand that. So I'm asking you to take a chance, Maeve. A chance on me,' he added softly, 'and on whatever *this* is.'

By *this*, he must mean the strange electricity in the small attic room, she decided, and tried to suppress the wobbly sensation inside that the mere sound of his voice seemed to have inflicted on her. And the fear that one of her legs had inexplicably grown longer than the other. For otherwise, why would she be listing so oddly to one side, her knees and assorted leg muscles and ligaments suddenly weak as limp spaghetti?

It was nerves, pure and simple. What else could it be? She was nervous about travelling home at last. Nothing to do with Leo Rémy asking her to accompany him to his family vineyard in Bordeaux.

How ridiculous she was being.

He was still waiting, his gaze steady on her face now.

Terror jolted through her.

And exhilaration.

Now it was her time to ask the difficult question.

'Why?' she whispered, all her fears and uncertainties and shining hopes somehow wrapped up in that one unpromising syllable.

Leo handed her the neatly folded dress. 'Because I think it would be a mistake to ignore what's been going on here. For both of us.' His smile was slow and filled her with heat. 'And because I think you feel the same.'

CHAPTER TWENTY-FIVE

They took the TGV to Bordeaux – the *'train à grande vitesse,'* as Sophie had explained helpfully while they were waiting to board – and it certainly lived up to its 'high speed' name. Maeve sat rapt in a delightful dream, watching the countryside flash past in ever-darkening shades of green and gold the further south they travelled. Quaint towns, hills and valleys, vast stretches of golden and verdant crops, all blurred into one recognizably French patchwork.

Leo sat beside her, pointing out landmarks and sharing amusing anecdotes or astute political remarks about the landscape they were passing through. 'That was the town where they wanted to elect a donkey as Mayor,' he commented at one point, nodding to a station name that passed too quickly for her to catch. 'Though, in my opinion, they already had one.'

His nieces Sophie and Marie were pleasant company too. She hadn't seen much of the twin girls during her stay at Château Rémy, since the bubbly teenagers had been out most days sightseeing with Madame Rémy. But she'd often heard them chattering in their room in the evenings or watching French films loudly. Now they sat opposite her and Leo on the journey, listening to music on their headphones or giggling together over social media posts. Sometimes they took selfies or reels, posing outrageously for their friends and followers on various platforms.

They had Club Quatre seats with a table, which allowed Maeve plenty of space to write observations in the notepad she'd bought at the station, using the emergency cash the bank had allowed her to withdraw. She was missing her phone and the laptop she used at home. But she'd been able to check her emails at least on Leo's laptop, reassured to see nothing too pressing in her Inbox.

Besides, doing without the internet had proved fairly relaxing so far. It was a digital detox she hadn't intended to take, but one she was actively enjoying now she'd got past the stress of wondering what she might be missing.

They were travelling first class, which felt wonderfully luxurious. The seats were wide and comfortable, with power-recline settings. She was surprised to discover that there was no food or drink offered with First Class tickets, although they did provide a café-bar compartment. Thankfully, Madame Rémy had kindly provided them with a picnic-style lunch, and they ate this instead, both girls apparently preferring her home-cooking to 'train food' anyway.

While they ate and chatted, Maeve couldn't help noticing that Leo seemed quite withdrawn, his smile perfunctory whenever she glanced at him.

'Are you okay?' Maeve asked him after they'd finished eating, careful to keep her voice down, although the girls were too busy discussing something they'd seen on social media to overhear their conversation. 'Tell me to mind my own business, but you seem a little unhappier today than last night.' Meticulously, she began clearing away the remnants of their train picnic. 'I thought everything was sorted amicably with your father.'

'I doubt that anything between me and my father will ever be sorted amicably,' Leo admitted with a weary smile. 'I'm sorry to be such poor company. I'm just worried about the exhibition, that's all.' He paused, gazing out at the sun-drenched countryside. 'I'm afraid Liselle was right to be angry with me.'

Having thrust everything into a paper bag ready for disposal, Maeve used a few wet wipes to clean her sticky fingers. But her mind was ticking furiously. She felt instantly on the defensive, hearing that. Liselle might be his manager, but what right did she have to judge him?

'Whatever do you mean?'

'By the time we get back from Bordeaux, the exhibition will almost be upon us,' he explained. 'And I only have three or four canvases that will be anywhere near finished by then.'

'But you've brought some painting equipment with you,' she pointed out. He had in fact carried an easel on board the train, along with his bag of paints and a portfolio case of blank canvases, ready for painting. 'Won't you be working while you're in Bordeaux?'

'Of course, and I intend to, it's just that…' He shook his head, his gaze returning to her face. There was a sombre glint in his eyes. 'I hate exhibiting my work. That's the underlying issue. I love to paint but I hate people seeing what I've painted. It's a real failing for an artist. Because if you can't exhibit and sell your work, you can't make a living.'

'But you spoke so lovingly of Bordeaux and the vineyard… Maybe it will provide some fresh inspiration while you're down there, so you produce work you're eager to show to the world.'

'Perhaps,' he agreed.

Their hands were resting on the train table very close to each other. Her little pinky was almost touching his. They looked down at the same time, as though both were abruptly aware of the proximity…

Nerves flared inside her, and she shifted her hand, fussing with the picnic rubbish again, though it was all ready for the bin. 'Tell me more about Henri and Beatrice,' she said hurriedly to hide her reaction, 'what are they like? I hope your aunt and uncle won't be horrified to see me with you. I mean, they're being expected to accommodate a complete stranger. It could be rather embarrassing.'

'Nonsense, they love visitors. Besides, you're a friend of the family now, so you'll be as welcome as any of us, trust me.' Leo held out his hand. 'Now, give me that rubbish and I'll take it to the *poubelle*.'

When he returned, he seemed more relaxed. He began to describe his Uncle Henri and Aunt Beatrice to her, chuckling as he retold humorous stories about them from his youth, while Sophie and Marie chimed in occasionally with jokes of their own. It was obvious that the two girls adored their parents, their fresh faces glowing with happiness the nearer they came to Bordeaux.

'Nearly home,' Marie murmured, checking her train app. 'I can't wait.'

'But won't you miss Paris?' Maeve asked her in French.

'Oh, yes,' Marie agreed with a sigh. 'All those amazing museums and art galleries...' She clearly had an academic turn of mind.

'And the designer boutiques,' Sophie added, a twinkle in her eye.

'But I'll be glad to get home too,' Marie admitted, smiling as she watched the countryside flash past. 'I miss my dear FrouFrou.'

Maeve arched her brows. '*FrouFrou?*'

'Her horse,' Leo murmured.

'He's incredibly old, so nobody rides him these days, but he's still a darling,' Marie told her enthusiastically.

'And I'll be happy to sleep in my own bed again,' Sophie said, stretching with a grimace. 'No offense, Leo, but that old mattress I had at the château was an absolute nightmare. I'm sure it was stuffed with straw, probably sometime back in the eighteenth century.'

And both girls fell about laughing at Leo's expression.

They arrived late afternoon, and were met at the station by Beatrice, a smiling, sun-tanned lady who looked about sixty, and a man whom she introduced as Pierre, her eldest son, who was driving a dusty, battered old minibus with *Cave Rémy* on the side. Pierre looked to be about forty years old. He was taciturn and moustachioed, with a thatch of pitch-black hair and olive skin the texture of well-tanned leather.

'We've always needed a large vehicle, not just to carry crates of wine about the place, but for all our children and their friends,' Beatrice told Maeve, seeing her surprised look as they climbed into the thankfully air-conditioned interior. 'Though they're nearly all grown-up now, apart from those two rascals, of course.' And she grinned round at Sophie and Marie, already seated at the back and poring over their phones as usual.

'How many children do you have?' Maeve asked.

'Nine.'

Maeve gasped. 'I'm sorry? Did you say, *nine*?'

'I know, I know, it's a large number.' Beatrice laughed. 'Henri and I didn't mean to have quite so many. We thought maybe five or six. But accidents happen, you know?'

Leo glanced drily at Maeve, who bit her lip.

'The girls are seventeen,' Maeve said slowly, thinking out loud. 'But that means –' She stopped, worried about offending the older lady.

'Sophie and Marie were quite a surprise, yes,' Beatrice agreed placidly. 'I thought I was long past childbearing age. Even my doctor thought it. Then suddenly, in my early forties, I started getting queasy and oddly fat. I thought it was the menopause at last, but it turned out to be twins!' She chuckled at the memory. 'It was a tough pregnancy, I can tell you. Carrying twins isn't easy at the best of times. I'd already had Michel and Jean-Luc in my late thirties, so I knew all about it. But it's especially hard when you're older.' She shrugged. 'But my older children were able to help out around the house and vineyard, so I got to spend most of my afternoons with my feet up. And I wouldn't be without my precious Sophie and Marie, of course.'

'They never stop talking though, those two,' her son Pierre said in a deep drawl, his hands resting lightly on the steering wheel as they took a sharp right-hand bend at speed. Rather too lightly, Maeve thought, clutching the seatback in front as the minibus swung violently around the corner. And at rather too much speed...

He finally hit the brakes as they approached a large sign declaring *Cave Rémy: Dégustation* and turned off the main road onto a narrow dust track.

The track ran past a large, stately warehouse with a shop at one end, which was clearly closed for renovations. The family's wine-tasting showroom, Maeve guessed, seeing how Leo turned to study the building with a frown as they passed.

'Such a shame about the fire,' Beatrice said unhappily. 'But Henri is confident the shop will be open again by the weekend.'

'That's good news, at least,' Leo agreed.

The girls were also peering back at the warehouse shop and exclaiming in horror, having been in Paris when the fire occurred.

Leo leant forward, saying quietly to his aunt,

'Henri told me you'd been unwell recently. I hope you're feeling better.'

'Oh, it's nothing serious. The doctor says... arthritis.'

'I'm so sorry.'

'It keeps me awake at night,' Beatrice admitted, sighing. 'I was in a great deal of pain. At the end of my patience, to be honest. But he's given me some exercises to do, and they do seem to be helping.'

Leo touched her arm. 'I'm glad.'

'Thank you, Leo. But I believe you've had some trouble too recently?' His aunt glanced round at Maeve, a furtive look in her face. 'We saw that photograph everyone was talking about... Oh, and then your father turning up out of the blue, and married to a woman *half his age*? Sophie and Marie told us all about it on the phone.' She tutted sympathetically. 'That must have been difficult. I know you and Sébastien still don't get on very well.'

'We've come to an agreement,' Leo told her. 'My father's going to live in Nice with Chanelle, and I'll continue running the business in Paris as before. With one big change.' He paused, smiling. 'Bernadette is going to be working with me, so I have more free time for painting. That was my condition for staying on.'

'How marvellous. She's such a capable woman. I never liked her being cut out of the family business.'

'But you know what my father's like. It's nothing to do with Bernadette herself. It's about his hatred for my mother. He just refuses to treat her like one of the family, knowing another man fathered her. And the law in this country is on his side.'

'It's a shame.' Beatrice shook her head. 'But I'm glad you've made this deal with Sébastien. Perhaps if the business starts turning a profit, he may change his mind and name her in his Will. She certainly deserves it, the hard work she's put into Château Rémy over the years.'

Maeve had been listening to this exchange with interest, fascinated by the internal machinations of the Rémy family.

But, as the minibus slowed to a crawl and they fell silent, she sat forward, peering eagerly out of the windscreen instead. The dust track had finally widened into a broad gravelled area, shaded by enormous cypresses, and within seconds they were pulling up outside the house itself, the girls quickly tumbling out of the vehicle.

Unlike the château in Paris, the Rémy house attached to the vineyard was a modern build, all glass and fancy brickwork, but with a charming terracotta-tiled roof like many of the older buildings she'd seen from the train as they travelled further south. The gardens were thick with lavender shrubs, several tall rows blooming a deep violet, a sea of bees drifting amongst the delicate flowers, their steady buzz audible even before they'd entered the gardens.

In an adjacent field, leaning over the gate with docile patience, was a large, dapple-grey horse. 'FrouFrou,' Beatrice told her cheerfully, having spotted her looking at the horse. 'The children used to ride her but she's too old for that now. Now she just gets lots of apples and hugs.'

Marie ran to embrace her beloved horse, while Sophie ran ahead of them into the house, shouting for her father. Soon, Henri emerged, a heavily bearded, jovial man who clasped both Maeve's hands in his and drew her close for the traditional three-cheek kiss. 'How lovely to meet you,' he said in thickly accented English. 'Leo told us you were coming and we were delighted. My wife has prepared a room for you. Oh no, please don't worry… We have plenty of space now that so many of our children have flown the nest. It's good to have new people in the house.'

While he and Leo spoke together about the fire that had devastated their showroom, Beatrice led her upstairs to a large room overlooking the vineyards. It had the prettiest pink curtains and a double bed decked out in lacy pink and white.

'My second eldest daughter Michelle loves everything pink,' Beatrice explained with an apologetic smile. 'Not my style. But what can you do?'

'No, I love it.'

'I hope you'll be comfortable, anyway. Please let me know if there's anything you need. I believe you lost all your luggage in Paris.'

'Yes, it was awful. I got my rucksack back in the end.' She slung it off her shoulder. 'But anything of any worth inside it had gone.'

Impulsively, Beatrice hugged her. 'I'm so sorry you came to our country and had such a bad experience. Let's hope we can make up for it, now that you're in Bordeaux. There's far less crime in our little corner of France than in the capital, and such beautiful countryside, you'll soon forget your troubles here.' She went to the door. 'I'll leave you to get settled in. There's a pool round the back if you'd like to swim.'

'How lovely.' Thankfully, she'd bought a swimsuit while waiting at the train station in Paris.

'We tend to eat late here, because there's always something to do in the vineyard, especially now we're coming up to harvest. But if you get hungry beforehand, please help yourself to anything in the kitchen.

'Thank you.'

'Listen out for the supper gong,' Beatrice added as she left, beaming back over her shoulder. 'You'll find us on the terrace.'

Once her host had gone, Maeve stood a long while at the window, staring out over the beautiful vista. The heat was so much more all-enveloping here than in Paris, and yet somehow fresher too, the air not hemmed in by brick and glass, but flowing freely across the fields.

The vineyard itself stretched far away, long dusty rows of dark green vines, heavy with fruit. Behind them, in the distance, rose the hazy bluish tinge of mountains, the piecemeal landscape in between punctuated by a few terracotta-roofed towns and avenues of tall, stately cypresses, perhaps grown in clusters to mark land boundaries.

Maeve sighed, hugging this spectacular view to her heart. She had come to France for a few days on her coach tour, expecting to see only Paris during her stay. The busy metropolis and river. The Eiffel Tower. The Louvre. She had seen all those, yes, but she had also travelled deep into the hinterland of this magnificent country.

It now seemed almost a blessing, what had happened to her when she'd stopped to help Madame Rémy. It had been dreadful, of course, as she'd told Beatrice. Even frightening, especially when she'd regained consciousness to find everything gone, including her money and passport.

Yet now, looking at this view and thinking how close she'd grown to the Rémy family, perhaps it was also the best thing that had ever happened to her?

Her life in England had grown narrow, dull and samey, she had to admit. She could no longer imagine returning to it after this adventure, or not with much enthusiasm. Especially now she knew her mother and grandmother were both still alive and in Paris. Her mother had made it clear she was not a clingy woman and wouldn't be pressing for a closer relationship now they'd been reunited. But perhaps she could visit Paris again next summer, to check in on her family... and perhaps see Leo too, if he was likely to still be interested by then? Or was that mere wishful thinking on her part?

Trying to live in the moment, rather than dwell on what might happen in the unforeseeable future, she took a shower and then soaked her hot, aching feet in cold water. Her body being unused to such intense heat, it felt like her feet had almost doubled in size during the long train journey. She had visions of needing clown shoes...

Afterwards, once her feet had returned to a daintier size, Maeve lay down on her bed in the stultifying summer heat to rest, just for a few minutes.

Only she began to dream of tall, dark Leo, standing before his easel, paintbrush in hand, the biggest paintbrush she had ever seen, and it was growing bigger and bigger the harder he painted...

CHAPTER TWENTY-SIX

Shocked by a loud crash, Maeve sat up groggily and realised she must have dozed off. Either that or she was still asleep and no longer dreaming of Leo and his enormous paintbrush, but of some imperial palace in China, where some dignity in rustling silks had just been announced and everyone was bowing down to them. Because she could have sworn that a gong had just been struck somewhere below her in the house.

A gong...

Hadn't Beatrice mentioned something about a gong?

She blinked, confused. How long had she been asleep? It was still sunny outside her window and she could hear birdsong. Yet there was a golden-orange glow to the light now that told her the time must be well into evening.

The gong sounded three more times, each resounding GONG louder and more insistent. She got the impression someone was standing there with a large gong mallet, enthusiastically whipping a large, gold-foil-wrapped after-dinner mint for all they were worth...

Come down to the terrace when the gong sounds. Wasn't that what Beatrice had said, or words to that effect?

Jumping up guiltily, Maeve splashed her face with cool water, using the handy corner sink in her room. Then she dragged a cool summer dress over her head and fastened a slightly loose pair of sandals borrowed yet again from Bernadette, before descending to the terrace as quickly as she could in flapping sandals without falling downstairs. Talk about clown shoes...

Embarrassingly, she found the whole family already assembled under burgeoning vines supported by a lattice structure of wooden slats and wire cables, soft purplish grapes dangling here and there, thick foliage providing gentle shade as everyone sat enjoying pre-dinner aperitifs on the terrace. There, a glass of some milky substance called 'pastis' was pressed into her hand, and she was introduced to Henri and Beatrice's other grown-up children, several of whom still lived at home and worked in the vineyard.

After much handshaking and cheek-kissing, followed by a gulp of the aniseed-flavoured pastis that left her gasping and spluttering, she was directed to a seat opposite Leo.

He grinned at her. 'Glad you could make it. I was nearly dispatched to find out if you'd got lost on your way downstairs.'

'I'm sorry,' she hissed across at him, 'I fell asleep. I was *tired*.' She frowned at him, trying not to be resentful of the fact that he still looked fresh and clear-eyed. 'Why aren't *you* tired?'

'I was, but I had a power nap,' he told her calmly, rising to shake hands with a late arrival, yet another of Henri and Beatrice's children, this one called Francois, a shambolic young man whom Leo introduced to Maeve in such a flurry of dialect that she was left without a clue what was being said.

The long dinner table was set with a cheerful, red-striped tablecloth and matching red linen napkins, with glassware sparkling by the light of many fat candles flickering inside glass containers. Bowls and dishes piled high with colourful salads, vegetables and succulent-looking meats had been arranged all the way down the middle, interspersed by water bottles and stoppered pichets of red wine.

Having carried out the last dish, which looked like trout sprinkled with almonds, Beatrice sat down, shaking out her napkin with a flourish and a comfortable smile. '*Bon appetit, tout le monde!*'

Following the others' example, Maeve began to help herself to salad and roast chicken, deeply aware of Leo's gaze on her face.

Okay, what was he looking at?

Paranoia began to work on her, aided and abetted by the milky pastis, which tasted less fierce after a few mouthfuls. Maybe her hair looked like a haystack. Or maybe she had red marks on her cheek from having slept so long and so deeply in one position…

Leo was looking strangely presentable in a crisp, short-sleeved white shirt opened at the neck to reveal a broad chest with a few manly hairs curling just within view. His shoulder-length sleek black hair had been recently washed, she suspected, and combed into a John Wick lookalike style. He had not shaved again though, so there was a faint dark shadow about his chin and jaw that gave him a broodingly sexy air…

A power nap, eh?

'I, um, hope the fire damage wasn't as extensive as you feared,' she said at last, addressing Leo in English while the others were chatting around them.

He broke apart a crusty baguette and dipped a fragment into a spicy bean mix dripping with olive oil. 'No, it wasn't complete devastation, you're right. And it's almost sorted now. They're just waiting on an inspector to check and sign off on the rewiring. Then the showroom will be back in business.' He ate for a moment, then poured both her and himself a large glass of water. 'The timing couldn't have been worse though.

Henri relies heavily on coachloads of tourists stopping here to taste the wine. Still, the place has only been out of commission a short time.' He grimaced. 'The insurance premium will be through the roof when we renew, unfortunately. But that can't be helped.'

Clearly having caught some of their conversation, Henri muttered something in agreement, and gestured her to try one of the pichets of red wine. 'Let me know what you think,' he told Maeve. 'It's drawn from a cask of our own Rémy label. Rich and earthy, with intense notes of raspberry and a lingering plum aftertaste.' He grinned as his son Pierre guffawed at this, and clapped him on the back. 'According to a recent review, that is,' he added with a wink. 'But I'd welcome your opinion.'

Feeling all eyes upon her, Maeve gingerly poured herself half a glass of the fragrant red wine, and took a cautious sip.

She wasn't a big wine drinker, it had to be admitted. Nor did she know the first thing about viticulture. But the knowledge that this had been produced on their own land, with grapes cultivated and picked by their own hands, lent a beguiling charm to the rich taste rolling around her tongue.

'I love it,' she told them, and raised her glass. 'Thank you all for welcoming me into your home so generously. Your health.'

'*Santé!*' they chanted in return, raising their own glasses.

Leo smiled at her across the table before drinking deep from his own wine glass, and she felt a blush creep across her cheeks at the look in his eyes.

He planned to paint while he was down here. And he'd told her that he intended to paint *her*, in particular. Maybe out in the vineyards.

Was it wrong to feel excited by that prospect? After this brief holiday in France, she might never see him again, even though he had politely offered to visit England. But she knew how things worked with these short-lived holiday romances. It all seemed so magical in the beginning. But once the holiday was over, the magic dwindled and was soon forgotten.

She felt a pang at the thought of all this magic and romance dwindling before it had even properly begun. But she was sensible Maeve, after all. She wasn't the sort of woman to throw herself into a fling with a Frenchman, however intriguing. Nobody back home would believe it possible.

No, she must not break the habit of a lifetime by doing something wild and foolish. Something she might quickly regret, and perhaps forever...

Dusk fell with surprising suddenness over that glorious landscape of cultured vines and dusty hills and cypresses piercing a violet dusk. The evening was thick with cicadas, their never-ending *chi-chi-chi* made by millions of insects out there in the shadowy landscape: invisible, omnipresent, loud. The family sat drinking on the veranda for over an hour after supper had finished, chatting amongst themselves, everyone relaxed and enjoying the evening's warmth.

Maeve listened to the French language weaving in and out of her ears, washing over her like a delightful piece of music, and looked up at the heavens as the first stars began to prick tiny silver lights across the thickening dark.

She was in love, she realised. In love with this country. In love with France itself. Oh, she still loved her cosy little corner of Britain. The everydayness of rainy streets and fish and chips and the school bell that she heard even in her sleep. France was more like a lovely dream to her, somehow perfect and magical in that moment, even though she knew it wasn't really like that, and that criminals like the mugger who'd stolen her bag existed there too, thieving passports and money and cards, and ruining people's lives. But just for that one evening at least, France was special. It was the mythical landscape she inhabited whenever she fell asleep and her subconscious took over…

'Care for a walk?' Leo asked softly at her elbow, startling her. He'd moved round to sit beside her when Sophie and Marie had disappeared upstairs to bed. 'I know it's getting dark but there's still enough light to see by.'

Maeve hesitated, pushing aside her empty wine glass and checking to be sure she wouldn't be needed. But apart from a few remaining glasses and pitchets of wine, the table was already clear. She had helped Beatrice carry the plates out to the kitchen, and the dessert bowls to the table and back again once consumed, and then had helped the twin girls load the dishwasher while Henri had collected the dirty cutlery. Now Henri and Beatrice were chatting together at the other end of the table, discussing a film they had recently seen, and there was nothing for her to do.

Yet still she hesitated.

She was afraid to be alone with Leo, she realised, shocked by this realisation. No, *afraid* was the wrong word. She felt… apprehensive. Not because she didn't like Leo or found him intimidating. Quite the contrary, in fact. She was nervous about being alone with him because she knew they would likely kiss again once nobody was looking. And in this wine-sweetened dream of dusty vineyards and warm night air, goodness knows where that might lead.

This was the land of romance, after all.

'I'd like that,' she said in typically contrary fashion, and even let him take her hand as they left the veranda with a soft farewell to their hosts, and wandered out along the dusty track in the purple gloom of evening.

She must be in a dream, she decided. Because people can do things in dreams that they wouldn't dare attempt when awake. Or perhaps she'd just had too much wine and was tipsy.

Embarrassingly, to add weight to this suspicion, Maeve hiccupped.

'We make good wine here, don't we?' he murmured.

'Delicious,' she agreed, and suppressed another hiccup as best she could.

Oh, for goodness' sake…

They walked for some time in companionable silence, and then around a bend where they were hidden from the house. They were a long way out in the countryside, she realised, listening to the quiet air. The evening would have been deathly silent if not for the incessant thrum of cicadas.

After another few paces, Leo stepped off the track into the dust soil of the vineyard, pulling her with him.

'Where are we going?'

'I just want to show you something.' He stopped at the vines growing closest to the edge of the track. 'Look,' he said, his voice low in the stillness, 'see these grapes, how dark they are, how well-rounded? This bunch is almost ripe. And the one next to it too. Only a few weeks now and most of these will be ready for harvest. Though we'll have been back in Paris a long time by then. And just as well. This place is utter chaos at harvest time. I know… I've been part of the workforce myself.' He brought her hand to the vine, her fingers rustling aside the warm leaves. 'Here, touch the grapes… Don't they feel round and firm and full of life?'

She choked. 'Um, yes, I suppose they do.'

It was almost dark but there was a soft glow to the sky that meant she could see his face clearly, even there in the gloom. He was staring directly into her eyes, both their fingers tangling around the warm, tightly-packed, nearly bursting bunch of grapes.

She felt breathless, and had to laugh despite herself. 'Do you often come out here at night to fondle the grapes?'

'This is my first time,' he admitted, and released her hand, drawing her close against his body. 'Maeve…' he murmured, and his arm slipped about her waist.

She tilted her head instinctively, her eyes closing as his mouth came down.

Oh goodness, she thought, as fireworks burst behind her eyes and her heart began to race.

His mouth worked persuasively on hers as they stood together, cuddling under a black velvet sky, the balmy night air caressing her bare shoulders. But she didn't just passively let him kiss her. She kissed him back, as she had done before, her own arms twined about his neck, pulling his sleek dark head down to hers, as if he needed any more persuasion.

It was just as well, she thought at one point, gasping as his hands moulded her body through the silky summer frock, that making love in a vineyard was not likely to be a terribly comfortable experience.

If they had been in an English meadow, for instance, she suspected they would probably have been rolling about in the clover long ago. Instead, they stayed discreetly on their feet and merely explored each other's bodies by touch and largely through clothing.

Talk about fondling, she thought hazily.

All the same, it seemed like a century before Leo pulled back, also breathless, and gazed down into her face. 'Wow.'

'Wow indeed,' she whispered back, hot-cheeked.

He glanced at the vines they'd been leaning against. 'I think we may have crushed a few grapes.'

'Your uncle won't be pleased.'

'You think you're kidding... Henri takes damage to even a single bunch of grapes very seriously indeed. He'd probably send us straight back to Paris.'

'I like him. And Beatrice.'

'They're a wonderful couple,' he agreed, smiling.

'*Nine* kids though...'

'I know.' With a sharp nod, Leo ran a hand through his hair, still badly mussed from where she'd been gripping onto it as though planning to yank the hair from his head, strand by sleek black strand. 'I wonder if they ever worked out what was causing that.'

She snorted with laughter, burying her face in his broad chest. His heart was beating as fast as hers. 'Probably not,' she said, her voice muffled. 'Though we could ask them for some pointers. Because I'm not sure I know what's causing *this*.'

'Yes, it's strange. I thought I had this under control,' Leo agreed, his voice uneven. He raised a hand to play with her hair as though mesmerized by it. 'You'll be going home soon too. It's insane to be making something out of this… And yet, I can't seem to help myself.'

'Me neither,' she agreed with a croak of laughter, even though it wasn't that funny. They were both grown adults. Yet they'd clearly lost sight of commonsense. Because this thing between them had to be impossible. He lived in France. She lived in England. He was a painter and a businessman. She was a teacher at a secondary school. And she taught maths, not even art.

In other words, they had zero in common. This relationship had disaster written all over it. Probably printed in triplicate, in capital letters and with red ink too. Yet neither of them seemed able to see the warning signs. Or were studiously ignoring them.

Leo said huskily, 'I think I'm in love with you.'

Her laughter died. She stared up at him blankly. 'I'm sorry, what?'

He swallowed before repeating in a dogged fashion, 'I said, I think I'm in love with you.'

'Oh good,' she somehow managed to rasp in reply, her throat dry. 'I thought that's what you said. But it didn't make any sense. So I was thinking, well, either I'm going mad or my hearing is failing. It's good to know neither of those were correct.' She bit her lip. 'But *you* may be crazy.'

He didn't smile. 'Love is a kind of insanity, it's true. Yet I've never felt saner.'

'Perhaps we could find a doctor to corroborate that.'

'I've been lost for years, wandering in the wilderness, unsure what I wanted for life. Then I met you and suddenly saw the right path, shining ahead of me.'

'And that's me, is it? The right path?'

'Undoubtedly,' he said solemnly, and took her hand, lifting it to his lips. 'I have no doubt, at any rate. Not anymore.'

The warmth of his mouth on her skin... The promise in his eyes... Her heart was thumping hard, loud enough to rival the cicadas.

'This c-can't work,' she stammered. 'You and me. It's impossible.'

He nodded. 'You think I don't know that? It doesn't stop me from being in love with you though. If anything, it makes me more determined to find a way through the difficulties.'

'But you said, you only *thought* you might be in love with me. Not that you definitely are.' She shrugged, watching him. 'I'm just saying…'

He kissed her again, and for a long time there was silence in the vineyard. Then he murmured in her ear, 'Pedant.'

'That's me.' So many people had called her a pedant over the years, she had become accustomed to it. It was almost a badge of honour. 'So you agree, what you said doesn't make sense. Or rather, I shouldn't take it too seriously.'

'No, let me rephrase,' he said briefly, and took a deep breath. 'Maeve Eden, I'm in love with you. For real and forever. I want to marry you.' He stuttered the last three words, his voice having started to shake. 'If you'll have me, that is.'

She felt as though someone had put a tube down her throat and sucked all the air out of her lungs. Though obviously she would have noticed that happening, so it had to be her own nervous system playing havoc with her head.

'Now my hearing is going wonky. I'm sorry. Did you just ask me to marry you?'

'Actually, I merely stated that I would like to marry you.'

'Pedant,' she whispered.

'If the shoe fits...' He was watching her closely, his hands hovering just above her shoulders but not touching. She sensed he wanted to kiss her again but was giving her a chance to reply to his proposal first.

But which way to swing?

'Oh. My. Gooodness,' she mumbled as the realization of what was happening began to sink in properly.

Marriage?

She couldn't seem to breathe properly. The world blurred to his dark face above her, a mauve-dark halo of night behind his head. Had Leo Rémy, a man whom she had only met, gosh, less than two weeks ago, really just proposed *marriage* to her? Or suggested it as a possibility, at least. Mentally, she went back through their last few exchanges... Yes, apparently he had. And now her brain was a hot mess of nonsense.

She groped for words that wouldn't come, and ended up making a strange bleating noise instead.

His brows tugged together. 'I beg your pardon?'

'*Meh...*' More bleating.

She'd definitely lost the use of human language. Hopefully, he wasn't against marrying a goat.

'I'm sensing my proposal may have come as a shock to you,' he mused, studying her thoughtfully.

A *shock*?

The man had such a talent for understatement,

Maeve was stunned into respectful silence. Which meant no more bleating, mercifully.

He bent his dark head, blotting out the sky. 'I seem to recall that kissing a woman in shock can be helpful,' he murmured just before their lips met again.

It was another long kiss. And by the time it was over, she had somehow processed the rapid influx of information – love, marriage, bleating – and come up with a more appropriate, adult response.

'We can't get married,' she told him flatly, pulling back from his lips, though still within the alluring circle of his arms.

'Why not?'

'Okay, let's see... We've only just met. We both have intensely complicated lives already without getting tangled up in someone else's complicated life. Also, you live in France, and I live in England,' she went on, carefully enunciating all the reasons she had already given herself to explain why this would not work. 'You're, like, really arty and a bit of a wild child.'

'A *child*?' His brows shot up.

'A bohemian, then.' She struggled to return to her list before he could kiss her again and commonsense fled in a rush of desire. 'And I'm just a maths teacher. I have equations living in my brain. People call me sensible. Pedant, remember? I'm completely ordinary. While you...' She sucked in a ragged breath. 'You're *extraordinary*. So this will never work, can't you see that?'

His smile had grown during her little speech, and now he shook his head. 'It will work precisely because of those things. Because we're such opposites. Have you never heard of the saying, opposites attract?'

'People only say that to explain really strange marriages.'

He threw back his head and laughed. 'Then let them say it about *our* marriage. Because it will be nobody's business but our own.'

'You father might have something to say about you marrying an Englishwoman.'

'He can hardly talk, given his recent choice of bride.' Leo paused, frowning. 'Though you're right about one thing.'

Maeve blinked. 'Good to know.'

'I haven't properly asked you to marry me. Not in the traditional manner. An omission I intend to remedy at once,' he insisted, then sank down on one knee in the dust of the vineyard, a bunch of purple-dark grapes nestling against his shoulder.

Oh my, she thought dizzily.

Gently taking both her hands in his, Leo gazed up at her through the gloom, though she wasn't sure he could possibly distinguish her features. Why, in this darkness she could be anyone...

But she was wonderfully glad that she wasn't.

Because her heart was flooding with love too.

Love for this man, this complex, talented artist. For this gorgeous country. Even for the night thickening around them, the scent of vines and dust, a slight breeze blowing warmly from the south and lifting her hair...

She just found it hard to express in words what she was feeling.

'Will you marry me, Maeve Eden?' Leo asked deeply, and when she tried to protest, shook his head. 'No, hear me out before rejecting me, please... I've spent my whole adult life wishing I could find a woman who would be my muse but also my friend. Someone to give me good advice but also excite me. I'd given up ever finding such a woman. In fact, I thought she didn't exist. Until I met you.' He drew a long, unsteady breath, going on earnestly, 'I knew almost as soon as we spoke to each other that first day that this would be something miraculous in my life. I wanted to paint you at once, which is very unusual for me. But I pushed those feelings away, because I was afraid what it would mean. I was afraid of how my world would change if I let you in. And it has changed. *I've* changed. But I realise now, that had to happen. This is a good thing. I'm embracing the changes... And I'd like to embrace you with it,' he added with a sheepish smile that rapidly faded. 'As *my wife*, not just someone I've known for a few days and may never see again.' His grip on her hands tightened, his voice hoarse. 'Will you give me a chance, Maeve? A chance to love you and maybe, just maybe, if you help me get this right, to make *your life* miraculous too?'

There were tears in her eyes. She was weeping with happiness. Either that, or she was allergic to their Bordeaux vines. Which would be awkward, to say the least, given what she was about to say.

'Yes,' she choked out breathlessly, 'yes, I will marry you, Leo Rémy. And maybe I'm a bit crazy too for saying that. Because everything I told you was true. This is a huge bloody gamble. But I don't care anymore. I want to take a risk for the first time in my life. I want to be the one who does the eccentric thing, the crazy thing, the wild thing, so that everyone tuts at me and wags a finger.' She gasped. 'I don't want to be *sensible Maeve* anymore.'

'Then you won't be,' he promised her. 'And I'll show you how that might work.'

He rose and took her in his arms. They kissed under the soft purple haze of nightfall among the dusty vines, the rhythmic chi-chi-chi of cicadas accompanying their love.

'Do those insects ever shut up?' she muttered between kisses.

'Never.'

She swore under her breath.

'You get used to them. After a while, you don't even hear them.'

'Like nagging wives?'

He laughed, and kissed her again. 'I can't wait for you to nag me, Maeve, *ma cherie, mon amour.*'

Maeve shivered in delight. 'Ooh, French love words.'

'You like?'

'J'adore.'

'There's plenty more what they came from,' he said easily, and began to make love to her with his tongue, so to speak, using all the French love words she knew and dozens more she didn't...

'I'm going to be so happy with you,' she whispered after another hot searching kiss, clinging onto him so she didn't fall over, because her head was spinning and her knees were frankly weak.

'We still have to tell Liselle,' he whispered back.

'Oh... Damn.'

Leo held her close for a while in the warm night air, his arms a comfortable support, his mouth nuzzling through her messed-up hair.

She knew they ought to return to the house. That would be the sensible thing to do. Henri and Beatrice would be wanting to lock up soon. Besides, with her delicate skin, she was probably being eaten alive by unseen mosquitos and would be covered in itchy red bitemarks by the morning.

But she wasn't sensible, dependable Maeve anymore, was she? Mosquitoes be damned. And she wanted to stay out here in the vineyard forever, loving Leo and being loved by him, and not thinking much beyond tonight...

'Do you really have equations living in your brain?' he asked.

EPILOGUE

A hand on his arm made Leo turn from contemplating the largest canvas in the exhibition, *Maeve Among the Vines*, to find Liselle standing behind him. His nerves jolted, his memory flashing back to the dangerous moment when he'd told his manager that he and Maeve were getting married, and she had literally bared her teeth at him. But to his relief she was smiling now.

The prospect of making big money from his paintings seemed to have a powerful effect on his manager these days. And if that made Liselle more inclined to relinquish the past, then he had no complaints. Especially since he would be making money too...

'This is your best work ever,' Liselle told him with soft satisfaction. 'Everyone is saying so. Even the critics, and you know how hard they are to please. Sascha is delighted. You already have ten confirmed sales, by the way. And Blanchy is here.'

His eyes widened, moving past her to search the small but crowded exhibition space, already jostling with buyers and art critics and invited guests. Blanchy was Belgian, and one of the biggest art critics on the Parisian scene. If he gave an artist the thumbs up, they were bound to be lauded everywhere. And if he ever gave an artist the thumbs down, their career could be finished in a matter of hours. In fact, someone should probably save everyone a great deal of heartache and simply remove Blanchy's thumbs...

'Did you invite him? I certainly didn't. He hated my last exhibition. He said it was like something from the 90s. And I think he meant the 1890s.'

'The art of the 1890s was massively influential,' Liselle pointed out calmly, studying the calculator she'd produced from her jacket pocket, but shook her head. 'No need to worry. I just left Blanchy looking at that odd little piece, *Maeve Distracted*. He stared at it for a good five minutes without speaking, then made a note on his phone. When I asked what he thought of it, he said... "Not bad. Not bad at all." Then he wandered off to look at that one of Maeve in Jean's café. The smaller piece with the fish in the background.'

'*Maeve Fish-Watching*?' Leo sucked in a breath, trying not to feel giddy with excitement. He wasn't a young pretender anymore. He was an artist in his prime and he needed to take such successes in his stride. Also, he would soon be a married man, with all the responsibilities that went with that. Talking of which...

'Have you seen Maeve?' He had arrived early tonight to oversee the final touches to the exhibition before the launch party for press and interested parties, and hadn't had a chance to check yet if his fiancée had arrived safely.

With a flicker of her eyelids, Liselle merely jerked her head over his shoulder.

Sure enough, there was Maeve, pushing her grandmother in her wheelchair, accompanied by a slight figure in a grey tracksuit and hoody, the face hidden in deep shadow.

Leo frowned, surprised. Maeve had not expected her mother to attend the exhibition, though she had invited her grandmother, of course. But they must have turned up together, and he could tell by the rapturous smile on Maeve's face that she was delighted to be able to show them both around the exhibition in person. They had stopped in front of one of his favourite canvases, *Maeve: A Study In Blue*. It was a portrait of Maeve lying in an immaculate white swimming costume beside the pool in Bordeaux, the dappled light from the water rippling over her body and face, even the costume overcast with it, so that she seemed almost as blue and fluid as the pool itself.

He recalled the day he'd painted that while Maeve posed for him, poolside. They had made love for the first time the night before, almost silently, not wanting anyone in the house to hear them, but with scalp-tingling intensity. And when he'd tried to capture her on canvas the next morning, that knowledge had shone from her eyes, her entire body exuding a bold new sensuality that was the dominant theme of the painting.

'What does Maeve think of the exhibition?' Liselle asked lightly, though he felt the weight of a more serious question behind her words.

She knew, better than anyone perhaps, how important it was for him that the woman in his life understood his art and appreciated it. Liselle had been his muse for a few years, though no more. And he still valued her opinion and input into his career. But she was a better person as his manager than she ever had been as his lover.

Now, he was able to look at her in a totally impersonal way and to count her as a friend, nothing more. And Liselle seemed to have embraced that new reality too. Yet they still shared one thing in common, and that was his art.

'Let's ask her,' he said with a smile as Maeve headed their way, pushing her grandmother up the ramp onto the raised platform dominated by his larger canvases.

Her mother, he noticed, had disappeared.

Maeve came to kiss him, and his arm curved naturally about her waist, pulling her close.

'Hello, darling,' he murmured against her lips.

Love and desire flooded him, as they did every time they kissed, and he marvelled at how strong the sensations still were. Part of him had been expecting this attraction to fade, especially once she had accepted his proposal of marriage. Instead, it seemed to be growing stronger every day, enhanced by each plan they made for their future together.

'Not here,' Maeve whispered, though with a chuckle. 'Maybe later?'

'Now there's a promise...'

She wriggled free, shooting him a smiling glance to soften her words, and hurriedly introduced her grandmother to Liselle.

While the two women exchanged a few polite remarks, Maeve whispered quickly to Leo, as though having read his mind, 'My mother couldn't stay. Too many members of the press here, apparently. She prefers to keep a low profile, she says. And she doesn't want us to have too much of a public connection, not now I'm going to be staying in Paris.'

He felt a distinct lightening of his mood at her words, for they hadn't yet decided where they were going to live full-time and he'd been concerned she might choose England. Wherever Maeve went, he knew he must follow. But moving to England would have meant immense upheaval for him, including the handing over of responsibility for his side of the family business entirely to Bernadette, who was capable but still learning the ropes.

'Paris?'

Her eyes twinkled up at him, catching the relief in his voice. 'Yes, alright, you win. Paris is the most sensible choice. Besides, I can easily get work here as a teacher of English, whereas it would be far harder for you to adjust to life in a new country. Your English is superb but you'd need to construct a whole new network of art contacts over there. And Liselle would never leave France, and I know how important she is for your career.'

'Plus, you must remain loyal to your idiom,' he murmured, unable to resist.

She wrinkled her brow at him. 'My idiom?'

'Being sensible,' he reminded her. 'I take it you're not quite ready to ditch the old Maeve in favour of a carefree existence as an artist's model?'

'An artist's wife,' she corrected him briskly.

'Of course. I apologise.' His lips quirked with humour. 'Yes, you are still...' He looked at her mouth, tempted to kiss her again. 'Deliciously *sensible*.'

She said nothing but arched her brows at him with wonderful hauteur.

Leo would have grabbed her, unable to resist, but Liselle had finished her conversation with Maeve's grandmother and was looking sternly at him. He also spotted a few photographers snapping candid shots of him and Maeve...

No, this was definitely not the time or place.

Not until the big announcement, anyway.

'Liselle wants to know what you think of my paintings,' he murmured, reluctantly taking a step back.

Maeve turned on her heel, taking in the whole exhibition. Her smile was tremulous as she looked back at him. There were tears in her eyes too, but they were tears of joy, or so he hoped.

'They're amazing,' she said in French, turning to Liselle. 'Quite incredible. I can't believe I'm the woman in these paintings. I mean, I can see myself... But it still doesn't seem real. I'm just a schoolteacher from England.' She threw up her hands. 'How did I manage to become anyone's *Muse*?'

'Now, Maeve,' her grandmother said, tutting her disapproval, 'we've talked about this before. Don't do yourself down. I can perfectly understand why Leo wanted to paint you. And look at this marvellous exhibition. With every painting you've shown me, I've heard other people exclaiming at his talent and how beautiful these portraits are.' Her smile was proud. 'And that's because of you.'

'Your grandmother is right,' he said, perhaps not very modestly, but then modesty was underrated in his opinion. It stopped people from realizing their true potential. And he had no intention of allowing that to happen. Not now that he'd found his mojo again. 'I couldn't have produced these paintings and put on this exhibition if you haven't sat for me and been such an inspiration. I was lost and confused when we met... Now I know exactly who I am and where I want to be.' He wanted to kiss her again, but everyone was looking their way now. It was nearly time for him to give his speech.

'Is your father not here?' Maeve asked.

He thrust his hands into his pockets, suppressing a laugh. 'I asked Papa to be here but he couldn't make it, apparently. He sent me a text just as the doors opened. Chanelle has a sudden hankering for Nice, he says. So they've brought forward their plan to move there. They went off on the train about an hour ago, on a house hunting mission. I don't think they'll be back anytime soon.'

'Not even for the wedding?'

He sensed relief in her voice and grinned. 'Yes, I texted him that question too. My father suggested he might be a little busy that weekend.'

'Oh dear, how very sad,' Maeve said without emphasis, but her eyes were dancing.

Bernadette came up behind them, with his grandmother and Nonna in tow. The two older women stopped to speak politely to Maeve's grandmother, who had come round to Château Rémy for coffee the previous day.

Bernadette turned to Leo and Maeve, and rolled her eyes with an exaggerated sigh because they were still gazing at each other, smiling secretly as they communicated without words.

'Erm, sorry to break up the lovefest, big bro,' Bernadette said pointedly, 'but it's time for your speech. Everyone's glasses have been charged with champagne, as ordered, and the podium is right over there. You don't want to keep your fans waiting.'

'I certainly don't,' he agreed, only belatedly noticing Maeve's tension. 'What is it, *cherie*? What's the matter?'

'Oh, Leo… ' Maeve gripped his arm, her smile vanishing. 'Do you really think it's wise to announce our engagement *tonight*?' she whispered furiously in English. 'It's bad enough having everyone staring at me in these paintings, but the media will go wild once they hear that. You told me I would be anonymous, remember? Instead, my name seems to be on every single one of these paintings!'

'I told you, being upfront about our relationship is the best way to deal with the press attention,' he assured her. 'There's already been so much speculation since that photo of us at Jean's place. Besides, if we'd tried to keep things quiet, not saying anything, one of them would have been bound to find out another way and make everything a thousand times worse. This way, we control the narrative.'

Liselle was nodding. 'Yes, let me handle all the publicity for you, Maeve,' she said calmly. He was glad that she'd come to terms with the news that they were going to be married. Although now Liselle was trying to turn it to their advantage, he sensed they might need to take their honeymoon somewhere far away, to avoid it turning into a media circus. Like the Arctic Circle, perhaps.

'Ah, you see,' Nonna said in French, jabbing a bony finger in Maeve's direction, though her smile seemed friendly enough, 'I told you, didn't I? You are perfect. The perfect Muse for our Leo.' She pointed significantly at one of the smaller canvases where he had painted Maeve almost – but not quite – nude, seated with a modesty-preserving lapful of flowers, a position which she had complained about constantly at the time, claiming the flowers were cold and prickly and probably had insects crawling all over them... 'I told you this would happen. Now you give Leo good babies, *hein*?'

Liselle inhaled sharply at this, pursing her lips.

Bernadette snorted.

Maeve muttered something in return that he didn't catch, not looking particularly gratified by this suggestion.

'Nonna, please...' Leo cleared his throat and put a hand over his mouth to hide his grin, pretending to scratch his upper lip.

Judging by Maeve's expression, she wasn't fooled.

'You're up.' Bernadette handed Leo a fresh glass of champagne and nodded him towards the podium. 'Good luck.'

Liselle tapped her glass with a pen to get everyone's attention. Quickly, the noisy hubbub of chatter died away as Leo strolled towards the podium.

'Thank you all for being here tonight, my friends, and for being among the first in the world to view these paintings of my new exhibition.' Leo looked across at Maeve, who was nervously gulping down the champagne she'd been handed instead of waiting for the toast, and smiled. 'Before I go on to talk about the inspiration behind this exhibition, and to thank all those who helped it happen, I would like first to introduce you to the woman who sat for these paintings. The woman you've been admiring as you've walked around the room. The woman who has graciously agreed to become my wife.'

A ripple of excitement ran through the room at this announcement, but he ignored it.

Leo raised his glass of champagne in a toast, his heart flooding, love trembling through his voice as he finished triumphantly, 'I give you... Maeve Eden, the love of my life.'

'Maeve,' most people responded, drinking her health, while others used their phones to snap pictures of the two of them.

The photographers set up a barrage of flashes, calling to Maeve to look their way and even to get up on the podium next to him.

'Come on... We want to see the happy couple together!'

Maeve's blush deepened at the shouts and whistles, but when he beckoned her forward, she didn't refuse, despite her obvious reluctance to be the centre of attention. As he put an arm about her waist, she raised her glass to Leo, even though there was only half an inch of champagne left at the bottom of the glass, and shyly murmured, 'I love you, Leo.'

I love you.

He had intended to keep his cool up to that point. To remain the elusive and enigmatic Leo Rémy he had always been in the past at exhibition openings.

But Maeve had never actually said those three little words to him before, even though she had agreed to be his wife. He'd hoped maybe those feelings would come in time, so hadn't mentioned it, fearing to have that conversation and be wounded by a cool, offhand answer. But Leo had wondered if she felt the same as him, especially once they'd made love. He'd thought perhaps she was still too 'sensible' to believe in love.

So, when he saw her mouth those special words,

his heart swelled, his breath tangled in his throat, and it was all he could do not to abandon the podium and seize her in his arms in front of all these people. Because nothing could be more perfect than his life at this precise moment.

Except perhaps the pitter-patter of tiny feet – or, more likely, ear-piercing wails emanating from tiny but powerful lungs – in the corridors of Château Rémy, assuming they were ever blessed with children.

Nonna would be pleased, he thought with an inner chuckle.

But that was a thought for the future.

'I love you too, Maeve,' he whispered back to her, raising his glass again, and the paparazzi went wild.

THE END

Printed in Great Britain
by Amazon